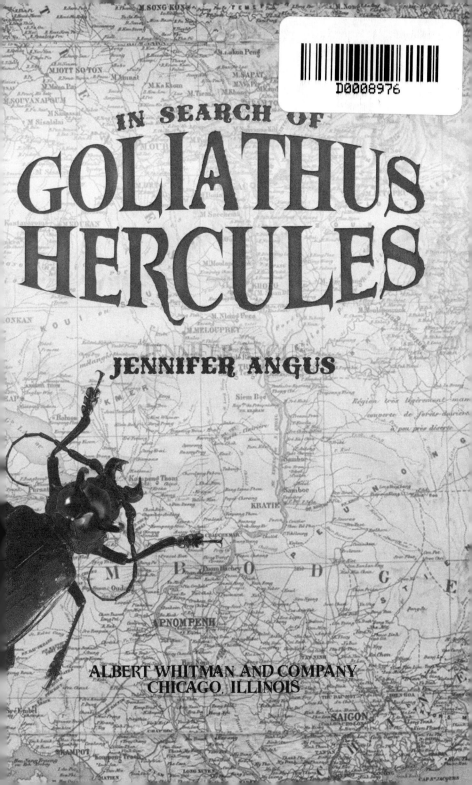

IN SEARCH OF
GOLIATHUS HERCULES

JENNIFER ANGUS

ALBERT WHITMAN AND COMPANY
CHICAGO, ILLINOIS

For my son, Sasa &
my father, William H. Angus
&
In memory of my mother, Anne W. Angus 1932–2002
Special thanks to Robert Apholz

Library of Congress Cataloging-in-Publication Data

Angus, Jennifer
In search of Goliathus hercules / by Jennifer Angus.
p. cm.
Summary: Ten-year-old Henri Bell discovers he can speak to insects and, as he travels the
world in search of a giant legendary insect, begins to metamorphose into an insect himself.
ISBN 978-0-8075-2990-4 (hardcover)
[1. Insects—Fiction. 2. Human-animal communication—Fiction.
3. Metamorphosis—Fiction.] I. Title.
PZ7.A58615In 2012
[Fic]—dc23
2011037135

Text and illustrations copyright © 2013 by Jennifer Angus.
Published in 2013 by Albert Whitman & Company.
All rights reserved. No part of this book may be reproduced or
transmitted in any form or by any means, electronic or mechanical, including
photocopying, recording, or by any information storage and retrieval system,
without permission in writing from the publisher.

Printed in the United States of America.
10 9 8 7 6 5 4 3 2 1 LB 17 16 15 14 13

For more information about Albert Whitman & Company,
visit our web site at www.albertwhitman.com.

PART I

Henri Bell
Age 10

HENRI BELL AND THE RESIDENTS OF WOODLAND FARM

1890

Henri sat by the window in Great Aunt Georgie's old, creaky house, gazing out to the pasture through the falling rain. All was quiet beyond the sound of the pitter-patter of raindrops and a fly's annoying buzz as it made futile attempts to gain its freedom by breaking the window's glass barrier. Stupid fly! thought Henri.

Henri is French for Henry. It is pronounced "On-*ree*." Henri thought it was inexplicable that his parents named him that. Neither of them spoke French, nor did he seem to be named after a distant relative. Everyone who knew him pronounced his name "Henry," but those who didn't often asked, "*Parlez-vous français?*"

Henri lived in the country on Woodland Farm with his Great Aunt Georgie, his father's aunt. It wasn't a working farm anymore. There was a house, a cheery two-story redbrick building that the ivy was threatening to disguise completely. The fields had lain fallow for years and the barn was empty. In short, the farm seemed to have fallen on hard times.

Despite the lack of activity, there were lots of places to explore—particularly down by the creek—and there were many good places to build forts. The problem was, there was no one Henri's age to lay siege to his fort. The only person he had to converse with was Great Aunt Georgie, whose primary interest in life was collecting buttons. Most of her conversation centered around buttons, which meant that their discussions were fairly one-sided since Henri didn't know anything about them. A typical exchange at dinner went like this:

"Henri, did you know that the earliest button was found five-thousand years ago?"

"No, I didn't."

"Did you know that buttons were first used to fasten clothing in Germany in the thirteenth century?"

"No. But if that's true, what did they use them for before then?" asked Henri, perplexed.

And so on and so on. Henri feigned polite interest, knowing that if he did not appear to be somewhat attentive, there would be little to discuss beyond the weather.

To Henri, Great Aunt Georgie looked like she must be a hundred years old. Whether she was or not, Henri would never know for sure because he knew it was impolite to ask a woman's age.

Now, many would expect an English boy with the name Henri to stand out or be remarkable in some way, but there was nothing in particular to distinguish him. He was just under five feet tall. He had brown eyes and brown hair that he parted in the middle. He didn't have any scars, although he wished that he had because there's always a good story that goes with a scar. Really, not very much had happened to him—just one thing: he was sent alone without his mother or father to live with ancient Great Aunt Georgie three thousand miles from home.

Prior to the long steamship voyage to America, he had lived with his mother in a small flat in London. It was just the two of them because Henri's father had departed nearly three years before to take up a position as a superintendent on a rubber plantation with the British East India Company in Malaya. Looking in an atlas, Henri discovered that Malaya was a tropical country, south of Siam, and nearly halfway around the world! Henri had to close his eyes and concentrate very hard to picture his father's face. It had been so long since there had been any news from him.

Henri gazed out the window and watched the raindrops hit the already-formed puddles. The fly continued to buzz in frustration at its inability to penetrate the window glass. Henri recalled happy memories of his father. His most cherished was his seventh birthday outing just before his father had left for Malaya. The family had gone to the zoo. They spent most of their time in the Asian pavilion because Henri's father wanted to show him the animals that were native to Malaya.

Henri had admired the sleek, majestic tigers that padded about their cage, ever watchful, as if waiting to pounce. Huge saltwater crocodiles blinked their eyes from time to time, which was the only way you could tell they were alive so still did they lie. When asked what his favorite animal was, Henri responded, "Elephants." One of the few postcards that Henri received from his father in Malaya showed a grand procession of elephants through a village.

Now he pulled a ragged stack of postcards tied with string out of his pocket. On top was a yellowed newspaper page, folded neatly, that Henri had kept because he had found an article entitled "Tiger Tales" about wildlife in the Malay jungle. He removed it from the pile and put it aside. He picked up the elephant postcard and turned it over. He didn't need to read it— he could recite it from memory. Anyway, it didn't say anything more than one expected from a postcard. It contained the usual sentiments such as "love you" and "wish you were here."

Henri turned back to the window. The rain seemed to be slowing down. The fly continued to buzz against the glass, looking for a way out. From time to time it stopped and, for lack of a better word, fidgeted. If a fly had hands, it would be scrubbing them together. It was a greedy type of movement, as if it were about to swoop down upon something particularly tasty. If Henri was to do that at the dinner table in front of a meal of roast beef, potatoes, and green beans, Great Aunt Georgie would surely rap his knuckles. Great Aunt Georgie was a devoted reader of *Beadle's Book of Etiquette* and often quoted passages she felt were relevant to Henri's proper upbringing. Salivating and "carrying on" were definitely considered bad manners.

He watched the fly as it continued to buzz about, stopping from time to time to fidget. The constant buzzing and scrubbing was annoying.

Finally Henri said out loud, "Could you stop that?"

From below on the windowsill came a faint sound, not buzzing. Henri would later realize it was a chuckle.

He looked down and there was another fly, but this one was quiet, not buzzing, nor scrubbing…It was moving quickly back and forth across the newspaper page Henri had set on the sill. Henri moved closer. Could it be? The fly appeared to be reading the newspaper!

"You know it's rude to read over someone's shoulder," said the fly.

7

"Sorry!" said Henri, greatly taken aback. Had he heard that right? In an effort to get the fly to speak again, he said, "Excuse me, I hope you don't mind if I ask, but…are you actually reading?"

"Yes, I do mind," said the fly. "Don't you think it would be proper if we introduced ourselves first?"

"Oh, I'm sorry," said Henri. "I am Henri Bell, and I am Great Aunt Georgie's nephew."

"Yes, I know. She mentioned you," said the fly.

"She mentioned me!" exclaimed Henri. "You talk to Aunt Georgie?!"

"Yes, of course. She is the owner of this house, and I am a housefly, after all."

"Oh, um…" How could he respond to that? "Um, you didn't mention your name."

"I am *Musca domestica*, but you may call me Dom," said the fly.

"I am very pleased to meet you," said Henri, and he actually meant it. Dom was the only person—or rather, thing—that he had spoken to since he had arrived at the house. Other than Great Aunt Georgie and her very unfriendly neighbor, the widow Black. The latter didn't count since she had spoken the entire time, not even allowing him a word in edgewise.

"Hmph," said Dom, which Henri took to mean that the feeling was not shared.

"And his name?" asked Henri, pointing to the other fly on the windowpane.

"That is my nephew, one of my thousands of nephews actually. You can just call him Nephew. Not unlike you, he is anxious to get outside and get a breath of fresh air. I have told him to settle down and wait for the rain to pass, but…young people. Always so impatient."

This last comment could have come straight out of the mouth of Great Aunt Georgie. "So you and Great Aunt Georgie are friends?"

"Yes, of course, boy! Why ever would we not be friends? We share this house, don't we?"

"Oh yes. It's just that most people don't seem to like flies in their house," Henri said reasonably.

"A common prejudice I fear to say, but Great Aunt Georgie is an enlightened woman, a great friend of the insect world, and really a very accomplished collector," said Dom.

"Oh, the buttons? Are you interested in them?" asked Henri.

"No, not particularly, although my friends and I have often posed for them," Dom answered with a note of pride in his voice.

"What do you mean?" asked Henri.

"Well, haven't you noticed? Most of the buttons in the library have been made by Great Aunt Georgie. She's quite a marvelous painter and sculptor. Nearly all the buttons there have insect themes. From time to time she asks me to pose or to invite one of my six-legged associates in for a sitting."

"Oh," said Henri, making a mental note to look at the buttons in the library the first opportunity he got. He put his head down on the windowsill, and from this vantage point, he had a better view of Dom standing on the folded newspaper. Henri gazed at his immense fly eyes and asked again, "Dom, can you read?"

"Of course!" said Dom. "Quite a fascinating article this is too! It's news from the Orient."

"Oh, the tiger article?" asked Henri.

"No, no. Below that. Look at this. It's news from the insect world." Dom pointed with a leg to a small headline that read "Vicious New Species of Insect Reported."

Dom read aloud: "From the highlands across Southeast Asia come numerous reports of a man-eating insect. The species, Latin name *Goliathus hercules*, is said to be nearly twelve inches long, with jaws capable of snapping off a man's finger."

"Barbaric!" exclaimed Dom. "This is the kind of individual that gives the rest of the insect world a bad name."

"Funny, I read the tiger article. I don't remember the one about the insect," said Henri.

"Never underestimate a creature because of its size, Henri. Though this one is huge by six-legged standards!" said Dom. The fly sighed—or at least it sounded like a sigh—and looked up at the other fly buzzing at the glass. "The rain has stopped. Nephew! You're getting on my nerves. Come along, you fool. You'll never get out that way. Follow me!"

And with that, Dom launched himself in the air and headed for the door. Nephew quickly followed him. Henri jumped up to pursue them, but they flew so fast from Henri's room, through the hallway, and down the stairs that it was quite impossible to keep up.

"Wait!" called Henri, but the flies paid him no heed.

Henri raced down the stairs in time to see the two black specks disappear down the hallway and toward the kitchen, where he knew the window was always open at least a crack.

"I'll never find them outside!" said Henri to himself. He sat down on the bottom step dejectedly. *What a strange day*, he thought.

The longer Henri sat on the step, the less sure he was that his conversation with Dom had really happened. In stories, people talked to animals like rabbits and dormice. Or they conversed with the various fairy folk, but not flies!

Henri got up and walked into the library. On one side were shelves from floor to ceiling filled with leather-bound books. Henri had browsed through them during his first week there, but the titles had not tempted him at all; however, now he noticed a book entitled *Insect Transformations*. He pulled it out to take upstairs for bedtime reading.

On the other side of the room were Aunt Georgie's many buttons. In fact, they covered all the walls of the rambling house from top to bottom, with only a few spaces left for painted portraits of long-dead relatives. However, Henri's room didn't have any buttons. He supposed that Great Aunt Georgie didn't completely trust him with her precious collection of buttons— her darlings, as she called them. If a small child were to enter the house, he or she probably would have thought it was built of buttons!

Henri considered leaning back against the wall in the hall so that the buttons would leave round impressions on his back. He would be spotted like a leopard. However, Henri didn't do it for two reasons: firstly, there was no one to see his leopard spots other than Great Aunt Georgie, and secondly, if she caught him, there would be big trouble.

There had already been trouble. She had found him one day in the living room touching a button that looked like it had a huge diamond in the middle.

"Look with your eyes, not your hands!" Great Aunt Georgie had said. His punishment was to sit and polish a half-dozen newly acquired cricket cage buttons. At first, cricket cage buttons sounded like fun. Henri thought he could go out, catch some crickets, then put them in the buttons and wear them on his coat. He would have friendly, chirping companions as he explored the fields of Woodland Farm.

However, it turned out that cricket cage buttons were actually miniature impressions of the ornate metal structures that the Chinese used to house their favorite cricket singers. It would have been quite impossible to fit a fly in one, let alone a cricket. So it was indeed a punishment to sit with the tin of Brasso, meticulously polishing each of the six buttons to Great Aunt Georgie's satisfaction.

It may sound like Great Aunt Georgie was a mean old lady. She was not at all, and Henri knew that. The problem was that when someone is a hundred years old—or at least looks like she is—and another person is ten years old, they don't have a lot in common.

Great Aunt Georgie felt sorry for Henri, so far from home and all by himself. The reason he was staying with Great Aunt Georgie was quite serious and sad. More than a year had passed since Henri's father had been heard from. No letters, no post-cards, no telegrams and no news. Henri's mother's inquiries to the offices of the East India Company produced no results beyond this reply:

> *Dear Madam,*
>
> *Due to the limited shipping traffic between British Malaya and England, it is not uncommon to have several months without communication from agents stationed in the colony. We are confident that everything is fine and that in time you will receive news. At present, it is best if you remain calm and patient.*
>
> *Yours truly,*
> *Richard Huntington*
> *Manager, London Office*
> *British East India Company*

This was hardly a satisfactory response, and Henri's mother could remain neither calm nor patient. She'd become more dis-traught with each passing week, and although Henri tried to assure her that everything was fine, he didn't believe it himself.

When they had not heard from his father for more than a year, Henri's mother announced with forced gaiety in her voice that Henri would be taking an exciting holiday to America.

"America?" Henri had replied. "I don't want to go to America!"

"Didn't you say that you would like to travel and see the world?" asked Henri's mother.

"Yes, but by myself? And only to stay with an aged great aunt I don't even know?"

"Well, don't you think it will be fun to live on a farm?"

"Well, yes, but…why don't you come along too?"

"No. I must stay in London and wait for news from Father."

Despite all his pleading, a steamer trunk was purchased. In addition, his mother bought him a diary to keep a record of his adventure. It was blue with gilt decoration and lettering that said *Five-Year Diary*. Five years! Was he to be away for five years?

"No, no," said his mother. It just *happened* to be a five-year diary.

"When will I come home?" Henri pleaded.

"When we have news from your father," she replied, and

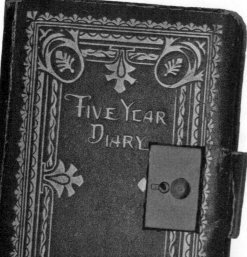

Henri could not bear to say anything, for it seemed quite possible that they would never hear from his father again, and he didn't want to cry. He threw the diary in his trunk and vowed that he would not write a single word in it because he knew that if he did, it would be like counting the days, and time always goes slower when you do that.

So that is how Henri came to stay with an aged great aunt that he didn't even know at Woodland Farm in the house of buttons. Henri never developed more than a passing interest in buttons, but what he did like about them was that each came with a story. He liked to sit by the fire at night and listen to Great Aunt Georgie tell him about how she came to acquire a particular button or the exotic place the button came from. It was at this time that Henri and Great Aunt Georgie had perfect understanding, for she was the storyteller and he was the eager listener.

One of Great Aunt Georgie's most precious buttons was from the coat worn by the Duke of Wellington in the Battle of Waterloo.

"Henri, are you familiar with the Battle of Waterloo?" she asked him one night at dinner.

"Yes, Great Aunt Georgie. We studied it at school."

"Tell me about it, please."

Henri gulped. He felt like he was taking an oral history exam. What would happen if he failed? "The Duke of Wellington was the commander of the English forces that battled Napoleon Bonaparte's troops. Um…the French suffered a humiliating defeat, and that brought an end to Bonaparte's career." Henri hoped she didn't want more detail because at the moment he could think of nothing to add.

"Indeed," said Great Aunt Georgie with a pleased look upon her face. "It just so happens that my godfather was a friend of the Duke of Wellington, and upon the Duke's death, the button came into his possession. He very graciously presented it to me on my sixteenth birthday. I already had quite a collection back then. Collecting is a passion, Henri. It can be a passion that connects a person with history and adventure!"

As Henri now gazed at the buttons upon the library wall, he saw they were just as Dom had said; they all had insects upon them—painted, sculpted, and embossed. There was even one that appeared to be a portrait of Dom himself (although it was hard to be sure since, to the average person, most flies look alike). All in all, he had no reason to doubt he'd had a conversation with Dom.

Henri headed to his room with *Insect Transformations* tucked under his arm. He lay on his bed and leafed through the book, taking special interest in a section titled "Order *Diptera*."

Henri learned that an order is like a family. Everything in nature is ordered. Well, not exactly. It was ordered by a man named Carl Linnaeus so that minerals, plants, animals, and insects could be identified by certain signs. Flies are in the order *Diptera*. In Latin *di* means "two" and *ptera* means "wing." Two wings! Flies have two wings! Finally those boring old Latin lessons were useful! At school everyone hated Latin class but now Henri had a real use, and he applied it to Dom's name. Dom had introduced himself as *Musca domestica*. *Domestica* means "house" in Latin, so Dom was a housefly!

Henri was engrossed in the book when Great Aunt Georgie called him for dinner. He was out of his room and down the stairs in a flash. It had just occurred to him that perhaps there was more than one talking fly in the world. Maybe his family had a special talent—they could talk to flies! Hmm…that didn't sound very impressive. Well, maybe they could talk to other insects too. He needed to ask Great Aunt Georgie about it.

Henri slowed to a walk as he entered the dining room, for he knew that if he didn't, he would be reprimanded with something like, "You are not a pig coming to the trough, Henri."

Henri waited until dinner was served, and finally he asked, "Aunt Georgie, do you know Dom?"

"What's that? Have I seen a palm? Well, many years ago when I was a girl. I think it was in the Mediterranean—Italy, perhaps. Why ever do you ask?"

"No, no, not a palm," Henri said, and Great Aunt Georgie picked up her ear trumpet and put it to her ear. In a louder voice, Henri repeated, "I said, do you know Dom? He's a fly."

"Is there any *pie*? Henri, we're having raspberry sherbet tonight. We can have pie tomorrow."

Henri decided to try again. "Um, Great Aunt Georgie, have you ever spoken to a housefly?"

"Have I seen a mouse die? I don't think so, dear. Why are you thinking about such sad and horrible things?"

This was why Henri usually let her do most of the talking. It made for less confusion. He decided to try one last time.

"Great Aunt Georgie, I was in the library today and I noticed a lot of buttons had insects on them. Did you make them?"

"Yes, I did," said Great Aunt Georgie. "Do you like them?"

not surprised that suddenly Great Aunt could hear him clearly and answered his question without hesitation. He had realized in his first week with Great Aunt Georgie that she had selective hearing. That is, she heard what she wanted to hear. If the subject was of interest, then her hearing was perfect. If it was not, then she pulled out the ear trumpet and nothing was accomplished.

"Yes, I like them very much," replied Henri. "I didn't know you were an artist. In fact, the insects look so realistic, I wondered if you actually drew from nature."

"Well, I am out in the garden quite a bit, and I try to sketch when the weather is fine, but lately it's been so dreary. I haven't done anything in quite some time," said Great Aunt Georgie.

Here was Henri's opportunity. "Perhaps you could work inside if the insects came to you," said Henri.

"I beg your pardon," said Great Aunt Georgie, and she held up the ear trumpet. Henri knew that he would get no further information from her.

He looked down at his plate. The food was cold now. He pushed it around to make it look like he had eaten some and then said, "Great Aunt Georgie, I have had enough. May I be excused?"

"Yes, dear," said Great Aunt Georgie, who seemed to have heard his request perfectly. "By the way, tomorrow we will make a visit to the widow Black. You will want to put on your smartest clothes and look like a proper young man."

Inwardly, Henri shuddered. Mrs. Black lived on Dutch Elm Farm to the west of Great Aunt Georgie's place, which made her their closest neighbor. The first time Henri met Mrs. Black was when she had appeared unannounced within hours of his arrival at Woodland Farm.

Great Aunt Georgie had been napping when the knock at the front door came. Feeling like a guest himself, Henri rather tentatively opened the door to greet the visitor. He'd been completely taken aback to see a woman over six feet tall, dressed entirely in black. She towered over him with her face set in a disapproving grimace, and Henri felt frozen to the spot. Her eyes scanned him up and down as if she were looking deep inside to the core of his being, and that was very unsettling.

"Close your mouth, or are you trying to catch flies?" she'd said. "You must be On-*ree* Bell. Quite an exotic name for such a sickly and pale-looking boy. London air, I suppose. Not healthy." She paused, looked directly into his face and said, "I am Mrs. Agatha Black. I live on the farm next door. I don't want to catch you climbing my fences or stealing my apples. If I do, there will be consequences. Welcome to America."

19

Then she'd turned and, with long strides, crossed the lawn and disappeared from view. Henri was left with only the swishing sound of her stiff skirt.

Further visits from Mrs. Black were no better than the first. Always she examined him from head to toe with her penetrating, somewhat beady eyes and seemed to find him wanting. Mrs. Black had a beak-like nose and black hair that was pulled back so tight that it seemed to have made the features of her face taut.

Henri rose slowly from the table, wishing he could come down with a case of chicken pox overnight. Any illness would be better than visiting Mrs. Black! He gave a little cough that he hoped might sound like the start of cold.

"Yes, Great Aunt Georgie," he said.

WIDOW BLACK

The following morning, Henri arose. He felt tired and cranky. At breakfast Henri ate very little and gave a few more coughs.

"I think I might be coming down with something," said Henri. "Perhaps I should stay home. I wouldn't want to make anyone else sick."

Great Aunt Georgie looked worried. She stood up and felt his forehead. "You don't feel hot," she said. "Maybe you just need a little fresh air. You were cooped up inside all day yesterday. I'm sure the walk will do you good."

Far too quickly, they reached the wrought iron fence that surrounded Mrs. Black's house and gardens. Henri opened the gate and motioned for Great Aunt Georgie to enter. Henri followed, and closing the gate, he thought that it was surprising that a ferocious guard dog had not greeted them since Mrs. Black seemed to so value her privacy.

"I'll ring the bell," said Great Aunt Georgie once they stood at the front door. Henri nodded and looked up at the tall brick house. At every window, the drapes were pulled. On the rooftop was a widow's walk—a kind of railed platform from which a person would have a spectacular view of the countryside. Henri let escape a snort as he thought of Agatha Black up there looking through binoculars, waiting, watching for anyone who dared pick an apple from one of her trees!

When Mrs. Black opened the door, she was dressed in one of her crisp black dresses, and had a look on her face like she had just swallowed a spoonful of bitter cod-liver oil. She forced the corners of her mouth up into an awkward smile.

"Georgiana. How lovely. I've been looking forward to your visit," said Mrs. Black with as much enthusiasm as Henri might have shown toward a Latin examination.

"It's kind of you to ask us, Agatha," Great Aunt Georgie replied. "Henri and I have been looking forward to it as well."

Ha! thought Henri. He would rather take the Latin exam than be here right now.

Mrs. Black's gaze turned to him now. "Ah. On-*ree*."

"It's pronounced *Henry*," he replied with a boldness he had not expected of himself.

"But it is spelled in the French way and the correct pronunciation is On-*ree*," countered Mrs. Black.

Before Henri could respond, Great Aunt Georgie stretched out her arm and wrapped it around Henri's shoulders, drawing him close to her. As she did so, she gave him a swift kick. "Your French pronunciation is excellent, Agatha," she said in an overloud voice. "It is obvious you've spent time on the Continent. Perhaps you can tell us about it over tea."

Looking slightly surprised, Mrs. Black apparently decided to let the matter drop. "Do come in," she said. Mrs. Black stepped aside to allow Henri and Great Aunt Georgie to enter and then firmly shut the door.

They stood in what Henri supposed was a hallway. It was so dark he really couldn't tell. Mrs. Black had all the drapes drawn; no natural light illuminated the space. It took a moment or two before his eyes adjusted and he started to make out the shapes of furniture and pictures on the wall. Mrs. Black ushered them into the parlor, where the tea service sat on a table.

"You're in for an interesting visit, Henri," said Great Aunt Georgie. "Agatha is a collector too!"

"What do you collect, Mrs. Black?" Henri asked politely.

Mrs. Black seemed to pause as if she was thinking about the question. "Seeds" she finally said.

Taking a seat beside Great Aunt Georgie on a very hard sofa, Henri gazed around the room. Seeds placed in patterns, landscapes, and portraits were framed and hung upon the walls. Larger pods were displayed in curio cabinets that stood on either side of the fireplace. A small selection of books all about seeds sat on the end table.

Clearly Mrs. Black was a learned woman, and although he disliked her, he was curious. "I would be very interested to learn how you began collecting seeds. Some of these are enormous. You must have traveled to some very exotic places."

"My dear departed husband, Dr. Black, was a great scientist—a zoologist. His specialty was bats, and the two of us traveled the world as he pursued his research. I began my collection during those trips. I accompanied him on all his expeditions."

"That must have been nice for him," said Henri.

Mrs. Black gave him a cutting look. "I should think so, but my job was not just to see to his comfort. I was his collaborator!" She stood up and walked over to the pile of books that Henri had noticed earlier. She pulled out a slim volume and passed it to Henri. In gilt upon the black cloth cover was the title, *A Monograph of the Bats of South America*, and in smaller type, "by Dr. Alistair Black, illustrated by Mrs. Agatha Black."

Henri gently opened the book to the title page, which showed bats swooping out of the jungle into the sky, a full moon illuminating their silhouettes. Leafing through the pages, Henri saw delicate, expert illustrations showing comparisons between various bats' ears, their heads, their teeth, and their wingspans, down to their clawed feet. There were other pictures in which a bat's belly had been sliced open to show the internal organs.

"Agatha, you are a marvel. The detail! Really, you are quite an exceptional artist," gushed Great Aunt Georgie with what Henri recognized was a kind of nervous intensity. How very strange. What was bothering her? The corners of Mrs. Black's mouth turned up as she attempted what Henri supposed was a smile. He doubted that she had much practice in smiling, as it looked more like she was showing her teeth to the dentist than sincerely showing her gratitude.

24

"Thank you, Georgiana. You are too kind."

"Did you draw these all from life?" Henri glanced down at the page, and upon seeing a bat sliced open from its neck to abdomen, rephrased his question. "I mean, from actual specimens?"

"Of course," Mrs. Black replied curtly. "I am a keen observer. I notice the details."

So fixed was her gaze upon Henri that he felt anxious. He wondered just what she was noticing about him at this very moment. Uncomfortable, Henri quickly glanced back down at the book and immediately regretted it, for upon closer examination his eyes beheld the sliced-open bat, its eyes wild with pain and fright, its heart exposed. Quickly, he shut the book and gave an involuntary shiver.

"I watch patiently and then I learn," said Mrs. Black with a dry chuckle.

"Just as all good scientists do. Patience is a virtue. Curiosity is another admirable quality in an inquiring mind," remarked Great Aunt Georgie in an anxious twitter. "Agatha, I must excuse myself and visit the powder room," she said, putting down her teacup.

Mrs. Black watched Great Aunt Georgie leave the room and turned her gaze back upon Henri. "What do you think, On-*ree*? Is curiosity a desirable characteristic?"

Suddenly the room seemed very hot. A bead of sweat trickled down his neck. He was sure this was a trick question. Reluctantly, he said, "I suppose that it is."

"Just don't forget, curiosity killed the cat!" She gave a raspy cackle. "You know your great aunt has been such a help to me with my collection. I trust she will continue to assist me. Thanks to her, I have expanded my collection of seeds to include scientifically related areas. Perhaps you will help me too?"

Help Mrs. Black with her collection? What a very odd request. "I wish I could help you," Henri said politely. "But I don't know anything about seeds."

"Well, perhaps you know about related fields?" Mrs. Black suggested slyly. "Such as insects?"

Henri felt tense as he thought of his conversation with Dom the fly. Avoiding the question, Henri said, "I didn't know that seeds and insects were related."

"Surely at school you studied that insects pollinate flowers, which in turn produce seeds?" asked Mrs. Black in an almost accusatory tone.

"Yes I did. I…I hadn't thought about it that way."

Rising, Mrs. Black said, "Come with me, On-*ree*. I have something I want to show you."

She led him to an adjoining room. It must have once been a conservatory for indoor plants, but the glass panes had all been painted black. There was no natural light. Henri could hear something that sounded a bit like the fluttering of birds' wings. Mrs. Black lit a candle.

Henri saw a shelf holding two glass tanks, like the kind people kept tropical fish in; but these contained no water. Mrs. Black ushered him closer as she held up the candle to the first tank. Staring out with unblinking eyes was a very large red, black, and white striped snake. Henri felt his heart speed up, and he took several quick breaths. The snake in turn seemed to stick out its forked tongue in time to the rise and fall of Henri's chest.

"It's a king snake," announced Mrs. Black.

Moving to the other case, she held up the light and said, "And this is a monitor lizard." Henri faced a gigantic lizard that was clearly too big for its tank. He had no desire to move nearer.

"And up here"—Mrs. Black raised her arm to a wire cage mounted on the wall—"are my beauties!" She said this with genuine enthusiasm. The fluttering sound stopped as the light hit the cage, and Henri could see at least six bats dangling from the top by their feet. "It's feeding time. I thought you would like to help me," Mrs. Black said. She grinned—or perhaps it was a sneer, Henri couldn't tell.

"Um…thank you for the opportunity. What do they eat?" he inquired.

"Their diet varies. Rodents, frogs, insects. Today they will be dining on crickets." Mrs. Black picked up a small wire box and pulled out a wriggling, very unwilling cricket. She moved to the lizard's tank. She was about to drop the cricket in when Henri heard a noise. It sounded like high-pitched wailing.

"Do you hear something?" asked Henri.

"No," said Mrs. Black as she dropped the cricket in. A second later, the sound was gone. Henri looked at the lizard in time to see it suck the cricket's last leg into its mouth, like a person slurping a length of spaghetti (not Henri, of course, since that was considered poor dinner table etiquette).

27

"Ready to give it a try?"

Henri moved forward and Mrs. Black dropped a struggling cricket into his hand. He quickly cupped his other hand over it so it could not escape.

The creature thrashed about in desperation, seeming well aware of its fate. Again Henri heard the high-pitched wail. "I hear it again! Someone's crying," said Henri. "Maybe it's Great Aunt Georgie. Perhaps she's fallen!"

"I don't know what you're talking about, On-*ree*. I hear nothing. Now, go ahead and drop that cricket in." Henri turned toward the tank, but the wailing was becoming even louder. The fluttering of the cricket in his hands sent tremors up his arms, and he realized that he could feel the insect's fear. "Do it!" commanded Mrs. Black.

Henri looked at Mrs. Black, blinked, and then felt himself falling. Suddenly everything went black.

THE ESCAPE

Henri opened his eyes. He was lying in his bed at Woodland Farm. Something wet and cold was on his forehead. He reached up and touched it. "Ouch!" It must have been a compress and underneath it was a very large bump. His head hurt! Just then Henri felt a tickle on his hand.

"Good. You're awake at last." Henri looked down to see a fly sitting on his hand.

"Dom?"

"The one and only! At your service."

Though it hurt, Henri couldn't help but smile because, after all, how could a fly be the one and only? And how could Dom possibly be of any help? Actually, he might be able to answer some questions. "What happened? Why am I here?"

"As I understand it, you fainted and cracked your head hard on the floor during your visit to Mrs. Black's house this morning."

"Oh yes. I remember. I was in the reptile room."

"Yes, apparently Mrs. Black thinks you fainted because you were afraid of a lizard."

"I was not afraid!" said Henri, sitting bolt upright in his rage. He instantly regretted it. His head ached and he felt woozy. Slowly he lay back down.

"Take it easy!

"I was not afraid," Henri firmly reiterated.

"Of course not. Good for you. Now me? I would be afraid because lizards have long tongues and excellent tongue-eye co-ordination. They'd pick me off in half a second and swallow me whole, not even bothering to see if I tasted good. Any insect in their right mind stays away from the Black house."

"The last thing I remember, someone was screaming, and then everything went dark," said Henri.

"Are you sure it wasn't you screaming?" asked Dom.

"Yes, I'm sure!" responded Henri, annoyed.

"Touchy, touchy. Well, since you don't seem to be in a very good mood, I won't linger here."

"Ugh!" mumbled Henri. It was true that he wasn't in a good humor. He rolled over on his side and closed his eyes.

When Henri awoke next, Great Aunt Georgie was sitting at the foot of his bed.

"Oh, Henri! I've been so worried! You told me you weren't well yesterday. I should have listened to you. You slept all through the afternoon and night. I feared you would never wake up again."

Henri sat up and felt his forehead. He could feel a trace of a bump, but his head was clear. "Aunt Georgie, I feel fine. I'm going to get up."

After much protest, Great Aunt Georgie allowed Henri to get up, but she insisted on helping him down the stairs to the dining room. She served him a cup of tea and bowl of porridge— "something soft," as she said. Henri felt amused. He'd hit his forehead, not lost his teeth!

After breakfast Henri declared that he was going outside. Alone. "Fresh air will be good for me."

Only after he promised to be back in one hour did Great Aunt Georgie at last agree. "Invalids should spend a little time outdoors but mustn't do anything to exert themselves."

"I am not an invalid!" exclaimed Henri in a voice loud enough that even Great Aunt Georgie could hear.

"Well, perhaps not, but you don't want to become one!"

Henri stomped out of the house. The garden backed onto a field that perhaps had been cultivated with crops at one time, but at present was a tangle of weeds, tall grass, and wild-flowers. The boundary of garden and field was marked by a white picket fence. Henri passed through the gate in the middle. He liked the abrupt change from the ordered garden to the chaos of the field. Henri started to run, heading for the creek that meandered lazily at the foot of the field.

He took off his socks and shoes at the creek and sat on the

bank and dipped his feet into the cool water. He thought about the last two days and how odd they had been. On two occasions now he had spoken with a fly! Or had he? Maybe the bump to his head had made him confused. Perhaps he was imagining the whole thing.

Henri sat, deep in thought. Around him on the bank, in the grass, and up in the trees, insects were chirping. It was a symphony of sound! The high-pitched squeal of cicadas was interrupted by the lower bass chirps of crickets.

Henri listened and slowly realized it was not just sound, but voices. Cicadas were entreating one another with calls of "I'm over here, I'm over here." And "Come closer, come closer, come closer." It seemed they never said anything just once. Over and over again he heard the beseeching calls. Meanwhile the crickets seemed to hum single words. "Careful, careful!" and "warning, warning!" Perhaps the crickets were warning their friends about him?

He was uncomfortable and a bit afraid. Henri realized he was not alone. There were hundreds, maybe thousands of other creatures here, and he could hear them. He could *understand* them! And then, just as suddenly as he had felt fearful, Henri felt excited. It was as if a haze had been lifted from his eyes and he could see properly. The whole riverbank was alive!

Now he understood that the sound he had heard the day before at Mrs. Black's house was the sound of a cricket, crying and begging for its life. Instantly Henri tensed. He realized that if he shifted his body, he might well hurt someone or something.

He felt like an elephant or "a bull in a china shop" as Great Aunt Georgie probably would have said.

Slowly and carefully, Henri stood up. Then, with a great leap over an anthill, he raced back to the house, socks and shoes in hand, to tell Great Aunt Georgie of his discovery!

Henri ran into the house, full of excitement and out of breath. He dropped his socks and muddy shoes by the back door. As he walked along the hallway, the polka dotted walls of buttons gleamed in the sun. He had come to think of the buttons as being a bit like books in a library. Henri could point to one, and Great Aunt Georgie would tell a story. He passed the black pearl button that had adorned a Japanese emperor's robe and then the turquoise button that came from deepest, darkest Peru. It was supposed to be lucky because it was believed that turquoise had healing powers that strengthened the wearer against sickness and disease.

"Henri, is that you?"

Henri stopped. He heard the ominous rustling of a stiff silk dress. He turned toward the parlor to see Great Aunt Georgie and...Mrs. Black. Henri shuddered, but he pulled himself together and said, "Good day, Great Aunt Georgie and Mrs. Black."

All thoughts of telling Great Aunt Georgie of his discovery left his mind. Instinctively Henri knew he did not want to share this information with Mrs. Black. There she sat in the armchair near the fireplace in her starched black dress. Her hair was drawn tightly back and wrapped in a bun that most unusually was held together with a very long, ornate hatpin. Despite the warm weather, she wore black gloves, and her bony hands made Henri think of claws. The rustling of the black silk dress seemed to create a charged, brittle energy in the room, and without knowing why, Henri felt nervous. He always felt nervous under her disapproving stare—guilty without having done anything.

Aunt Georgie smiled and Henri felt encouraged. "How are you today, Mrs. Black?"

"Adequate, I suppose," she said, which was followed by a little cough. "But the more pertinent question is: how are you? That was a nasty fall yesterday. I didn't mean to frighten you."

"I wasn't frightened!" Henri said a little too forcefully.

"Of course not," she replied with a knowing smile to Great Aunt Georgie. Then she turned to Henri and her eyes fell to his bare feet.

"Mrs. Black is taking refuge from her home while the farm workers burn off the straw stubble in the fields," Great Aunt Georgie said. "The wind shifted, and all the smoke is blowing directly at her house. Very bad for the respiratory system and constitution. And, of course, she was concerned about you, Henri." The latter was said in such a way that Henri knew he was being warned to remain polite to Mrs. Black.

"Surely you should be recuperating in bed," Mrs. Black pointed out. "What have you been up to? Where are your socks and shoes?"

Henri gulped. He was starting to feel guilty, but then he

reminded himself that he hadn't done anything wrong. The problem was, he had a secret, and Mrs. Black seemed to suspect that he was hiding something. Though it made no sense at all, Henri decided to lie. He knew it was wrong, but he couldn't stop himself. "I just polished my shoes, and I didn't want to scuff them up, so I took them off."

Great Aunt Georgie smiled as if he were the perfect little gentleman she was training him to be, but Mrs. Black said, "I see. Are you going to a fancy gathering this evening?"

"Well, no. I just like them shiny." Henri knew that didn't sound very convincing, but if he could just get out of the room quickly…

"And your socks? Was it necessary to remove them?" inquired Mrs. Black.

"Um…well, I didn't want to get any polish on them. So I took them off…" He could feel his face getting hot.

"I see. Do you normally shine your shoes when they are on your feet?" But before Henri could dig himself a deeper hole, Mrs. Black said, "Georgiana, I do not think this young man is telling the truth. I believe he has been over at my farm. I expect he is interested in the fire. Well, let me tell you that if you play with fire, you will get burned!"

"I haven't been at your farm!" exclaimed Henri. "I didn't even know you were burning the fields." He knew that he shouldn't speak to Mrs. Black that way.

"Hmm," Mrs. Black said calmly, but her face showed a frightening fierceness that Henri had never seen before. She moved her arms up to adjust her bun, pulling out the sharp hatpin. For a moment it was poised in the air, and it occurred to Henri that she could easily throw it at him like a dart. "Well, why don't we see those nice shiny shoes then, On-*ree*?"

Now he was cooked! With little choice, Henri silently turned and exited the room. As soon as he was in the hallway, he started to run, pausing only for a moment to pull the turquoise button off the wall.

He was really in trouble now. Mrs. Black would see his muddy, scuffed shoes and accuse him of trespassing on her farm and who knew what else? Great Aunt Georgie would be furious that he had taken the turquoise button, but he was scared and figured he needed its special powers. Anything to protect himself from Mrs. Black!

Henri reached the back door and found his less-than-shiny shoes. He picked them up, and in a moment he was running, but not back to the parlor.

Out the door, through the garden, and down to the creek Henri ran. He sat down dejectedly on the bank. He had escaped Mrs. Black for the moment, but what was he going to do? What would Great Aunt Georgie do? Maybe she would send him home to London. That would be good, but he didn't want to hurt her feelings. Really, she had been nice to him. Why were Great Aunt Georgie and Mrs. Black friends? They weren't alike at all. It felt as if Mrs. Black was always lurking about.

As Henri stared down at the water, deep in thought, his ears once again began to distinguish the voices of insects. The cicadas and crickets still cried out their entreaties, but there were other high-pitched voices coming from upstream. A moment later, a small boat came into sight. It was a toy boat, really; one that looked like it had been discarded or forgotten by a child long ago. The paint was peeling, and it looked less than seaworthy. The occupants were a motley assortment of insects—a grasshopper, a stick insect, a couple of mantises, and some kind of beetle.

One of the mantises called out instructions: "Keep her steady, more to the right. Hey, tell us what's coming up in front." The beetle was weeping inconsolably and the grasshopper seemed to be trying to calm her. "Don't worry, I'm sure they got out. There was enough time," he said.

"I wanted to go back, but the flames…It was so hot, and the smoke, it made my eyes water." She started to cry again as the boat drifted out of earshot. Henri got up and started walking along the bank of the creek so he could follow the boat. He realized that these insects must be refugees from Mrs. Black's fields. The fire merely inconvenienced Mrs. Black with its blowing smoke, but it was endangering the lives of these creatures and destroying their homes.

Henri continued to follow the boat. Up ahead he could see that the stream ran faster. Surely the boat would capsize in the rapids. He needed to help them! But how? At the same time, the stick insect lookout saw the rapids too. "Reverse course, reverse course!" he yelled. There was screaming and the sound of confused voices from the boat. They managed to escape the fire. Now Henri had to help them through this latest peril. He didn't want to scare them, though. He called out, "Watch out! There are rapids ahead! Your boat is too light. It will capsize!"

The beetle cried out, "It's a man, an insect killer, following us!" And she wept harder, her head bent low. The other insects said, "What? What's he saying?"

"No, no! I want to help you. You need ballast, something to make the boat heavier so that it won't tip over." Suddenly Henri had a burst of inspiration. From his pocket he pulled out the turquoise button. Taking careful aim, he threw the button as gently as he could toward the boat. "This will help! Duck!" he yelled.

The little group saw the button flying toward them and scurried for cover. *Plop!* It landed in the center of the boat, causing it to tip dangerously back and forth. Everyone held on for dear life. As the boat steadied, the grasshopper that was the oarsman called, "That's it! I've got more control now!" And with that, the little boat entered the rapids. Henri ran along the riverbank, to where the water became less turbulent, and waited. He couldn't see them among the rocks and white water. Suddenly, they catapulted forward, spit out by the angry water. They were a little wet, but everyone was accounted for.

"Hooray!" called Henri. "You made it!"

The mantis standing on his long hind legs seemed to be saluting. "Thank you, young sir! We shall never forget this act of kindness. What is your name?"

"Henri. Henri Bell."

"Henri Bell, I salute you! We will tell our grandchildren of the human who saved us on this dreadful day."

"Keep the button. It's lucky. You may need it!" called Henri. He stopped. He could go no farther along the bank. Dense bushes blocked his way. "Good-bye," called Henri. "Good luck!"

"Good-bye, Henri Bell!" they all called, and Henri stayed until they disappeared from sight down the stream.

NEWS FROM HOME

Henri returned to his spot near the anthill on the riverbank. There was a frantic urgency in the air. The crew of the small boat was not the only one trying to escape the fire. The sun was obscured by clouds of insects taking to the air. There was a shrill, loud call repeated again and again by a multitude of voices. "Fly, fly, fly for your life!"

Henri felt drawn to the fray, but he knew it would be unwise to set foot upon Mrs. Black's property. Anyway, what could he do? The insects in the air probably had a much better view than he did from the ground. No, there was nothing more he could do, and he was very sad.

Slowly he turned from the moving sky of insects and trudged back toward Great Aunt Georgie's house. He decided to take the long way around and go through the front door. As he walked into the front hall, he noticed that the parlor was empty. He saw Great Aunt Georgie had brought in the mail, and he walked over to the hall table. There was a postcard from his mother! Underneath was a flyer that he supposed Great Aunt Georgie had put in the pile, thinking it would be of interest to him.

Stealthily, Henri climbed up the stairs, avoiding any creaking steps, and scurried as fast as he could to his room, silently shutting the door. He threw himself down on the bed and breathed a deep sigh of relief. So far, so good. No Mrs. Black. Then he heard a voice.

"Ah, you have returned! My boy, I must say congratulations! What a stroke of brilliance!"

"Who's that?" said Henri in a nervous voice. "Dom?"

"Yes, over here on the windowsill."

Henri sat up and moved to the chair by the window. Dom paced back and forth—like any fly—but it was clear he was tremendously excited.

"What are you talking about, Dom?" asked Henri.

"I'm talking about the way you helped those insects, the ones on the boat! You saved their lives. You're the talk of the town, the savior of the stream, the angel of all insects, the conqueror of the creek, the hero of the—"

"OK, enough!" said Henri, though he felt a warm glow. "How do you even know about this?"

"I was there—you know, 'a fly on the wall,' so to speak. I overheard your Great Aunt Georgie when she discovered you were missing, so I decided to check on your whereabouts. She was worried about you."

"Is she angry? What about Mrs. Black? Is she still here?"

"Georgie's not angry, just worried. As to Mrs. Black, she has left. Henri, you must not tangle with Agatha Black."

"Why?" asked Henri, his tone more anxious than he'd meant it to sound.

"It's not for me to say. Anyway, time to get ready!"

"Ready? Ready for what?"

"Visitors!" announced Dom cheerily.

"What, more visitors? Oh no. Mrs. Black was more than enough for one day."

"Not human visitors; your admirers from the insect world. News travels fast. We're all abuzz, no pun intended."

"What? Dom, I only managed to help the insects in the boat. I couldn't do anything for the rest of them," Henri said sadly.

"Yes, but that's more than any human has ever done before! Henri, today men set fire to fields and destroyed the homes of thousands, callously and with no consideration whatsoever. No one came to their aid but you. It is a first. All we have ever known from man is brutality—the swat of a newspaper, the poison vapors of a spray, the crushing blow of a boot heel, a pin through the heart just to add an insect to someone's collection." The last two words were said with extreme distaste. "You have shown a kindness unheard of, and when you told those boaters to keep the lucky button…you wished them well. You wanted them to survive!"

"Of course I did!" said Henri with both surprise and indignation.

"Not everyone feels as you do, Henri. It makes you special, that and the fact that you are also able to communicate with us six-legged folk. Now, tidy yourself up. They'll be here soon!"

Imagine being told to clean yourself up by a fly! Henri walked over to his dresser and picked up his comb. As he sat down on the bed and began to smooth down his hair, he picked up the postcard from his mother. On the front was a picture of her in a traveling suit, and she appeared to be boarding a train. Henri turned the card over and read:

Dearest Henri,

Don't I look smart in my new traveling outfit? As you can see, I am about to embark on a journey. Sadly, there is still no news of Father, and thus I have decided that I must take matters into my own hands. To-night I am boarding the Orient Express to start my journey overland to Malaya and search for Father myself. Darling, do not worry. I will write regularly and let you know of my progress. I am sure you understand that I could not sit still any longer. Meanwhile, I know you are safe and sound with dear Great Aunt Georgie. Please be a good boy for her.

All my love,

Mother XOXO

Henri's eyes smarted, and he could feel the tears welling up. Never had he felt so alone. There had been comfort in imagining Mother back in London in their cozy apartment, but now she was setting out into to the unknown. Father had disappeared. Perhaps his mother would too.

But before Henri could sink into the true depths of misery, Dom's voice brought him back. "They're here! They're here! Open the window!"

No sooner had he opened the window and stepped back than Henri heard the remarkable sound of the gentle beating of two thousand butterfly wings. They flooded in through the window, a dazzling kaleidoscope of color. They fluttered about in groups that seemed like breaking waves upon the air. The butterflies were followed by darting dragonflies, which appeared to be carrying out prescribed military-like formations. Their jewel-like colors caught the light, and they glistened like glass ornaments. Next, singing insects—crickets, grasshoppers, and cicadas—entered the room. Their movements were less graceful, but their joyous voices sang, "Henri Bell, Henri Bell." A miscellaneous assortment of wasps, bees, flies, beetles, and mantises brought up the rear. It was clear that some of the latter weren't very good fliers. They seemed to barely land on the windowsill, and then staggered around for several moments before they moved on to let others in. Henri was touched by the tremendous effort they had made to come to him.

At last, everyone had arrived and found a place on a piece of furniture or upon the wall. Every surface was covered, and individual insects were indistinguishable from one another. They made little movements, a slight flutter of wings or a shifting of feet. The result was that the whole room—walls and furniture—appeared to be breathing like a pair of lungs, in and out, in and out. The room was so quiet, you could have heard a pin drop. "Say something!" came Dom's familiar voice.

"Um…thank you very much for coming."

"Hooray for Henri Bell! Hip, hip, hooray! Hip, hip, hooray! Hip, hip, hooray!" chorused the insects.

As the insects cheered, Henri's mind raced. He was only ten years old, so he didn't have much public speaking experience. It seemed that he should say something. Something like how he was just doing his duty and he would work hard to right any misunderstandings between humans and the insect world. Wait a minute! He sounded like a politician! Before Henri had time to give it further thought, there was a knock on the door.

"Places, everyone! Evasive action!" cried Dom's voice.

Suddenly there was a rush of color and a soft brushing against Henri's cheek. It seemed as if every insect in the room was in the air. It wasn't possible for them all to exit the window at once.

Then Henri realized they were not leaving. They were adjusting their positions, moving into formations that created patterns upon the wall. They were creating living wallpaper! Anyone who had not entered the room before would assume he had highly colored and geometric wallpaper. It was amazing! It was fantastic camouflage!

When he was certain everyone was in place, Henri went to the door and opened it. There stood Great Aunt Georgie with a very worried look on her face.

MAESTRO ANTONIO'S AMAZING FLYING FLEA CIRCUS

Uh, hello, Great Aunt Georgie," Henri said awkwardly.

"Henri, I was greatly worried when you did not return to the parlor in a timely manner," began Great Aunt Georgie. "May I come in?

"Uh...yes." Henri took a deep breath and opened the door wider to let Great Aunt Georgie pass.

"Really Henri, I do wish you would ask my permission before pasting up fancy papers on your wall. I don't mind if you make it your own, but it would be polite to ask before doing so."

"Yes, Great Aunt Georgie. I'm sorry. I'll take them down today," and Henri couldn't help smiling a little.

"Henri, let me come to the point. Today you were very rude to Mrs. Black."

The smile on Henri's face disappeared, and he dropped his head. "I'm sorry, Aunt Georgie. It's just that...she doesn't seem to like me very much, and…" Thoughts of the harm Mrs. Black had caused the insect world that day churned in his head. Looking up he said, "And really I don't like her. She's…she's evil!"

Great Aunt Georgie did not look surprised, nor did she seem offended. "Henri, if you don't have anything nice to say, then it is best you say nothing at all." Great Aunt Georgie gave a deep sigh, and then, appearing to summon all the strength that her frail body could muster, she said, "I am in debt to Mrs. Black for a number of reasons, mainly financial ones. It's very distasteful to talk about money, and I do not wish to burden you with my problems. You can see the farm is not what it used to be, and then there's the family home back in England. It's a lot to keep up, and, well…it is not appropriate that I go into detail, but I implore you, do not anger Mrs. Black, or there may be some unpleasant consequences for both of us."

These last words were almost a cry, and Henri was afraid and sorry to have caused Great Aunt Georgie such anguish. "Yes, Great Aunt Georgie," and he rose from his seat and gave her a hug that he hoped would comfort her.

"Thank you, Henri. Now, did you pick up your mail?"

"Yes, I did. There was a postcard from Mother. She's leaving London. She's going to search for Father. I wish she had taken me along," he said sadly, and then quickly added, "Not that I'm not having a good time here with you, but I miss my family."

"Of course you do. Henri, I know it's hard not to worry about your father and now your mother too! Well, she's doing what she thinks is best. In the meantime you and I will have to wait for news, but I'm sure we can find some amusing distractions. By the way, did you see the handbill?"

"Oh, I haven't read it yet."

"Mrs. Black gave it to me. The circus has come to town! She thought you might enjoy it. Would you like to go this afternoon?"

"That would be great!" exclaimed Henri. He had imagined he was going to be punished, but instead he was going to the circus!

Once Great Aunt Georgie had left the room, Henri turned back to his very colorfully patterned walls. None of the insects had moved yet. As everyone was quiet, it seemed like a good time to resume his speech.

"Um, as I said before, thank you all very much for coming. I wish I could have done more to help today." Henri paused, unsure of what more to say. At last he said, "I would like you all to know that the insect world has a friend in Henri Bell. If I can ever be of service, please do not hesitate to call."

His words brought a tremendous chorus of chirps, high-pitched calls, and a general flapping of wings from the assembled insects. The sound was a bit like a dozen bottle rockets going off in his room, and Henri was relieved that Great Aunt Georgie was hard of hearing.

When the noise died down, Henri heard Dom's voice. "Unfortunately it's time for you all to be on your way. I know you would like Henri to recount his courageous act in detail, but he has many urgent matters to attend to. Such is the busy life of our hero, you know!"

There was a collective sigh of disappointment, and gradually the insects alighted from the walls. Henri stood near the window, nodding and waving good-bye as they slowly made their way out. When almost all were gone, Dom rose into the air from his position on the windowsill, alighting on Henri's nose.

"Don't do that!" complained Henri. "I'll go cross-eyed looking at you."

With a huff, Dom rose again and Henri felt a tickle on his hand. He raised it up and held his hand close to his face to stare into Dom's huge eyes. "What urgent matter needs my attention?" Henri asked.

"Nothing," replied Dom. "Do you want to go the circus today?"

"Well, yes," said Henri.

"They would have kept you here for hours telling and retelling the story. It's the most exciting thing that's ever happened in our world, but I'm a domesticated housefly, somewhat more worldly than my brethren," said Dom with pride. "I know the ways of humans. You're a boy. You want to go to the circus, and you deserve to have some fun. And to be honest, they have work to do. There are larvae to nurture, queens to feed, and colonies to defend. So you see, it was time for them to go home."

Henri smiled. "Thanks, Dom. You're a...a..." Henri struggled to find the right words. Finally he said, "You're a very civilized fly."

"Why, thank you, Henri!"

A short time later, Great Aunt Georgie and Henri stood at the entrance to the circus grounds. The big top rose beyond them, its red and yellow stripes dominating the view. Around it were smaller tents with banners advertising the amusements held within, such as *World's Tallest Man*, *Fernando the Fire-Eater*, and, most intriguing, *Human Caterpillar*.

"Now here's a little pocket money for you, Henri. I know you won't want to join me. I'm going to have my tea leaves read and perhaps visit the crystal ball reader." Henri could not believe how excited Great Aunt Georgie sounded, almost like a little girl. "I will meet you at the big top for the three o'clock show. Now, be careful of con men and those games of chance. They're rigged! Now, off you go, and have fun!"

And with that, Great Aunt Georgie turned and, with surprising speed for someone nearly a hundred years old, headed for the tent with a brightly colored banner reading, *The Future Foretold by Madame Noir*.

For no particular reason other than to enjoy his independence, Henri decided to go the opposite way. He passed on the *World's Strongest Man* and the *Elastic Woman*. Looking closely at the poster for the *Human Caterpillar*, Henri decided the figure looked more like the *Human Sausage*. Finally, Henri came to a tent with a banner announcing *Maestro Antonio's Amazing Flying Flea Circus*.

The announcer wore a bowler hat and had a very extravagant and neatly trimmed handlebar mustache. He entreated the crowd: "Step right up, ladies and gentlemen, to see the world's smallest circus. Yes, indeed! Those pesky vermin are trainable! See the flying flea on the trapeze! Be amazed at the balance of the lovely Sophia as she stays atop a rolling ball! Think fleas aren't strong? Well, watch our mightiest, tiniest flea strongman as he pulls ten times his own weight. How much to see this once in a lifetime show? Only five cents! What a bargain! Step right up!"

Henri looked up at the large painted banner that showed fleas being ridden as if they were racehorses or show jumpers. They had men upon their backs! Unless the world's tiniest man was in the circus too, this was a joke. Still, Henri was intrigued. He paid his five cents and went in.

The tent was dark, except for a center spotlight under which was a glass case surrounded by spectators' seats. Henri was the first to arrive, so he took a chair directly in front. Inside the case was a miniature three-ring circus. In one ring sat a ball painted yellow with a red star. In another was a tiny, golden Roman-style chariot. In the last ring was a cannon! Above it all hung the trapeze.

Henri sat gazing at the apparatus, wondering how the fleas could possibly perform tricks. Slowly he realized he could hear a dull murmuring. Henri looked around the tent, but other than a rather mangy-looking dog in one corner, no one was there. Henri soon realized the sound was coming from inside the glass case, so he stood up and looked down inside it. He could see some little black specks moving. Of course! Those were the fleas! To the right of the circus case was a large magnifying glass with a horn handle. Henri picked it up and looked through it. Now he could see clearly. There were perhaps four fleas moving about in a disconsolate way. Still another was hanging upside down from the trapeze, and one more was tethered to the chariot.

"I'm starving!" said the flea in the ring with the ball. "I haven't had a good meal in days."

"We're all hungry, and talking about it just makes it worse," said a flea standing on top of the cannon. "I have a headache after hitting my head on the glass wall three times already today. I'm so tired of the maestro yelling too. I can't understand a word he says no matter how loud he shouts. Anyway, I know he's unhappy because he wants me to hit the target."

Henri looked across to the glass wall opposite the cannon and saw a painted target of red and yellow with a little gold bell over it. "Ha-ha, he's not going to be happy until you go splat in the bull's-eye!" This came from the flea hanging upside down on the trapeze. "Anyway, no one's got it worse than me. I'm glued up here! All day, upside down. You think that's a picnic?"

"Did someone say picnic?" asked the first hungry flea.

"Quiet, everyone! Complaining is not helping. We have to make a plan, an escape plan." This came from a flea that appeared to be wearing a pink tutu. He was becoming engrossed in their conversation when a few more people entered the tent. Henri quickly put down the magnifying glass and sat back down in his seat.

Soon the tent had filled up, and the man with the bowler hat and handlebar mustache walked to the center and announced, "Ladies and gentlemen, I am Maestro Antonio. Welcome to my amazing flying flea circus! Now gather around." The audience members were handed opera glasses to have a better view of the performers.

"Let the show begin!" the maestro announced. "Our first act is a show of great balance and grace. Please welcome the lovely Sophia!" And with that, the ringmaster set the ball spinning. With tweezers, he picked up Sophia and dropped her on the ball. It was not difficult for the flea to stay on the ball while it spun, but as it slowed down, the ball began to roll. Sophia managed to stay atop the ball, but Henri would hardly have called it graceful. She lurched back and forth, and when the ball came to a stop, she toppled off and lay still. There was a smattering of applause.

Maestro Antonio began his next introduction. "And now meet Giovanni, the strongest flea in the world! Giovanni will pull this chariot, which weighs more than ten times his weight, around the ring. Imagine, folks, if we could harness all the fleas in the world! Make them useful rather than a pesky nuisance. Giddy up, Giovanni!"

Maestro Antonio snapped his fingers, and Henri was sure that he saw him drop some kind of powder into the back of the chariot. Immediately, Giovanni sprang into action and began to pull the chariot wildly. Around and around the flea went at top speed. The crowd cheered him on, although eventually the shouts died down and it was clear that everyone wondered when he would stop. Finally, there was a spectacular crash. Giovanni had managed to pull the chariot up and over the ring and straight into the side of the glass case. The chariot lay on its side, the hapless flea on its back with its feet in the air.

"Uh…moving along. Cast your eyes above the ring to see the

duo of Maria and Leonardo perform on the trapeze." The flea glued to the trapeze bar started to swing. "Watch as Maria jumps and is caught in midair by the debonair Leonardo, the flying flea!" Back and forth Leonardo went in the air. With a point of the maestro's finger, Maria the flea in the tutu leaped into the air…and missed the outstretched legs of Leonardo!

"No problem, no problem!" said Maestro Antonio. "Let's try that again shall we?" Maria staggered from the ground—there was no safety net—and took her place again. This time the trick went off without any mishap. There was a short round of applause. "And now, upon my cue, that daredevil Maria will drop down and into this tea cup." The maestro placed a tiny cup from a children's tea set into the middle ring. "And here we go! One, two, and three!" With a point of his finger, Maria dropped from Leonardo's grasp and…missed the cup!

"Boo!" someone shouted. The audience seemed to be getting a bit bored.

"And now for our grand finale!" said Maestro Antonio, wiping some sweat off his brow. "Cast you eyes to ring three. Fabio will be shot out of the cannon, hit the target, and ring the bell! Are you ready Fabio?"

It didn't appear that Fabio was ready because he tried his best to evade the tweezers in the maestro's hand. At last he was captured and stuffed into the cannon. Striking a match and holding it to the miniature cannon's fuse, Maestro Antonio counted, "Three, two, one!" There was a pop, like the sound of a toy cap gun. Henri couldn't see if the flea had been shot out, nor did he hear the bell ring. There were some puzzled whispers and then someone yelled, "There he is! On the trapeze!" Sure enough, Fabio was in the air holding on to Leonardo. With a wave of his hand, the maestro magically set the trapeze moving again and said, "No bull's eye, but not bad!" The tone of his voice, though, indicated that he was not particularly pleased.

"And that concludes our show. I trust you enjoyed yourself and do tell your friends to come and see Maestro Antonio's Amazing Flying Flea Circus! Thank you."

There was a bit of polite clapping, and the audience rose from their seats. Henri hung back, and when everyone had left he walked up to the maestro. "Maestro Antonio, my name is Henri Bell, and I think I can help you to make your flea circus the greatest show on earth!"

FLEA WRANGLER

Maestro Antonio looked down at Henri. "Really. Do tell." His voice was not sarcastic or unkind. He sounded amused, like an uncle humoring a young child.

"Well, your show was good." Henri thought it best to start with a compliment. "But I think it could be a lot better."

"That's an understatement," said the maestro. "That cursed flea and the chariot. He always goes crazy. He just doesn't know when to stop. And Fabio! How hard is it to be shot out of a cannon?"

Quite hard, thought Henri.

"Why can't he hit the target? He's pointed right at it," continued Maestro Antonio.

"Um…exactly," said Henri. "The show needs some fine-tuning, and I can do that for you."

"What's your name, boy?" asked the ringmaster.

"Henri. Henri Bell."

"Henri, you're not from around here. I can tell by your accent. You have some experience with a flea circus?"

"Actually, yes. Yes, I do. Back in London, I worked with my family's flea circus." Obviously it was a lie, but Henri knew he had only one chance to convince Maestro Antonio.

"Really?" The maestro suddenly looked much more interested. "What brings you to America, Henri?"

"Um…I'm living with my great aunt on a farm near here."

"An orphan. Sorry to hear that, kid. That's tough, really tough."

Henri decided not to correct him. He looked down, pretending to be sad, and said, "Yes, I miss my family, and I'd really like to be back in the circus business. It would remind me of home." What a whopping lie! "Maestro, if you'll just give me half an hour with your fleas, I'll prove how useful I can be to you."

Maestro Antonio looked down at him, sizing him up. Finally he said, "OK, kid. Just promise me you won't kill any of them. They're my bread and butter. No fleas, no show." Henri nodded. "OK, I'm going out to sell tickets for the next show. Good luck," and he turned and headed out of the tent.

Henri turned to the glass case. What to do first? Introduce himself, of course. He knew the fleas were hungry, so feeding them might well earn their loyalty. But he knew that fleas consume just one thing: blood! He looked over at the mangy, sleeping dog. No, he couldn't do that.

Henri picked up the magnifying glass and cleared his throat. "Um…excuse me." All the fleas looked up and into his face. They looked terrified.

"It's not the maestro. Who is this new one? I can understand what he's saying!"

"Shut up, everyone," said Maria, the flea in the tutu.

"Ah, sorry to bother you. I'm Henri, and I have come to help Maestro Antonio with the circus. I know you're all hungry. I overheard you talking before."

"You got that right!" said the hungry flea, Sophia.

Taking a small penknife out of his pocket, Henri opened it and raised it to his thumb. He made a small cut. It didn't hurt much. He actually had to squeeze it to make the blood come out. He let three drops hit the floor of the center ring. There was a frantic scurrying as the fleas ran toward the blood.

"It smells so delicious!" said Sophia, and she jumped to the edge of the pool of blood and stuck her head in. Fabio the flea cannonball leaped into the center ring, joining her, and the two of them gorged themselves. Maria approached and daintily took a sip. Out of the shadows, another flea approached. It moved very slowly and Henri realized that this one had not performed in the show.

"Come on. Move out of the way and let Umberto have a bit," Maria said to the other fleas.

"What about me?!"

"And me!"

Henri moved the magnifying glass around and realized he had forgotten about Leonardo, glued to the trapeze, and Giovanni, still attached to the chariot lying on its side.

"Oh, sorry!" said Henri. "Don't be afraid. I'm just going to pick up the chariot and put it back in place. Let me know if I'm hurting you at all."

Slowly, Henri put his hand down into the case and carefully picked it up. He gently placed the chariot, with Giovanni still tethered to and dangling off of it, back in the center ring. As he did so there was a great deal of coughing and sputtering.

"Hey, get that stuff out of here!" one of the fleas said.

"Yeah, it's making me nauseous!"

"What?" said Henri.

"The chariot!" And then Henri remembered that the maestro had dropped a powdery substance into it. Taking out his handkerchief, Henri wetted a corner with his tongue and wiped out the back of the chariot.

"Ahhh…What a relief," Henri heard a flea say.

"Yes, yes. Much better."

Henri brought the handkerchief up to his nose and smelled it. Camphor! It was used in mothballs, and fleas must not like it. That would be why Giovanni charged around like a mad flea trying to get away from the strong odor.

"Hey, I'm still hungry up here!"

"Oh, sorry. Are you ready?" and Henri positioned his thumb above Leonardo and squeezed a large drop of blood onto the flea's head.

"Bon appétit," said Henri.

The blood was quickly consumed, and all the fleas looked up expectantly at Henri.

"I'm sorry," said Henri. "I know it wasn't much, but if you're too full, you'll feel sleepy and won't want to perform."

"I don't want to perform regardless of whether I'm hungry or not! I like the quiet life, but it's not like I have a choice. Perform or get squished," said Sophia.

"Oh," said Henri. "Well, perhaps in the future we can have auditions? The fleas that perform will be here of their own free will. What do you think? Also, I think we can tie a good performance to a reward of a good meal. How about that?"

There was a general murmuring of agreement.

"OK. Now we have to get ready for the next show. There was some sloppy work in the last one."

"That's not our fault," said Maria. "It's the maestro. His timing is off. When he points his camphor-smelling finger at me, I have to jump. I just can't stand the smell. If he let me choose when to jump, Leonardo would always catch me and I'd land in the teacup every time. And by the way, Leonardo is a girl. Maybe she should be called Liora?"

"Maria is right," said Giovanni. "The camphor is choking me. If you just give me a cue, I'll pull the stupid chariot. Just let me know how many times to go around, and I'll do it. Anything but the camphor."

"OK, so noted. Leonardo shall now be known as Liora, and no more camphor," said Henri. "Sophia, I'm impressed with how you stay on the ball, but could you do it a bit more gracefully?"

"How graceful would you be if you had just been spun around a hundred times at high speed? It's everything I can do not to vomit all over the stupid ball. I'm strong. I could roll it myself if the maestro let me. And the tweezers! I don't like the tweezers. They squish me."

"Well, I'll speak to him about it," said Henri. "Now, Fabio, can you make a bit more of an effort to hit the target?"

"Effort! It's not about effort. It's physics, boy! The cannon's got a curve. The idiot maestro points it directly at the target, but it shoots me to the left every time. Just point the cannon a bit more to the right, and I'll ring that bell."

"OK!" said Henri. "Excuse me." He moved the cannon as the flea suggested.

"All right, the show's going to be starting soon, and I know we have a lot more to talk about, but we'll do that after. Remember: put on a good show, and there'll be a tasty meal for everyone!"

The fleas nodded in agreement. "Oh, I almost forgot," said Henri. "What about Umberto? Is he in the show?"

"He used to ride the trapeze, but when he was pulled down, the glue left two of his legs up there," said Maria. He's managed to hide from the maestro; otherwise he would have been squished a long time ago."

"Ouch! Sorry to hear that, Umberto. Do you think you could ride in the chariot and wave a flag?"

"I could do that if someone helped me up," came Umberto's feeble voice. They helped Umberto up, and Maria ripped a piece off her tutu and gave it to him for a flag.

"Great!" said Henri. "Places, everyone!"

The audience for the next show was slowly trickling in. Henri knew he must have a word with Maestro Antonio before it began.

"Sir, we're ready," Henri whispered. "Just one thing: I'll need to be standing beside you to speak to the—" Quickly Henri thought better of telling the ringmaster that he was speaking to the fleas. That would sound crazy. "I mean, to prompt the fleas."

Maestro Antonio frowned and then said, "It won't look very good. I'm the ringmaster, after all."

"You can say I'm your assistant," replied Henri with a smile.

"Well, fine, but you'll need a costume. Don't have one right now, but I'll get you a hat."

He found a round, flat-topped hat, the kind Henri had seen an organ grinder's monkey wear. He felt foolish, but this was not the time to be fussy about his appearance.

"One other thing," said Henri. "You won't need to use any camphor. Don't worry! Everything will be fine."

Maestro Antonio didn't look happy. He shrugged, but he said nothing.

"Ladies and gentlemen, welcome to Maestro Antonio's Amazing Flying Flea Circus. I am Maestro Antonio, and this is my assistant Hen— I mean, Enrico!"

"Take a bow," whispered the maestro.

Henri took a deep bow, holding on to his hat so it wouldn't fall off. Maestro Antonio began to introduce the graceful and lovely Sophia. Henri leaned over and said, "OK, Sophia! Your turn!"

Sophia leaped onto the ball and began rolling it with masterly control. Frontward, backward, sideways, and around the ring. Maestro Antonio, who had been about to pick up the tweezers, looked shocked. Then, in his booming voice, he said, "How's that, ladies and gentlemen?" and the audience went wild with applause. Henri leaned down and said, "Good job! Can you finish it up with something a little special?"

"You bet!" said Sophia. She brought the ball to a stop, and with a flurry of her legs, set it spinning. Then, with a great leap, she sprung up in the air, did a flip, and landed on the still-spinning ball. The audience clapped and yelled, "Bravo, bravo!"

Giovanni was up next. On cue, he began to pull the chariot around the ring. Henri had told him ten laps would be good enough. As he whizzed around the ring, Henri said to the audience, "Not only does he pull ten times his own weight, but take a look: he has a passenger. The Great Umberto is waving a flag at you!"

The spectators focused their opera glasses, and up went a cheer. Henri looked at Maestro Antonio, who smiled and whispered back, "Good job, kid, but I do all the announcing."

"OK," whispered Henri. "Then tell them that Sophia has just jumped on too," for she was now waving madly from the chariot next to Umberto.

The former Leonardo—now Liora—and Maria's act went off without a hitch. Maria landed in the teacup and crawled up to the rim to wave to the crowd. Fabio hit the target and the bell rang. There was a big round of applause, and when the show ended, Henri overheard people saying that it was the best act they had seen at the circus.

"Well, I don't know how you did it," Maestro Antonio said

when the tent was empty, "but you turned this flea circus around. Henri, I would like to offer you a job. How about room and board and a dollar per week? I'll throw in the costume too. Do you think your aunt would let you?"

"Wow!" said Henri. "Sure, I think Great Aunt Georgie won't mind."

"Well, ask her. I don't want anyone accusing me of kidnapping you. The circus will be leaving town at nine o'clock tonight. If you're coming, I'll expect you back here this evening."

"Right!" said Henri. "Thank you, sir."

AMBASSADOR TO
THE INSECT WORLD

Before he left the tent, Henri, true to his word, squeezed out three more drops of blood for the ravenous fleas on the circus floor. Another drop went into the waiting mouth of Liora on the trapeze. He congratulated everyone on a job well done and told them he had to go home and pack his bag. They would have to bumble through two more performances without him, but he had asked Maestro Antonio to knock on the glass, which would be Sophia's cue to start the show.

Then Henri stuffed the hat Maestro Antonio had given him into his coat pocket and exited the tent. It was only two o'clock. There was still another hour before he was to meet Great Aunt Georgie but he had no intention of making this rendezvous with her. Instead Henri quickly walked the two miles back to the house alone hoping he wouldn't meet anyone he knew and certainly not Great Aunt Georgie.

As he walked, he thought about the adventure he was about to embark upon. He could ask Great Aunt Georgie for her permission to join the circus but he felt quite sure she would never agree. His mother had found that she couldn't sit still and wait for news of Father—well, neither could he! Maybe once he was on the road he could find his way to Asia too and help somehow.

The days at Woodland Farm had been dull until three days ago when he first conversed with Dom. Now he knew he had a calling, a gift. His ability to understand and speak to insects was his ticket to an exciting journey and maybe a little collecting!

The house was silent. Quickly Henri went upstairs and gathered his belongings. He gently packed his tattered postcards from Father and almost as an afterthought, he threw in the five-year diary. Lastly, it seemed like a good idea to borrow the *Insect Transformations* book.

Henri put the bag in the hallway and went down to library, where he took out paper and a pencil from Great Aunt Georgie's desk. Then he pulled from his pocket the hat Maestro Antonio had given him. There was a small brass button on the hat, and Henri cut it off with his penknife. He picked up the pencil and began to write.

Dear Great Aunt Georgie,

Thank you very much for looking after me. I have been offered a job with Maestro Antonio's Flying Flea Circus, and I have decided to take it. I will be his assistant. You see, I can talk to insects. I think you can too.

I know it is better if I leave because I keep getting into trouble with Mrs. Black, and I don't want to upset you and cause problems. Please don't worry about me. I will be fine. I will write to you often and let you know how I am and what I am doing. Maybe I will have some adventures and stories to tell, just like you!

Aunt Georgie, I didn't tell you before, but I took the turquoise button, the one from Peru. I didn't mean to steal it. I was just going to borrow it, but I had to give it away to someone who needed it more than me. I'm really sorry. I know it means a lot to you. I can't replace it, but here is a new button for your collection. It's from my circus costume. Maybe one day I'll be famous. I don't know what I'll be. Maybe one of those people who studies insects—an entomologist, I think they are called.

Your loving nephew,
Henri Bell

Henri left the note and the button on the bedside table in his room. He looked around the room and found Dom on the windowsill.

"Dom!" said Henri. "I'm really glad to see you. I'm leaving."

"So I see," said Dom.

"I have a job with the flea circus. They need me because I can talk to the fleas!"

"I don't like fleas," said Dom. "They're bloodsuckers."

"You know, for a fly, you're very judgmental. It's not their fault they drink blood," said Henri.

"To each his own," responded Dom. "So, you're setting out on an adventure. I knew you would. It was only a matter of time. Where are you going?"

"Oh, I didn't ask where the circus is heading," said Henri. "You know, Dom, it feels good to just be going somewhere, anywhere.

I feel like I'm doing something, getting closer to my father, not just sitting around and waiting like a helpless little boy."

"I understand. He's in Southeast Asia, right? You know that beast, what's its name? Oh yes, *Goliathus hercules*! That's where he resides. Maybe you can meet him. If anyone can do it, you can. You've got the special ability." And Henri was sure the fly winked, if such a thing were possible.

"Dom, you're right! Maybe I'll be a famous entomologist who captures *Goliathus hercules*!"

"Good to set goals," said Dom. "But go easy on him, Henri. He's probably not as terrible as he's made out to be."

"I could never again kill an insect," Henri said. As soon as he said it, he realized it was as much a confession as a proclamation. It was then that Henri noticed a butterfly, a moth, and a green beetle all lying dead on the windowsill.

"What happened here?" asked Henri.

"Hmmm…Overexcitement from your hero's welcome, I think." Henri looked upset. "Not to worry, not to worry. It was their time. They died happy," Dom reassured.

Henri had a thought. "Dom, do you think it would be OK if I kept them?"

"You mean like in a collection?" said Dom.

"Well, sort of, but not in a disrespectful way. I told you I will never kill another insect, but if it dies naturally…Dom, I have a chance to educate humans. I think my job in life is to be an ambassador—an ambassador to the insect world."

"That's an interesting idea, Henri. I hadn't thought of it that way before," said Dom. "Tell you what: I leave, I mean, I bequest my humble body to you upon my death," he said.

Henri was touched. "Thank you, Dom." He pulled out the five-year diary from his bag and tore out three pages. Then he carefully wrapped the insect bodies in the paper. He pulled out an old cigar box from under his bed containing a motley assortment of trinkets—a scratched marble, three jacks, a few bottle caps. He dumped those out on the bed, then carefully placed the shrouded bodies in the box.

A new thought had occurred to Henri. "Dom, will I see you again?"

There was a moment's hesitation, and then Dom responded, "I expect not, Henri. You see, my life is already more than half over. Compared to a human being, the life of an insect is but a fleeting moment."

Henri's face turned grave. "I'm sorry, Dom."

"No need to be sorry. When I kick the can, I will have led a full life. A fly can do that in Great Aunt Georgie's house since there are no fly swatters," Dom said jovially. "And Henri, though I may not be here when you return, my descendants will know you and welcome you because you are famous in the insect world! When you come to this house next, they will dive-bomb your ears in celebration!"

"OK, Dom! Thanks." Henri laughed. "I've got to go now." He picked up the cigar box with its precious contents and stowed it in his bag.

"I'll see you to the door," said Dom.

Henri went down the stairs and opened the front door. Something light tickled his hand, and, looking down, he saw Dom. He brought his hand up to his face, and looking directly into Dom's huge fly eyes, he said, "Good-bye, Dom."

"Good-bye, Henri, and good luck." And then Dom flew off Henri's hand and back into the house.

As Henri walked down the steps, a carriage raced by on the road, leaving a billowing cloud of dust. It was headed toward town and the circus. Although he wasn't certain, Henri thought he saw the pale, pinched face of Agatha Black looking out at him from the carriage. He hoped he was wrong.

He stopped, took a deep breath, and paused for a moment. From the trees, the flowers, the bushes, and the sky came a million voices all calling, "Good-bye, Henri Bell. Good luck."

And with that, Henri set out down the road.

PART II

"Perhaps if I had seen the fortune-teller at the circus, she would have foretold that Henri would run away, and I could have stopped him!" cried Great Aunt Georgie. She sat upon Henri's bed with his note in her hand.

"Rubbish!" said Dom the fly, standing on the windowsill in Henri's room. "Fortune-telling! Absolute rubbish—and a fly knows rubbish! Good thing she wasn't open for business so you weren't able to throw your money away. Anyway, you know he had to leave. Really, it's for the best."

"But I am responsible for him. His mother entrusted him to me, and now he's gone, run off with the circus! He's only ten years old!"

"Yes, that's true, but he is quite mature for his age. Imagine if he were an insect and ten years old. He would be the wisest, most knowledgeable of our kind!"

"Dom, you are digressing! Besides, no insect lives that long," replied Great Aunt Georgie.

"Not true! Goliathus hercules is supposed to live a very long time," said Dom in a rather know-it-all voice.

"Really, Dom! You are quite obsessed with that creature. It is  probably just a fairy tale, a monster made up to frighten disobedient children," said Great Aunt Georgie in a rather exasperated tone.

"Maybe, but I don't think so. Henri will find out if it exists," replied Dom. "He's going to become an entomologist, and he's going to seek Goliathus hercules and bring one back alive."

"Why would he put his life in danger on such a foolhardy quest? It's preposterous!" argued Great Aunt Georgie.

"The fact of the matter," said Dom, "is that he was probably in more danger when he was here on Woodland Farm than he will ever be on the road with the circus or searching for Goliathus hercules."

Great Aunt Georgie cast her eyes down. Tears slowly rolled down her cheeks. "You're right, Dom. Of course, you're right. I didn't know he had the gift. If I had, I would never have let him come here. I worry so much, but at least he will escape Agatha Black! Eventually she will find out that he is gone. When that day comes, we must deny any knowledge of his whereabouts. I will burn this note."

"Yes. Destroy any evidence," agreed Dom. "What do you think she is up to? What does she really want?"

"I'm not sure. You know, I thought I had met a kindred spirit in Agatha because she loves collecting as much as I do. She seemed like such a dear friend, and I confided in her! Every day, I regret that moment of weakness when I told her of my money troubles. When she offered to lend me money so I could save the farm, I was without any other option." She let out a sob.

"Now, now, Georgie! Don't upset yourself. You couldn't have foreseen it," Dom told her.

"I should never have revealed my ability to speak to insects. I felt so indebted to her that the least I could do was help with her seed collection. I naively thought that calling a few six-legged friends to her house would help Agatha acquire a few special seeds, perhaps those gallnuts that some wasps lay their eggs inside." Great Aunt Georgie sighed. "She fooled me at first, asking me to summon insects so she could observe their habits. But then she started collecting them—putting pins through them!"

At this, Dom shuddered.

"She told me not to be so sentimental, that it was all for science," said Great Aunt Georgie. Again and again I have been forced to use my gift to do her bidding. Any insect that responds to my call but is already in her so-called collection, she feeds to her pets. Whenever I refuse to assist her, she threatens to call in the loan, and then I will lose the farm and the family home in England!"

"Georgie, I've told you before that you needn't defend yourself to me. I know that you are a friend to the insect world no matter what. I know you have no choice. We will keep trying to think of a way to free you from her grasp!"

For a moment, they sat in thoughtful silence. It was Great Aunt Georgie who broke it. "Dom, do you think I should have admitted to Henri that I have the gift too?"

"It might have helped him understand, but I don't know. It might have frightened him too. You did what you thought was right," replied Dom.

"Yes, I was just trying to protect him from Agatha, but you know that she sensed it the moment she met him. Dom, I don't want Henri to be part of Agatha Black's collection!" and she started to cry again.

"Now, now, Georgie, don't fret. Let's go to the parlor and burn that note."

Great Aunt Georgie stood up, the note clasped in one hand and the button from Henri's hat in the other. "Yes, I must pull myself together! I wonder where I should put this button. Should it be where the turquoise button used to be?"

"It should be in a place of honor! Beside the Duke of Wellington's button, I should think."

"Of course. You are absolutely right, Dom."

"Again!" the fly said smugly.

AUDITIONS

Six months had passed since Henri had transformed himself from Henri Bell of London, England, to Enrico Bello, flea-wrangler in Maestro Antonio's Amazing Flying Flea Circus. During the day, he stood in his costume and greeted spectators entering the tent with, "*Buongiorno, signore e signori!*"

in a rather poor imitation of an Italian accent. However, no one appeared to notice he was a fake. The audience was caught up in the excitement of the circus and seemed to have checked any disbelief at the door.

"I feel a bit silly in this costume," Henri told Maestro Antonio one evening. He was convinced the maestro had purchased it from a hotel bellhop.

"The main thing is that you are not to be confused with paying customers."

"That certainly will not happen," said Henri, lowering his chin and gazing down the front of his red jacket with gold buttons to his blue trousers with gold side-stripes. He still thought he looked like a trained monkey in his hat.

"Henri, we are a sideshow act," said Maestro Antonio.

Henri had quickly learned that there was prestige in having a fancy costume. The more elaborate the costume, the more important the performer, and the most important performers were in the big top.

"Now, that's not to say that I think the big top acts are any better than us," continued Maestro Antonio. "In fact, Henri, if there were a competition today, I believe that our little show would win first prize because it's quite simply the most entertaining and novel act of the lot!" Maestro Antonio's last sentence was said in his most theatrical voice, as if he were announcing it from his ticket podium in front of the flea circus's tent.

Henri laughed and, for the moment, forgot his costume concerns, although the fact of the matter was that he would like to be respected by his circus peers. So far, they were not very welcoming. They seemed suspicious of him and made fun of his English accent. In Henri's opinion, if there was anyone to be suspicious of, it was Madame Noir, the fortune-teller, who didn't appear to socialize with any of the circus folk.

One day, curious to catch a glimpse of the mysterious seer, Henri had stealthily poked his head through the gauzy silk that draped the entrance to her tent. The tent was very dark and reeked of incense. As his eyes adjusted to the dark, he made out the figure of Madame Noir seated at a small table. Her pale face was covered with a veil and her eyes were closed. Henri was about to withdraw his head when, suddenly, Madame Noir's eyes opened, and in a low growl with a trace of a French accent, she spoke: "The crystal ball foretold that you would pay me a visit."

Henri jumped. "Sorry, wrong tent!" he muttered and ran away as fast as he could.

While Henri was unlikely to become fast friends with Madame Noir, Maestro Antonio was kind. After a few days on the road, he had told Henri to just call him Tony.

The circus moved from town to town by train. When they reached the next town, the big top was raised and the smaller tents were always set up around it in the same order and placement. There was also a daily routine. "There are six shows per day," the maestro explained. "More, if we think we have an audience. After the last show, you'll be in charge of moving the benches so we can lay out our bedrolls. All meals will be taken in the mess tent. We have a set mealtime, Henri. Don't show up earlier and don't show up later."

"Yes, Maestro Antonio, um…I mean…Tony."

Henri found that, at mealtimes, the most extraordinary and unlikely people sat together. Hope and Charity, the Siamese twins, were great friends with Gertrude the Fat Lady. Usually Henri and Maestro Antonio sat with Andre the World's Strongest Man, Herbert Kramer the Lion Tamer, and his assistant, William, more commonly known as Billy. The maestro introduced Henri to his colleagues as "Henri Bell from London, England; stage name, Enrico Bello.

"The lad comes from a fine circus family, and the innovations he has brought to my flea circus—well, really, you must come and see for yourself! Drop by anytime, and if there's a vacant seat, you are welcome to watch the show at no charge. But I must tell you that these days, it's standing room only!" the maestro bragged.

Henri felt proud, for indeed, just as Maestro Antonio said, it was he who was responsible for the flea circus's success. Ticket sales had doubled, nearly tripled. It helped that Henri was a keen observer of nature. He noticed almost immediately that the thing the fleas did best was jump. Not just little leaps but great bounds nearly one hundred times their own height. Henri wanted to capitalize on this amazing ability with an act that showed off their true talent.

Henri also knew the fleas would be happier in the circus if they were there by their own free will, so on his first full day of work, he met with them to discuss who wanted to stay and who wanted to leave.

"I've had it. I don't like the limelight," said Sophia. "Count me out."

"But Sophia, you're so good," cajoled Henri. "No one else seems to understand showmanship—I mean, showfleaship. You know how to make the act exciting! Remember that time you jumped onto the chariot with Umberto and waved to the crowd? It was great. You have natural instincts."

"Sorry, Henri. I like the show, but I don't like the pressure of performing."

Despite all his compliments, Sophia could not be persuaded to change her mind, but she did agree to stay on as trainer and choreographer. The rest of the fleas had agreed to keep performing, but auditions would have to be held to replace Sophia.

"Where can I find some recruits?" Henri asked the fleas.

No one responded. Finally, Maria said, "I'm afraid we don't know, Henri. We never leave this tent."

"Right. I'll figure something out." Henri noticed Rex, Maestro Antonio's mangy old dog who always napped in the tent. Since sleeping was all Rex appeared to do, it seemed to Henri that the least the dog could do was donate a few fleas. Carefully combing through Rex's fur, Henri managed to gather about a half-dozen fleas. He dropped them into the glass case. Right away he noticed that Rex's fleas were smaller than the performing fleas. They huddled in a corner together, cowering from the gaze of the circus fleas who seemed to find something very, very amusing. Henri felt himself turning red when he had to ask, "What's so funny?"

"Ho, ho, ha!" Fabio finally managed to say, "We can't work with them! They're so small!"

"OK, so maybe they're a little young. They have some growing to do, but I am sure they have potential," replied Henri.

Finally, Maria stepped forward and said, "Henri, they are dog fleas."

"Um, I don't mean to be rude, but aren't *you* dog fleas?"

"No! We are human fleas. That is, we generally reside on people. We are the largest type of flea there is," said Maria.

"And don't forget—the smartest!" piped up Liora. "We can't work with those simpletons."

"Oh." Henri wanted to argue that, given the opportunity, the dog fleas would probably be every bit as intelligent as human fleas, but there was little point. The dog fleas were so tiny, they would be even harder for the audience to see. As he scooped up the little group, still crowded in the corner, he realized that fleas had their own prejudices and were no more open-minded than people.

Returning the fleas to Rex seemed a bit mean, so Henri stepped out of the tent and, seeing a rat lurking near a rubbish bin, tossed the dog fleas in the rat's direction. He hoped they would find a new home in its gray fur. "Sorry," he said as he threw the fleas. "It turns out we won't be needing your services after all. Thank you. Best of luck in your future endeavors."

Where was he to get human fleas? Fortunately, or unfortunately in this case, he didn't have any himself. Henri imagined walking up to the various circus folk and asking, "Do you have any fleas you can spare?" All he was likely to get was a punch in the nose! Well, at least he could ask the maestro.

"Sir, bad news. We'll need a replacement for Sophia. Do you have any spares?"

"Fleas are hard to come by, Henri," said Maestro Antonio. "You need the right circumstances, if you know what I mean."

"Yes, I think I do, sir. It's a delicate matter."

"Exactly! Well, I have a couple. Recently received them. Shipped by a friend of mine who lives in a warmer climate. They're a little easier to get down there. Really, it is amazing how you can just post them in the mail. Just a minute."

Maestro Antonio rummaged in his trunk and then pulled out a matchbox. Henri opened it and saw two rather groggy-looking fleas.

"Now, be careful with them, Henri."

"Yes, sir, I mean…Tony." Henri took the new recruits back to the glass case and dumped them out of the matchbox. He could see they were exhausted and obviously famished. Pulling out his penknife, he made a small incision in his left thumb and squeezed out two drops of blood to feed them.

"Hello. Welcome to Maestro Antonio's Amazing Flying Flea Circus. My name is Henri and I'm, um…the trainer."

"I'm Pedro, and this is Pablo," said one of the fleas.

"Gentlemen, it's a pleasure to meet you. You have arrived at precisely the right time to audition for our world-renowned circus."

"What's an audition?" asked Pedro.

"What's a circus?" asked Pablo.

So much for human fleas being bright, thought Henri. "A circus is a performance in which fleas, in this particular case, perform tricks. An audition is a kind of test in which we see if you are good enough to perform with the troop."

"Oh," said Pedro. "No, I don't think I want an audition."

"Me neither," said Pablo. "It sounds like a lot of work."

Henri had not anticipated this response. He looked at the other fleas, but of course they were too small so he couldn't read their expressions. He decided to try another tactic. "Pedro, Pablo, did you enjoy that meal you just had?"

"Sure did. Could do with some more."

"Well, let me tell you that all working fleas receive a hearty meal after each performance. And, um…those fleas who choose not to perform are asked to leave and, of course, are not entitled to partake in the rewards that come with the job."

"Hmm…I changed my mind," said Pedro.

"Me too," said Pablo. "I want an audition."

And with that, Pablo and Pedro auditioned successfully and became the newest members of the flea circus. The veteran fleas began to show them the basics; however, Henri could not imagine either of them taking over Sophia's balancing act. As he sat watching them practice, he heard a small voice. It was Maria.

"Henri, may I offer a suggestion?" she whispered.

"Of course," said Henri.

"Well, this may not sound very good, but…generally speaking, I think that you will find that female fleas are better performers. I'm not sure why. I suppose we love to jump. I think that you'll discover that the boys are, um, a bit lazy, and I mean no disrespect to Fabio, Umberto, and Giovanni, but it's we girls who carry the show."

"Thank you, Maria. Pedro and Pablo appear to be proof of your point," Henri replied. He watched Pedro make a leap for the moving chariot and miss because his jump was too short.

BREAK A LEG

Problems! Why were there so many problems? Henri decided to write them down on paper and put them in order according to urgency:

Replace Pedro and Pablo. They are terrible!

Find something Pedro and Pablo can do without injuring themselves or anyone else.

After Henri had written these down, he realized that everything pointed to the fact that he needed not just more fleas—he needed *talented* ones.

Despite nearly a week of training, neither could balance on the ball, and one night they almost ruined the chariot act when Pablo got himself wedged in the spokes of one of the wheels. The chariot had come to a grinding halt, causing Giovanni to crash and Umberto to tumble out, head over heels. Still, as a veteran of the flea circus, Umberto did manage to make it look like a planned tumbling routine, so that the audience didn't seem to recognize that this was a complete disaster. After the show, Maestro Antonio said, "Henri, I commend you on adding a new twist to the routine, but in the future, would you inform me of any changes to the program prior to the start of the performance?"

"Yes, Tony, sorry about that," Henri replied. He had to remove the stuck Pablo from the wheel with the dreaded tweezers. Groaning, Pablo complained that his back was broken, although this clearly wasn't the case since he moved as quickly as any of the others when the blood droplet meal was served.

Pedro, on the other hand, really had managed to maim himself. Henri felt some guilt over this accident. Having sat in on a few performances in the big top, Henri had watched Herbert Kramer the Lion Tamer coax his big cats through rings of fire. Amazing! thought Henri. He decided to adapt that trick for the fleas with a set of miniature rings.

The fleas had been less than excited. "It sounds dangerous, Henri," said Maria.

"It's not, really." Henri replied. "Look, you can see for yourselves! I'll take Maria and Sophia to the big top to see the show."

They'd agreed to hide in Henri's hair with the firm understanding that they were not to bite him. And so the two fleas attended their first non-flea circus. Henri found a spot under the bleachers where he could point things out to Maria and Sophia without drawing attention to their presence. When the show began, the two fleas came out of his hair and rested upon his forehead for a better view.

The two fleas were absolutely delighted with the performance. They chortled and cheered with the rest of the crowd at the antics of the clowns, the daring of the trapeze artists, and the precision of the acrobats. They watched the lions jump through hoops of fire, and when they saw that the big cats were unharmed, they admitted to Henri that if those furry lions could manage to get through the flames unsinged, then so could they!

"We have to be brave like the lions," said Maria.

"Well, we're much better jumpers than those cats," said Sophia. "It would be easy to jump through twenty rings."

Henri laughed. "That would be great, but I don't think we'll have room for that many. I think six rings would be good, and then it should be easy enough for even Pedro and Pablo to jump through them."

"Good point," said Sophia. "Those two nincompoops!" he heard her mutter.

Just then Henri heard the sound of scuffling shoes behind him. He turned around and saw a clown watching him from a few feet away. Sophia and Maria scurried for cover in his hair as he had instructed them to do if anyone came around. He wasn't sure whether they had been fast enough, though.

"Talking to yourself?" the clown asked.

"Um, yes," stammered Henri.

"That's a sign of craziness. Are you going mad?" the clown jeered.

Henri realized first that the clown was a girl, and second, that she was probably no older than him. He didn't feel so intimidated now.

"That's right. I'm the crazy flea boy!" and he made a leap toward her.

She laughed. "So I see. And was that flea language you were speaking? I couldn't understand a word you said."

Henri had never really thought about it before. Speaking to insects came so naturally to him that he had never stopped to think that it might sound any different than English. "Well, yes, of course it was." For her amusement and also to warn the fleas, he said in what he now realized was insect talk. "Maria, Sophia, keep yourselves hidden. I think the girl may have spotted you."

And, indeed, she had. She laughed again and said, "You're weird. You really are the flea boy. Henri, right? Do you always carry your fleas around with you? It's kind of disgusting. People won't want to be around you if they know."

Henri's face fell. Drat! This was not going to improve his reputation at the circus. He decided to tell the girl the truth, though she certainly wouldn't believe him. "No, they don't usually travel on me, but we're working on a new act. The fleas are going to jump through hoops of fire just like the lions. They were scared and thought it was too dangerous, so I brought them to see the show and prove to them that they can do it too."

"Sure, sure. OK, stop it. You don't need to make up a big story."

"I knew you wouldn't believe it," Henri said. "But let me prove that I really am speaking to the fleas." To Sophia and Maria he said in insect language "Girls, you can come out now. Just walk out onto my forehead." The clown girl listened and watched him with interest. Slowly, the fleas came out, appearing

87

as two dots on his forehead. Then Henri held out his hand and said again in insect speech to them, "Would you mind jumping onto my hand?" In a second, the two fleas sat in the palm of his hand.

"Wow! I don't know how you did that. I can't believe you're really talking to them. You must be some kind of magician. Good job! I'm Robin, by the way."

"Pleased to meet you, Robin. Why don't you come by the flea circus sometime and see our show. If you come tomorrow, you can see the new rings of fire act, and then you'll know that I was telling the truth."

"You really want me to believe you, don't you?"

"Well, yes, I suppose I do, but mostly I don't want the circus folk to think I'm some dirty, flea-bitten boy."

She laughed again. "I wouldn't worry about that too much. Lots of people around here have fleas. People don't like to talk about them for obvious reasons. You know Billy, the lion tamer's assistant?" Henri nodded. "He's got fleas, for sure. I always see him scratching himself, but I don't think less of him. It's a—what do you call it? My dad told me…an occupational hazard!"

"What does that mean?" asked Henri.

"It means it's a danger, an annoyance that comes with the job. I gotta go now. I'm on again in five minutes. See you, Henri."

"OK. Bye." And as an afterthought he said, "Break a leg!"

Robin turned and smiled. "Thanks," she said and hurried off. Henri had learned in his first week that you never wish a performer good luck because if you do, they believe quite the opposite will happen. So you wish something bad on them—like breaking a leg—instead.

Returning Sophia and Maria to his hair, Henri smiled. Three good things had happened. First, the fleas were now convinced that they could jump through the rings of fire. Second, he had met Robin, who didn't seem to look down on him, and in terms of the circus hierarchy, she was far superior since she was a performer in the big top. And finally, he knew where to get fleas! Billy! But he would have to figure out a way of getting them without making Billy feel bad.

The following day, Maestro Antonio announced, "And now ladies and gentlemen, a world premiere! Let me introduce a pair of brave daredevils…Pedro and Pablo! These two will launch themselves through not one, not two, not three, no, not four, not even five, but six, yes, six rings of blazing fire. Enrico, prepare the rings!"

Henri was a little concerned. Despite his suggestion yesterday that the two fleas rehearse, both had decided that it was so easy it wasn't necessary. Henri leaned over to set the rings ablaze. As he did so, he whispered to Pedro and Pablo, "Break a leg!" Pedro looked startled but braced himself and launched his body into the air. Through the hoops he flew, but Henri could see his jump was off-center. He landed at the other end and collapsed! Pablo was up next, but it was clear he was frozen with fear. Luckily, out of nowhere, Maria jumped through the hoops and landed beyond Pedro with a flourish. The audience roared with delight. Of course, they had no idea which flea was which, so it was all the same to them. Two fleas had made it through the rings of fire.

When the show was over, Henri quickly turned his attention to Pedro. "What happened?" asked Henri.

"You told me to break a leg! I didn't break a leg. I burned one off! This is all your fault!" he howled.

"Oh, quiet!" said Sophia. "It's nobody's fault but your own, you idiot. You should have practiced the way Henri wanted you to."

"What am I going to do now?" Pedro wailed. "I'll never work again."

"The only reason you won't work is because you're so lazy!" Maria retorted.

"OK, OK, everyone. Calm down. Pedro, I am very sorry you were hurt," said Henri. "Maybe I could make you some crutches? Or an artificial leg? That's what they do for soldiers who have lost their legs in battle."

"Now, *that* I would be interested in," said Pedro.

"Henri, don't be ridiculous," said Sophia. "Pedro, you still have five good legs. You are exaggerating! Look at you, you've been moving around almost normally."

It was true. In his anger, Pedro had bounded about the circus stage just as he always did. "But the pain!" he howled. "I'll be in agony for the rest of my life."

"Tsk, tsk," said Maria. "I've seen better acting by the clowns in the big top show! Sophia is right. You're exaggerating!"

It was impossible for Henri to know if Pedro was really in pain or faking it, and so he said, "Pedro and Pablo, I am going to make arrangements for both of you to be shipped home tomorrow." And with that announcement, Henri realized that more than ever he must hold auditions.

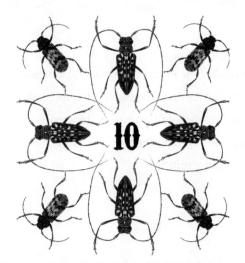

FACTS OF LIFE AND DEATH

Pedro, Pablo? Where's home for you?" asked Henri.

"Here," they replied in unison. "Not that it's a great place," said Pedro dejectedly.

"I mean, before coming to the circus, where was home?"

"Oh, now that was a nice place," said Pablo. "Wasn't it, Pedro?"

"Sure was. I remember it well. Nice juicy flesh. Blood had an outdoorsy type of taste…like a breezy summer's day by the seaside."

"Yes," continued Pablo, "but there was a hint of citrus too and such a sweet aftertaste."

"I think that his name might have been John," said Pedro.

"No, it was Jean!" said Pablo.

"I was thinking the country or the town you come from, not the person you resided on! Just forget it!" said an exasperated Henri. Based on their names, Henri had to assume that Pedro and Pablo were from Spain, or maybe Italy. He felt an obligation to them, for no matter how hopeless the two fleas had been, the fact remained that Pedro was now an amputee. Since they were unable to give Henri any better idea of where they came from, he decided to send them to Valencia, Spain. They had mentioned that their host had a taste of citrus, and Valencia oranges were famous. He put the matchbox inside a bigger box and addressed the label:

c/o General Post Office

Valencia, Spain

Henri posted the package and checked his mail but there was nothing. From time to time Great Aunt Georgie sent him letters. He had mailed her the circus's schedule so that she could send mail to the post offices in the towns where they stopped. He had been very nervous opening her first letter, fearful that she would be angry or hurt at his departure from Woodland Farm; however, quite to the contrary, she had written that she understood his need to travel and to learn as well as his desire to help in some way to find his father. "Besides," she wrote, "what child wouldn't want to join the circus? If I were ninety years younger, I would do it myself!" She did caution him to be careful, though. Still, she never mentioned Henri's ability to speak to insects. And she made no mention of Mrs. Black.

Henri decided to walk to the town library. The circus had only arrived that morning, so there would be no show until the following day. He wanted to do some reading, particularly on fleas and generally on insects. In the library, Henri gazed at the shelves of books, wondering where to begin. Eventually he selected a number of volumes and took them to a table, pulling out the paper and pencil he had brought along. He had considered bringing the five-year diary to make his notes in, but he felt miserable whenever he looked at it. It reminded him of home and his mother and father. Great Aunt Georgie forwarded him any mail that came from his mother.

Rarely did his mother send letters. He supposed that since she didn't have any good news to report, a postcard was easier and less painful to fill. They were postmarked British Malaya. As was his habit, Henri pulled out the stack of worn postcards from a canvas bag. It had grown so big that it would no longer fit in his pocket. He undid the string and read through the two most recent cards containing messages that he could practically recite.

Darling Henri,

Arrived at Father's rubber plantation today. His assistant, a local man, says that one day Father was there and the next day he was gone! No notice at all. Most unlike the man we know and love. Nonetheless I think you will agree that in some ways no news is good news! Do not give up hope.

Love as always,
Mother

My Dearest Henri,

My journey takes me to Kuala Lumpur where I will meet with many of Father's business and personal acquaintances. I expect they will be able to give me several clues as to Father's whereabouts. It is even possible that one of them will lead me directly to him. Perhaps he is in a local hospital, too ill even to write. Not to worry, I will nurse him back to health!

All my love,

Mother

Henri tied up the postcards and put them away. He sighed and then opened one of the books on fleas he had selected. As he read, he jotted down facts that he found to be of interest. He wasn't exactly sure what he would do with the information, but he knew that if he wrote it down, he would remember it better.

Fact #1: Some fleas can jump 150 times their own body length.

Having watched Maria, that didn't surprise him at all.

Fact #2: Fleas are often confused with other pests such as lice and ticks.

Funny, he never really thought of the fleas as pests. OK, maybe Pedro and Pablo, but that was because they were useless performers.

Fact #3: A female flea can lay up to two-thousand eggs during her lifetime.

Wow! He wondered if Sophia, Liora, and Maria had any desire to become parents.

Fact #4: A female flea can consume fifteen times her own body weight in blood each day.

Ugh! He didn't want to think about that. Since he had joined the circus, his blood was the sole source of nourishment for the fleas. If more were to join the troop, he would have to ask the maestro to start contributing at mealtime!

Fact #5: Fleas can live up to three months.

This was something he would have to learn to get used to. The life of an insect, no matter what kind, was short compared to his own. A mayfly lives less than twenty-four hours. A stag beetle might live up to three years. Cicada nymphs, while living underground for up to seven years, could measure their adult lives in weeks. The fleas were his friends. He was attached to them, and he would be sad when they died.

Most of the letters Henri received from Great Aunt Georgie were filled with inconsequential thoughts on the weather, a neighbor's new recipe for apple pie, and highlights of the previous Sunday's church sermon. But in one of her letters, she mentioned that she had gone into his old room to put any belongings he might have left behind into safekeeping. She'd found a few items—a marble, some jacks, and bottle caps. "Also upon the windowsill was a fly," the letter continued. "He was dead. I have carefully wrapped up his body and will save him for you. I understand you are building a collection of sorts and he is to be added to it."

She was of course letting him know of Dom's death, his friend and hers too. Her note confirmed that she too could speak to insects, for Dom must have told her to save his body for him. Henri had cried when he read the letter, but he could not share his grief with anyone at the circus. Who cries over a fly?

Henri gazed into space as he sat in the library and recalled the letter. He turned back to his flea facts.

Fact #6: Fleas can live up to one hundred days without eating.

No need to worry about Pedro and Pablo on their voyage home!

Fact #7: Fleas are known spreaders of disease. The bubonic plague, or the Black Death, was spread by fleas that lived on rats.

This was worrying. He hoped all his fleas were disease-free. Would they foam at the mouth and jump around like mad fleas? How would he be able to distinguish that from their regular jumping?

Henri decided to move on from fleas. He had one truly burning question. Why—or was it *how*—was he able to talk to insects? He went back to the shelves and discovered a book titled *Insect Communication, or My Life with Talking Beetles* by Dr. Daniel Young, Entomologist.

Henri was excited as he took notes. It turned out that Professor Young had spent his life studying *Odontotaenius disjunctus*, more commonly known as patent-leather beetles. Professor Young had found that the beetles had fourteen distinct sounds they used to communicate with one another. The professor had discovered that by mimicking the sounds, he too was able to communicate with the beetles.

Henri could barely contain himself. Perhaps Professor Young could explain why he was able to speak to insects! He would write to the professor. Henri jotted down the information from the book. Perhaps in his letter he would ask the professor about *Goliathus hercules* too.

Henri left the library and returned to the circus tents pitched in a field on the outskirts of town. It was a sunny day, and wildflowers dotted the grounds. Fluttering about the purple and pink blooms were butterflies of lemon yellow, golden yellow, yellow with orange spots, and white with yellow spots. Henri stopped to watch their joyful flight, and it occurred to him that it had been a while since he'd spoken to any insects but the fleas. He cleared his throat and said, "Good afternoon. What a beautiful day it is."

There was a twitter, and then he heard the butterflies say in unison, "Good afternoon, Henri Bell."

Henri was shocked. They knew his name! "How do you know my name?"

One of the larger yellow butterflies flew toward Henri and rested on his shoulder. "Everyone in the insect world knows of you. Your deeds are told to our children and passed from generation to generation. Our offspring are numerous, and thus the tale travels quickly. We are honored to meet the Hero of the Creek," she said.

"Oh," said Henri, feeling somewhat embarrassed. "Well, thank you. It's my honor to meet you too."

"If we may be of any service, do not hesitate to call." And with that, the butterfly took flight into the air.

"Thank you," called Henri. "Likewise, let me know if there is anything I can do for you!"

Henri heard a chorus of thank-yous and general chattering. "He's here! He's right here in our field. Oh, I must go and tell my brother. He won't want to miss this!"

Feeling even more embarrassed now, Henri turned away. Helping the little boat on the creek seemed the smallest of gestures at the time, but to the insect world, his actions were deeply significant, a kindness they had never known. He would need to work harder to be deserving of the gratitude that the insects showed him. He envisioned himself with a calling card that would read

HENRI BELL

INSECT INTERPRETER AND MEDIATOR

ALL QUESTIONS AND PROBLEMS RELATED TO THE INSECT WORLD

WILL BE CONSIDERED

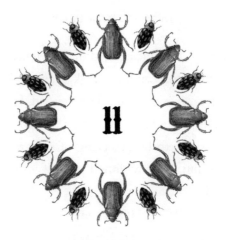

ROBIN

Two days after he had met Robin, she appeared in the flea-circus tent for the final show of the day.

The audience and the maestro had already left when Robin approached the glass case where Henri was serving the evening meal. She watched, fascinated, as he provided a blood drop into the waiting mouths of each hungry flea. Robin looked very different without her clown makeup. She had long brown hair with rather severe bangs in front. She was about the same height as Henri, maybe an inch shorter. She wasn't exactly pretty, but there was something about her that was compelling.

"That was a really good show, Henri. I don't know how you manage to get the fleas to do that stuff. It's amazing!"

"I told you. I talk to them." Henri had to ask himself why he was telling her the truth. Until he had met Robin, his instincts had told him not to confide his secret to anyone. Despite the excitement of the circus, he was lonely, and there was something about Robin's smile that made him want her to be his friend.

"Come here," said Henri. "I'll introduce you to everyone. Hold up your opera glasses so you can see them. Everyone, I would like you to meet Robin. She's a clown in the big top. She said she really enjoyed the show." One by one, he introduced Robin to the fleas, who appeared to be quite excited that someone from the "big show," as they called it, had admired their performance. Robin was quite charmed as Sophia and Maria curtseyed to her and the boys, in turn, bowed. Liora, who was still attached to the high trapeze, waved to her. (Henri was still trying to figure out how to get her down without losing her hind legs as had happened to Umberto.)

After the introductions, Robin looked up at Henri and said, "You really are speaking to them, aren't you?"

"Yes, I told you I am. Do you need more proof?"

"Yep, I do. Why don't you teach me to say hello in insect language?"

"Well, I can do that, but I've recently learned from the fleas that a more appropriate greeting in the insect world is, 'Are you hungry?' Their lives are short and they don't have time for formalities. They have very immediate needs, food being the primary one."

"So, if we were insects and I hadn't seen you for a week, I wouldn't say, 'Hello, what have you been up to up to?' I'd say, 'Are you hungry?'"

"Right! It's like learning the customs in another country," said Henri. "You'll make a good impression on them if you ask. Of course, they will say yes because they always want to eat."

"Yes, I wouldn't want to make a bad impression." She rolled her eyes. "Am I going to have to give them my blood when they say yes?"

"No, no. They'll just be happy you asked about their well-being."

"OK, teach me," Robin said.

"All right, it's like this." And Henri made a short combination of hisses and clicks.

"Um…Can you do that again?"

Henri repeated it several times, and Robin repeated it back to him. Finally he said, "I think you've got it. You have a strong accent, but I think they'll understand."

Robin stepped up to the case, and seeing Liora on the trapeze, she stammered out the series of sounds. "I think she made a sound back! I'm not quite sure."

"She did. She said she's famished," and Henri laughed. Robin beamed. She sought out each of the fleas with Henri's help and asked each of them if they were hungry. Henri translated. "They all say you're very polite. They're flattered that you asked."

"Well, I'm just going to have to believe you because I could only hear a few faint sounds, and I certainly couldn't understand."

Henri paused and then said, "I never really thought about it, but I guess I have developed really keen hearing. I could hear them perfectly." Strange, thought Henri, that he hadn't noticed that before. "Do you need more proof?"

"Yes," she said with a smile. He knew she didn't, really. She believed him already, but she was having fun.

"OK, come outside." They walked away from the circus tents to where Henri had spoken with the butterflies the day before. The butterflies were still clustered around the wild-flower blooms. Henri made a few barely perceptible sounds that Robin wouldn't have otherwise noticed at all. Rising en masse from the flowers, the butterflies began to fly in tight formation around Robin's head. She giggled as she caught sight of the colorful wings.

Henri grabbed her hand and led her to the mirrors outside the fun house tent. Robin caught a glimpse of herself and gasped to see the butterflies cir-  cling her head like a hovering wreath or halo. "They're beautiful. Oh, Henri! I look like I'm a fairy queen."

Henri laughed, sharing her delight. She started to skip around, glancing at herself in the mirrors from time to time. A crowd was starting to gather to watch Robin as she leaped about with her colorful entourage. She seemed to be testing to see if the butterflies could keep up with her. Henri decided that perhaps she was attracting a little too much attention. A faint whisper from his lips, and the butterflies stopped following Robin and began their flight back to the meadow.

Robin came back to Henri, out of breath. She grabbed his arm, saying, "That was wonderful! I looked beautiful."

He laughed. He wanted to say that she didn't need butterflies to look beautiful, but that would be embarrassing to say out loud. They headed back to the flea circus. Robin had a million questions. "When did you first learn you could speak to insects?"

"I guess it would have been about six months ago. That's when Dom—he's a fly—spoke to me."

"Was he your teacher?"

"Not exactly. I didn't need a teacher. I never studied. One day it was raining, and Dom was sitting on the windowsill reading…"

"A fly was reading! Oh come on, Henri! Stop it! How gullible do you think I am?"

"It's true! I'm not making this up. Do you want me to answer your question or not?" Henri said a little huffily.

"Pretty please. I won't interrupt anymore."

"All right," said Henri grudgingly. "So…where was I?"

"Dom was reading," said Robin quickly. "What was he reading?"

"The newspaper."

"Can all insects read, Henri?"

"You said you weren't going to interrupt anymore," Henri reminded her.

"Sorry…but can they?"

"I don't know for sure, but I think the answer is no, although they may have the ability. It's a bit like if you never went to school, would you be able to read?"

"No, I guess not," responded Robin.

"Dom lived with my Great Aunt Georgie. They're friends. She may have taught him to read. She's a bit...um, eccentric. Anyway, so I saw Dom was reading, and I asked him what he was reading about. Just like that. I didn't even think about it. I just seemed to know what to say, or how to say it...I don't know."

"Wow, that's amazing! It's also kind of peculiar. You're a little bit weird, Henri Bell, but that's OK. Everyone around here is strange, which means that you're normal. You belong here."

"Um, thanks," said Henri with a small smile.

"Can you speak to any type of insect? Do they all speak different languages?" Slowly Henri answered each of her questions. Back at the tent, he pulled out the old cigar box and showed her the insects that hadn't survived the celebration in his room after the rescue on the creek. Since then he had added a few more. Using the *Insect Transformations* book, he tried to identify their species. When he did, he made a little label with name, date, and the place they were from. If he knew their first name, he'd added that too.

"Some day I'm going to be a famous entomologist," said Henri.

"A famous what?" asked Robin.

"An entomologist. That's a scientist who studies insects."

"What makes you think you're going to be famous?"

"Because I'm going to capture *Goliathus hercules!*" A puzzled look appeared on Robin's face, so Henri elaborated. "He or she, I guess, is a mysterious insect which lives in Southeast Asia. No one has ever caught one, and a lot of people don't even believe it exists, but I do."

"Mysterious like Bigfoot?"

"I suppose, but I would hate to make that comparison because I think Bigfoot is a phony."

"Me too. I wouldn't be surprised if one day Bigfoot joins the circus!"

They both laughed. Eventually Robin began to ask Henri about his family. When he told her about his missing father and how his mother had gone to look for him, she looked very grave. "I'm so sorry, Henri. You're really brave to be so far from home and all on your own. I've never been separated from my family, not for a single night."

"Tell me about your family," said Henri.

"There's not much to tell," Robin replied. "My mother's and father's families were both in the circus business. Mom's family were high fliers—you know, trapeze artists—but Dad's were clowns. Now Mother works on costumes. I have an older sister, Eunice. She's fourteen and thinks she knows everything. My younger sister, Olive, is eight years old, and she's nothing but a pest. I'm sure you've seen them. They're clowns too."

"Do you like being a clown?"

"Never really thought about it. As soon as we could walk, we joined the act. It's not really a choice. It's, um…what do you call it? Oh yeah, an obligation. Everyone has to pull their weight." She sighed.

"Would you rather do something else?"

"Well, everyone wants to do the trapeze. They're the stars of the show. I kind of have it in my blood from my mother. I don't know…I don't think about it much 'cause it's never going to happen."

"You never know," encouraged Henri.

She gave him a half-hearted smile. "Anyway, did you know there's going to be fireworks in town tonight? Do you want to go? My family's going."

"Sure, that would be great!" Fireworks. That gave Henri an idea.

"Robin, would you be willing to help me out with something?" He knew she would say yes. She was that kind of friend.

He explained that he needed more fleas to audition. "You said Billy, the lion tamer's assistant, has fleas, but I don't want to embarrass him or hurt his feelings. Maybe we could invite him to the fireworks, and while he's distracted, I could send Sophia and Maria over to the hair on his head to see who might be interested in trying out."

"Good idea! I'll go right now and invite him. Meet you after dinner at my family's tent, OK?"

"Great. I'll see you then."

After dinner, Henri collected Sophia and Maria from the flea-circus tent. They jumped up and hid in his hair. As he walked over to Robin's tent, they demanded a full description of exactly what fireworks were. When he arrived, Henri was very pleased to see that Billy was standing with Robin's family and ready to go.

"OK, girls. On my cue…as we discussed," said Henri to Maria and Sophia, and he walked over to join the group.

MADAME NOIR

Henri could only recall having seen fireworks once in his life. It had been a long time ago—New Year's Eve in London, he thought. Tonight he was just as excited as everyone else, although he tried to stay focused on the job at hand. He sat with Robin's family on a blanket. In fact, most of the circus folk had congregated on the hill overlooking the town to watch the fireworks display.

Henri had strategically placed himself behind Billy, while Robin sat to Billy's left. She was prepared to keep up a continuous commentary during the fireworks to distract Billy, if necessary. At the blast of the first rocket, Henri would tip his head toward Billy, and Maria and Sophia would leap onto the hair of the unsuspecting boy. Then the two fleas would wander on top of Billy's head in search of recruits. They were to do this as quickly as possible. When they were ready to return, they would call to Henri, who would cup his hand near the back of Billy's head. The fleas would jump into it, much like a safety net.

Despite any loud bangs from the fireworks, he knew he would hear their voices. Since earlier in the day, when Robin had drawn attention to his sensitive hearing, Henri realized that this was not the only improved sense he seemed to have acquired. His sight was astonishing. He really didn't even need the magnifying glass any longer to see the fleas. And when he pricked his finger to dole out the blood droplets, he could smell its rich scent himself. All of this seemed to have happened so gradually that he had not even noticed it until that very day. Now he was aware that no one else was experiencing the world with quite the same intensity as he was.

Henri had fretted over how to transport the new recruits back to the circus. "I don't think I can trust these newcomers to travel in my hair and not bite," he told Maria and Sophia.

"What's a little nip? Never killed anyone," said Sophia casually.

"Sophia!" exclaimed Maria.

"I was just joking. You knew I was joking…right, Henri?"

Finally it was agreed that everyone, including Maria and Sophia, would travel back in a matchbox.

Then there had been the question of what to do with any fleas that did not successfully pass the audition. "Easy," said Fabio. "Return them to Billy, their home."

"I can't in good conscience do that," responded Henri. "Billy's my friend."

"We're you're friends too," piped up Giovanni. "Are you saying you like Billy better than us?"

"Yeah! Is he better than us?" chimed in Liora.

"This has nothing to with what we're talking about. I like all of you and Billy equally. You are all my friends. What we're discussing is finding a new home for those fleas who don't have the talent to join the show."

"So you're saying you only like talented fleas?" asked Fabio.

"Yes. I mean, no!" sputtered Henri. "We can't keep every flea who auditions for the circus. There's simply not enough blood in my body to feed so many hungry fleas." This at last made an impression on the fleas. A threat to their food source was serious. Finally, they reached another compromise. He would not return them to Billy but would find another human host. This presented a bit of a dilemma for Henri. There wasn't anyone whom he felt deserved such punishment.

As they had walked over to the fireworks, he whispered his predicament to Robin.

"Oh, I can think of loads of people who deserve them," she giggled. "I'd like to put them in Eunice's underpants and watch her scratch! She sewed up the legs of my costume yesterday so I couldn't put my feet through. No, wait! You know what would be really funny? Put them on Madame Noir! She thinks she's better than everyone else, the snooty old biddy. I'd like to see her do a bit of undignified scratching!"

Putting her nose in the air and attempting a French accent, she imitated Madame Noir's cold and forbidding voice. "I don't want to catch you children near my tent or interfering with my business. If I do, there will be consequences!" A cold chill went down Henri's spine as he remembered Mrs. Agatha Black, Great Aunt Georgie's neighbor, saying something very similar.

According to the banner hanging outside her tent, Madame Noir foretold the future through palmistry, crystal ball gazing, and tea leaf reading. Since he had poked his head into her tent, he had only seen her on two occasions. Normally most performers met at the mess tent, so Henri supposed that she cooked for herself and took her meals alone.

Madame Noir mostly wore long, black satin dresses with a band of a bright red or purple at the hem. She wore octagonal-shaped spectacles with tinted blue glass, which suggested she had sight into some other world. With her hooked nose, she was not a beautiful woman, and her hair—well, it was the wildest hairdo Henri had ever seen. Her hair was frizzy and striped black and white, much like a skunk. Henri thought of the *Insect Transformations* book and how some caterpillars are brightly colored as a defense against predators—a warning to birds that says, "Keep away!

Poison!" Madame Noir was like that. She looked so strange and frightening that he had absolutely no desire to go anywhere near her.

"Putting the fleas on Madame Noir would be asking for trouble," said Henri.

"Oh, I bet she's all bark and no bite," replied Robin.

Henri didn't answer. He didn't want to sound like a chicken, but he really didn't think it would be a good idea to provoke Madame Noir.

The first blast of a rocket went off. "Wow, look at that, Billy! It's like a million tiny gold and ruby stars. Isn't it beautiful?" asked Robin.

"Sure is," said Billy.

As Billy answered, Henri leaned forward. "Jump!" he called to the two fleas.

"Ooh! Look at that one. Emeralds!" and Robin started to chant, "Diamonds, rubies, emeralds, and gold."

To the fleas, Henri whispered, "Did you make it?"

"We're here," he heard Maria call as the screech of a bottle rocket filled the air.

Henri gave Robin a nudge and the thumbs-up sign, then sat back and enjoyed the show with everyone else. After about fifteen minutes, he heard Sophia calling his name. He gave Robin a shove with his foot to indicate that she should distract Billy again.

"Don't you wish we had fireworks every night, Billy?" Robin asked, while Henri held up his hand to the back of Billy's head.

113

"If we did, then it wouldn't seem special anymore," responded Billy. "Maybe once a month would be good."

"No, I would love it every day…" Robin prattled on. Henri counted in his head as the fleas jumped into his cupped hand: one, two, three, four, five, six, seven, eight, nine, ten.

"Ten. There are ten of you, including Sophia and Maria?" Henri whispered into his hand.

"Right, ten of us," Henri heard Maria say. Gently, he placed the fleas into the waiting matchbox, hoping that no one was watching him. Everyone's eyes should be upon the sky. Henri closed the box and put it in his pocket. As he looked up to see a burst of red and blue stars, he gave Robin another nudge. She turned and beamed at him. Of course, Henri could not help but smile back.

After the fireworks display ended, the crowd on the hill lingered. Many of them were circus folk, chatting about the next day's journey, which would take them much farther south.

Robin turned to Henri and Billy. "Look at Madame Noir," she said. "What's she doing?"

"Dunno," said Billy.

Henri looked over to where Robin had pointed. Madame Noir was not chatting with anyone. Instead she was stealth-ily moving between trees and bushes. From time to time, her hand reached out with lightning speed and grabbed something. "Looks like she's collecting something," said Henri.

"Come on, let's spy on her!" Robin jumped up, and before Henri or Billy had a chance to respond, she was moving across the grass in the direction of Madame Noir. Billy shrugged and then set off behind them while Henri reluctantly followed. They caught up to Robin, who was crouched behind a bush. They were perhaps thirty feet away from Madame Noir, who continued to glide about in search of something.

"What is it she's picking?" asked Billy. "Maybe it's leaves she's going to brew into a tea for her tea leaf reading?"

"No, can't be," said Robin. "Why would her hand come out so fast? It's not like a leaf is going to run away. She's catching something—but what? I wish it weren't so dark."

Henri gazed at Madame Noir. Robin was right. She was catching something. And he knew what too. "She's catching insects," he said with shock in his voice, for Henri's eyes were sharp and it no longer made any difference to him if it was night or day. He could see her clearly.

"Why would she catch insects?" asked Robin, but Henri didn't answer for he had just seen something else. As Madame Noir caught the moths, crickets, and mosquitoes, she put some in the pocket of her dress, but others she popped directly into her mouth. No! That can't be, thought Henri. At that moment, Madame Noir looked directly at the bush they were hiding behind.

In the dark, Robin and Billy could not see that Madame Noir was staring at them. Henri, though, was frozen to the spot. He stared back into the rigid, frowning face of the fortune-teller, and then he noticed her earrings. A wave of nausea hit Henri as he realized that her earrings were made of insects. Dead insects. He turned and retched. This startled both Billy and Robin.

"Henri, what's wrong?" asked Robin in a concerned voice, completely forgetting to whisper.

"Henri, are you OK?" asked Billy.

He looked up, past their frightened faces, to where Madame Noir had stood moments ago. She was gone.

"I don't know. I suddenly felt ill," Henri mumbled.

"Let's get you home," Billy said kindly.

With Robin on one side and Billy on the other, Henri was escorted back to the flea-circus tent.

"Hope you feel better," said Billy. "We've got a long journey tomorrow."

"I'll come and check on you in the morning," said Robin, and then she whispered, "I know you saw something and you're not telling."

"Thanks. I'm sure I'll be fine," Henri said to them both.

The following day, Henri was packing up his bedroll when Robin burst into the tent. She was out of breath and she had tears in her eyes.

Startled, Henri said, "Robin, what's wrong?"

"Come, come with me! You have to see!"

Together they raced across the field. No one noticed them in view of all the activity. The tents were coming down and being packed up for the long journey south. Robin led him to the wildflowers where the yellow butterflies had danced the day before. She pointed her finger toward the ground, and Henri saw the torn wings of hundreds of butterflies lying in the dirt. Robin burst into tears again.

"Who would do this, Henri? It's so cruel and terrible."

Henri did not answer. He called out to the field in insect language: "Who did this?" His call was met with silence. There was not a single chirp or a peep. Henri frowned.

"Madame Noir did this. I think it's a warning."

PLOTS AND PLANS

Once the circus locomotive started moving, Robin came back to the car where Henri sat with Maestro Antonio and Andre, the World's Strongest Man. Henri sat, dully watching the two men play cribbage, lost in thoughts of his own. Robin signaled to him from the carriage door. He got up and went to her.

"We need to talk," she whispered. There had been no chance to discuss the previous evening's fireworks event or the butterfly massacre they had discovered that morning. Everyone had to pitch in when the circus moved.

"We can't talk here," said Henri.

"We can't talk in my family's carriage either. I know—let's go to Billy and the lions."

As the lion tamer's assistant, Billy's job was to travel with the lions and tigers. He had to sit by their cages and keep the big cats calm. They didn't like train travel very much.

"I don't know if I want to bring Billy into this," Henri said hesitantly.

"What do you mean?" responded Robin.

"I mean, I don't know if I want to let him know that I can speak to insects."

"Nothing that happened last night or this morning has anything to do with that," said Robin.

"I wouldn't be so sure of that."

They made their way through the train, past Gertrude the Fat Lady, who was gossiping with Hope and Charity, the conjoined twins; through the carriage of the elegant flying Peppiano family, the circus's trapeze artists, until they reached Billy, all alone with the big cats. He was lying on a crate with a pillow and reading a comic book. As soon as Henri and Robin entered the car, one of the tigers let out a roar causing them to jump. Billy looked up from his reading.

"To what do I owe this honor?" he said. He looked pleased to have company.

The stink of the lions and tigers in the car was very strong. Billy carried a whiff of them wherever he went. Unlike Henri, he really was an orphan. His mother had died giving birth to him, and his father—the former lion tamer of the circus—had been killed by one of his own tigers. When Herbert Kramer joined the circus, he had agreed to raise Billy and train him to be a lion tamer. He had a lot of responsibility caring for the lions and tigers and was not as free to wander about as Henri and Robin.

Billy was a head taller than Henri. He had curly brown hair and was rather skinny. Henri couldn't imagine one of the big, hungry cats taking a chomp out of him. He would be all bone and gristle.

"OK, Henri. Spit it out," said Robin. "You said Madame Noir was collecting insects, but I don't think that was all you saw. Come on, fess up."

"Ah, well…she was catching moths, mosquitoes, some crickets. You know, the things that come out at night."

"And…" cajoled Robin.

"Well, she was putting some in her pocket."

"And…" Robin would not give up.

"And some she was putting in her mouth."

"Eating them?" exclaimed Robin incredulously.

"Disgusting!" said Billy. "Are you sure, Henri? It was really dark."

"I know what I saw."

"Why wouldn't she eat normal food like everyone else?" persisted Billy.

"Maybe she's some kind of witch," suggested Robin.

"Or she's the latest sideshow act! Ladies and gentlemen, I present Madame Noir, the Human Lizard Lady!" announced Henri.

"You know what?" said Robin. "I think we should start spying on her. See what the old hag is really up to. We didn't tell you, Billy, but this morning Henri and I found hundreds of butterfly wings all torn and thrown to the ground. Henri thinks Madame Noir did it!"

"Really?"

"I think the butterfly wings are a warning—a warning for us to stay away," Henri replied. "Last night I'm pretty sure Madame Noir knew we were watching her. We seem to have caught her at something, although exactly what, I have no idea. If we start following her, there'll be trouble…guaranteed."

"Well, I'm not going to be put off so easily," declared Robin. "I think we should start by seeing what's in her tent."

"What are you going to do? Go and have your tea leaves read?" said Billy with a laugh.

"No, I mean investigate when she's not there."

"That'll be hard," said Henri. "She always seems to be in her tent."

"Well, we'll just have to wait for our opportunity and be ready," Robin declared.

They sat in silence, each considering what kind of opportunity was required and when that might possibly happen. At last Robin announced she should be getting back to her family. Billy looked disappointed. "Want to play some cards, Henri?" he asked.

"Sure. I'll play a couple of hands, but then I'll have to get back. I have a letter to write tonight."

When Henri returned to his seat, the maestro and Andre were still playing cards. Henri took out a piece of paper and began to write.

Dear Professor Young,

Let me introduce myself. My name is Henri Bell. I recently came across your book Insect Communication, or My Life with Talking Beetles. *I found it fascinating. I am an amateur entomologist with an interest in insect communication …*

Henri had done his best to write the most formal letter he could in the hope that the professor would reply that he was willing to meet. He had decided not to mention outright that he could speak to insects. Nor had he told the professor that he was just ten years old.

Sometime in the middle of the night, the circus stopped at its destination. In the morning, Henri disembarked from the train and noted how warm and humid the air was. The roustabouts had been up for hours, and the tent city was already half up. Henri walked into the town and mailed his letter. The circus flyers had been posted all over town, but he noticed other posters advertising a completely different kind of show:

FIREWORKS DISPLAY
MOTHER NATURE'S OWN CREATION
SYNCHRONOUS FIREFLIES
GREEN RIVER NATURE RESERVE
AT DUSK FOR THE ENTIRE MONTH OF SEPTEMBER
ADMISSION FREE

Henri ripped down one of these posters, folded it, and put it in his pocket. Robin had wished for another fireworks display. It wasn't exactly the kind she had in mind, but it might work as a diversion to get Madame Noir away from her tent.

Back at the flea-circus tent, the fleas had been familiarizing the new recruits with the act and the equipment.

"All right. I'm back now," Henri said as he walked over to the glass case. "Shall we start the audition?"

"Ready!" called Sophia. She had worked out a kind of obstacle course in which the fleas would demonstrate balance, strength, speed, jumping ability, and grace. Sophia, Maria, and Henri would be the judges evaluating each flea out of a possible ten points. As they came up one by one, Sophia announced their names.

"First up is Martha," said Sophia. "Any time you're ready, Martha, go ahead."

Martha started the course and completed it in a mere ten seconds. Henri was impressed. She had balanced well and he liked her style. Henri awarded her a nine out of ten. Next up was Lucy. She was a great jumper, almost as good as Maria. Again Henri awarded her nine points. Lucy was followed by Elizabeth, Myrtle, Ethel, Louise, Susan, and Bertha, who was certainly the largest of all the fleas. As far as Henri was concerned, every one of them had been excellent. He put his hand down into the case, and Sophia and Maria jumped on. They had agreed to consult privately and pool their scores before announcing the results.

"Good job, girls!" Henri told Sophia and Maria. "You chose well. I thought everyone was fantastic! I'd like to keep them all."

"Yes, they all did very well," agreed Sophia.

"Did you notice something they all had in common, Henri?" asked Maria

"Hmm...What?"

"They're all girls! I told you so. Girls are better performers."

"Yes, you told me," admitted Henri. "What about Bertha? She's huge!"

The two fleas laughed. "Henri, she's pregnant!" giggled Sophia. "When we spoke to her, she said she wanted to give her children a better life, more opportunities."

"Well, I think that's great. We'll find something not too demanding for her in the beginning. We don't want her to get hurt." Henri rejoiced to himself. He would have no shortage of performers for quite some time.

Henri was happy that the circus had now traveled to a warmer place. He could hear the crickets singing in the field, and he was excited about the firefly show that night. It gave him another idea—maybe he could add sound and light to the show! He walked over to Robin's tent to tell her about the fireflies. Since there was no circus performance that night, they would all be free to go and watch.

Perhaps Madame Noir would go too. This could be Henri's opportunity to learn more about the mysterious fortune-teller.

MONSTROUS

Robin and her sisters had taken on the task of telling everyone about the firefly show that evening. "What are synchronous fireflies?" asked Olive, Robin's youngest sister.

"I looked it up in a book I have," responded Henri, "and it means the fireflies flash their lights in unison. You know, at the same time. Actually they aren't even flies, they're in the beetle family. Some people call them lightning bugs." *Ugh! I sound like a teacher*, he thought.

"But why do they flash at the same time?" asked Olive.

"Scientists aren't sure why, but they think that it might have to do with a mating ritual. Basically, the boys are trying to impress the girls and be the first to flash their lights. Regular fireflies just light up whenever they want. There are only two places in the whole world where these synchronous kinds are found, here and in British Malaya."

Despite being in a tent surrounded by Robin's family, he felt a sudden pang of loneliness. He wondered if his father or his mother had ever seen synchronous fireflies.

Word of the evening's entertainment passed quickly among the circus folk. To make sure Madame Noir would be in attendance, Robin told her mother that she had noticed that the fortune-teller wasn't looking well lately. Perhaps she needed a little cheering up. While not very fond of Madame Noir, Robin's mother was a compassionate woman. She took it upon herself to personally invite her.

"Imagine if she sits with my family! Ugh! That would be terrible," exclaimed Robin.

Billy chortled. "I don't know why you went to the trouble, Robin. If she really is an insect eater, she'll be there!"

He's right, thought Henri, and he suddenly felt terrible. What if she gobbled up all the lightning bugs? It would be like stealing Christmas.

Dusk approached. Henri arrived at the reserve ahead of time with Robin and Billy. Twilight is a wonderful time when the daytime insects are heading for bed and the nocturnal ones are just beginning to rise. Henri thought he might be able to find some insects that would be willing to join the flea circus and ask them to come by the tent tomorrow if they were interested.

Luckily, the buzzing of locusts kept Billy from overhearing Henri's conversations with passing butterflies and bounding crickets. Henri was thrilled when a passing luna moth said that he would be honored to work with *the* Henri Bell. In fact, every insect Henri greeted responded to him by name. He couldn't help but marvel at how quickly he had become known in their world. By the time they reached the Green River Nature Reserve, Henri was a little worried that he might have invited too many to join the flea circus.

The plan was for Henri, Robin, and Billy to make sure that Madame Noir was there. When the fireflies began flashing and the crowd was caught up in the sparkling magic of the moment, the three of them would sneak away to investigate her tent. It was difficult to know how much time they would have. Someone would have to stand guard and be ready to warn the other two.

At about seven the first light flashed. The crowd suddenly became quiet. Slowly, more and more tiny lights appeared at each flash. The fireflies were in the air and in the trees. Sometimes they all flashed together, but on occasion the fireflies appeared as a wave of light, beginning at the top of the forest canopy and cascading to the earthen floor. When this happened, it was if they were one entity rather than millions of tiny shining beetles. Each wave of light brought sighs from the gathered spectators.

"Oh, it's so beautiful. If I were a princess, I would ask the prince to have the fireflies perform for me every night," gushed Robin.

"Sorry, you'd have to be a queen to make that happen," said Billy. "Girls! Can't you just enjoy it for what it is and not get all romantic about it?"

127

Henri laughed. Billy was right. Robin was mostly a tomboy, but every once in a while she got all dreamy and started talking about fairy princesses and enchanted lands.

Henri was just as entranced by the fireflies. He could have stood in the forest all night long watching them, but he felt a tug at his sleeve.

"Come on," whispered Robin. "It's time to go."

Slowly, they edged away from the crowd. A handful of stray fireflies were just arriving at the scene, and impulsively, Henri invited them to join the circus. Billy heard his strange whispers and looked at him, but Henri just acted like he was clearing his throat. "Little nervous," he said.

Once they were away from the reserve, they broke into a run until they had made some distance. As they slowed to a walk, Billy said, "You know, if Madame Noir is a fortune-teller, maybe she knows we're about to break into her tent."

"She might if she thought about it," agreed Robin. "But she's a greedy old witch and there's not any profit in reading her own future!"

Henri and Billy chuckled. "Well, just in case, we need to make this quick. Who's going in and who's standing guard? I'd like to go in," said Henri.

"Me too," said Robin.

"OK, I'll stand guard," said Billy. "I just had an idea. What if I stop and get Licorice, you know…the black panther? He enjoys a walk and I could just pretend we were out strolling if anyone comes around. You'd hear me talking and know you had to get going. Just slip under one of the tent's sides."

Henri and Robin looked horrified at this suggestion. "Oh, come on!" exclaimed Billy. "He wouldn't hurt a flea—no offense intended, Henri!"

"Are you sure he's that tame, Billy?" asked Robin in a quavering voice.

"Tell you what, I'll put him on a leash if you like."

"Oh, why would you want to do that? He's just a harmless pussycat," said Robin sarcastically. "Of course you'll put him on a leash!"

"Great. I'm glad we're agreed that it's a good plan."

They were now at the field where the circus tents were pitched. As they entered the menagerie tent, one of the lions let out a roar. This set the elephants trumpeting, the horses whinnying, and the dogs barking. "Just shut up, all of you! It's only me," yelled Billy. When they heard Billy's familiar voice, the noise died down. "Thank you," said Billy. Grabbing a collar and leash hanging from one of the tent posts, he went to Licorice's cage. "Hey boy, we're going for a walk."

"Oh, be careful, Billy!" whispered Robin.

"Don't worry. OK, he's ready!"

As they walked toward Madame Noir's tent, Billy and Licorice led the way while Henri and Robin followed at a respectful distance. When they arrived, Billy said, "Licorice, sit!" and the big cat sat. Only his amber eyes were visible. The rest of his body was disguised by the night.

There was no light or sound from inside Madame Noir's tent.

"OK, we'll be out here patrolling. Anyone comes along, you'll hear one of us," laughed Billy.

Robin pulled out two candle stubs and a box of matches from her pocket. Henri lit the candles, and Billy held open the tent flap for them so they could go inside.

Madame Noir's tent was divided in two by a paisley curtain. The front was where she did her readings. One table held a crystal ball, and on another table sat a very ornate tea set and a couple of tea canisters.

Henri lifted the dividing cloth, and they both passed through to Madame Noir's living quarters. Robin gave a little gasp as she looked around, for the scene that met their eyes could have been taken right out of the *Arabian Nights*. The candlelight picked up the gold thread, beads, and sequins of elaborately embroidered tapestries that adorned the tent walls. Luxurious silk cushions abounded on both her bed and the floor, which was covered with a silk oriental carpet.

The bed had an elaborately carved wooden headboard. It was a jungle scene. Among the curving, leafy branches were hidden various animals both large and small. There were rats, squirrels, monkeys, tigers, elephants, and even insects like cicadas, grasshoppers, and stag beetles. It was like the Garden of Eden, except that in the sky of the carved tableau were bats—hundreds and hundreds of bats. They flew toward a chiseled full moon. In this world, the bats were clearly rulers.

"I wouldn't want to go to sleep with that above my head," whispered Robin. "I'd have nightmares."

Henri nodded. There was something eerily familiar about the scene. He recalled an illustration he had seen of bats silhouetted against a nighttime sky. Where had he seen that? Perhaps a book in the library the other day. Looking away from the bed frame, they saw a wardrobe carved with the same lush tropical leaves. Robin opened it, but all that hung there were Madame Noir's long silk dresses. A light breeze caused the dresses to sway on their hangers, and the silk made a swishing sound. Henri felt himself tense. Now, *that* sound; it was familiar. Where had he heard it before? *Think!*

"Nothing here." Robin quietly closed the door.

To the left of the wardrobe was a table with a pile of books. Henri picked them up, and as he leafed through the volumes, he realized that they were all about Southeast Asia, its geography, its peoples, its plants, and its animals. How odd, thought Henri, that he and Madame Noir should share an interest in that part of the world. His father and now his mother were there in British Malaya. And *Goliathus hercules*, the supposed man-eating insect said to be native to the region. Why was Madame Noir interested? As Henri stood thinking about this remarkable coincidence, the silence was broken.

"Henri!"

Henri jumped. "What?" He looked at Robin's white face.

"That plant behind you!" She pointed a shaky finger at it. "It was going to bite you."

Henri turned quickly. He held the candle up. The plant was still. "What are you talking about? Plants don't bite."

"Henri, it was. It had its mouth or jaws or whatever you call them open."

Henri examined the plant. "Robin, I think this is a Venus fly-trap. It's a carnivorous plant."

"See! It was going to eat you!"

Henri laughed. "It doesn't eat people. It eats insects. That would explain why Madame Noir was collecting insects. She was going to feed them to these plants." Henri felt pleased that he had come up with an explanation for her eccentric behavior. It made him feel a little less nervous.

"Yeah, well that doesn't explain why she was eating them *herself*. Henri, move away from that plant. I know what I saw."

"Oh…if it makes you happy, but really it doesn't eat people. Look…" and he poked at one of the podlike leaves. As he did so, it suddenly opened up and then closed its serrated jaws around Henri's finger. "Ow!" yelled Henri. He pulled his finger out with little difficulty, but he was shaken. "It's not supposed to do that!"

"Get away from it, Henri! Let's get out of here."

"No, we've come this far. Let's see what's in these boxes."

Robin had found a jewelry box and a larger wooden box. Henri opened the jewelry box first. Sitting on top were the beetle earrings that Madame Noir had been wearing the night before. He felt the sick feeling rising in his stomach once again. "Those are what she was wearing last night," he mumbled. He couldn't bear to touch them. Robin picked them up.

"They're sort of pretty, but kind of grotesque too. And look at this."

She pulled out a necklace of metallic green beetle wings strung onto a cord. They looked a bit like long, green, pointy fingernails. Between each beetle wing was a white button. Robin put down the necklace and pulled out a bracelet also made of beetle parts, and another still in which small blue-green beetles were encased in glass. There was a crack in the glass.

"All of this stuff is made of insects. Henri, are you OK?"

Henri stood with his hands over his stomach. "No, not really. I don't know. When I see that jewelry, I think it's the dead insects that make me feel nauseous. Put it away, will you? Is there anything else in there?"

"Yeah, some mourning jewelry. You know, the kind of things you wear when someone's died. They put a lock of hair or a picture of the dead person on it. Creepy, if you ask me."

Robin returned the items to the box, closed the top, and turned to the bigger wooden box. Henri took off the lid. There lay a collection, an insect collection—but not an ordinary one. There were all manner of insects—beetles, butterflies, grasshoppers, and cicadas. However, they were not pinned or labeled in any traditional way. The insects were threaded on long hatpins, as if they were on a gruesome shish kebab. An image flashed to Henri's mind of a hand holding a long hatpin, which was poised like a dart in the air.

The fancy silver, glass, and pearl heads of the pins gleamed in the dark. The labels beside them, written in a tight script, made no sense. Henri read *Ethel W., Niagara Falls, 1880* and *Mildred M., Kenya, 1875.*

Henri's eyes scanned the box. What was this monstrous collection? And then his eyes alighted upon a large beetle. He wasn't sure what kind it was—a rhino beetle, perhaps. The beetle had been stabbed with a pin, a mourning pin. It had a picture.

The picture was of Henri's father. The label read, *George B., British Malaya, 1888.*

Henri let out something between a gasp and a wail. He was certain he was going to vomit.

At that very moment, there was a rustle, a swish—like the sound of a stiff silk dress in motion. A second later, they heard a deep, rumbling roar.

En Francais

J ust what do you think you're doing?" asked Madame Noir.

"Walking Licorice," responded Billy.

Madame Noir's eyes narrowed. "Is it really a good idea to walk a dangerous animal that blends into the night at this hour?"

"Licorice isn't dangerous. Are you, boy?" Billy gave him an affectionate scratch behind the ear, and Licorice purred in his deep growl.

"He's a nearly two-hundred pound black panther!"

"That's right," said Billy cheerfully. "You really know your cats, Madame."

"Oh! Stand aside, you idiot. I don't want to catch you walking that beast near my tent again. Do you understand?"

"I don't know why you've taken such a dislike to him. He hasn't done anything to you. What about Peppermint the Siberian tiger and Butterscotch the lion? Can I walk them by your tent?"

"You cheeky, impertinent boy! I will speak to Herbert Kramer about you! Move out of the way or there will be consequences."

"No need to get yourself in a tizzy, Madame. We'll be on our way. Good night! Come on, Licorice. We'll go some place where you're more appreciated," Billy said in a loud voice.

He heard Madame Noir let out a frustrated "Ugh!" as she swept into her tent with a swish. He hoped he'd given Henri and Robin enough time to get out. He also hoped that she wouldn't follow through on her threat to speak to Herbert. The lion tamer wouldn't mind Billy walking the cats, but he wouldn't be happy to hear that Billy had been rude to Madame Noir.

Fortunately, the time she'd taken to tell Billy off had given Henri and Robin the seconds they needed. They were able to replace the lid on the insect collection and slip under the tent wall undetected.

Then they ran. Instinct made them stick together. When they neared the flea-circus tent, they slowed. Henri leaned over, his hands on his knees, and threw up. Robin stood beside him, not knowing what to do. When he straightened up, Henri said, "You better get back to your tent."

"Will you be OK?"

"I think so."

"All right. See you tomorrow. Bye."

It took Henri a long time to fall asleep. Over and over again he went through an inventory of what he had seen in Madame Noir's tent. First and foremost, there was the beetle stabbed with the mourning pin containing the picture of his father. It was labeled with his father's name and the location he was last seen, British Malaya, and the date of 1888 was approximately the time he went missing. What did it mean?

"Henri, can I come in now?" Maestro Antonio called from outside the tent the next morning.

Henri turned to Robin and Billy. "You've got to leave! We'll talk more tonight," he whispered.

"Come on," said Billy, and he and Robin dropped to their stomachs and slid under the tent wall.

"Come in," Henri called, "but we're not quite ready to show you the new routine. It'll take a bit more rehearsal," replied Henri. He had told Maestro Antonio that he and the fleas were working on some new tricks, and he wanted it to be a surprise. The maestro was happy to oblige and stay out of the tent. Henri ran the whole show now. All Maestro Antonio had to do was sell tickets, make the announcements, and count the money at the end of the day. He was pleased to wander about the circus, catch up on any gossip, and maybe have a few rounds of dominos with Andre, the World's Strongest Man.

"You know, the show is running really well," the maestro said as he came inside. "Don't know how you do it, Henri. You've got a real gift!"

"Thank you, Tony. Actually, I'm hoping to bring other insects into the show." In fact, first thing that morning, the insects he had spoken with the night before had started to show up in the tent. They came out of dark corners, they crawled under the tent walls, and sailed in when a gust of wind caused the tent flaps to rise. It seemed that every insect he had invited had taken up his offer and was anxious to begin rehearsal.

He showed Maestro Antonio the glass case, which was crammed with all manner of insect life.

"Wow! If this works out, we may have to get some more traveling cases for these critters," the maestro said. "Speaking of travel, Henri, I have news. After our run here, the circus will be splitting up until next spring. The big top folks are going to winter in Florida. All the sideshow acts, we're going to Mexico. I think the flea circus is going to do really well down there. What do you think? Excited?"

"Splitting up?"

Maestro Antonio could see that Henri looked a bit glum, although he couldn't imagine why. "I'll bet there's lots of new insects down there for you to see. You'll enjoy that, I'm sure," he said encouragingly. He was well aware that Henri's interest in insects extended beyond fleas.

"Yes, sir. I'm sure it will be fascinating," Henri said.

"Well, I'll let you get back to rehearsing, then," said Maestro Antonio, and he walked out of the tent.

Henri sat down, overwhelmed. He finally had some friends, but now the circus was splitting up and Robin and Billy would be in Florida while he'd be in Mexico. *In Mexico with Madame Noir.* Henri shuddered at the thought.

That morning, he and Robin had told Billy about seeing the insect and mourning jewelry in Madame Noir's tent, but Henri hadn't told them that one of the photos was of his father. Why? It felt as if once he said it aloud, it would be true. *Father is dead.*

All Robin and Billy could make of the frightening insect collection was that it was eccentric. "What do you think the labels with people's names on them mean?" asked Henri.

"Maybe that particular person caught the insect?" suggested Robin.

"I think that usually a label is supposed to have the name of the species, the place it was collected, and the date of collection," said Henri. "I've never heard of including the name of the collector. It's very odd." He thought how lovingly he prepared his own collection of former insect friends and associates compared to the brutality of the fortune-teller's skewered victims on hatpins.

Again, Henri's mind flashed back to a black-gloved hand holding a sharp hatpin in the air as if ready to strike.

Robin was more concerned about the Venus flytrap. "Why do you think that plant attacked you?" she asked.

"It didn't attack me. I stuck my finger into the trap."

"Maybe it thought Henri was an insect?" Billy said with a laugh.

Henri laughed and then stopped. The plant should be interested in insects, not people. None of it made any sense.

139

That night, after the last show ended, Henri was anxious to meet with Robin and Billy, so he went to the menagerie tent. As he entered the tent, he smiled to hear Billy singing to the cats. He followed Billy's voice to Licorice's and Peppermint's cages.

"*Le petit chat noir!*" Billy sang as he finished the song.

"Bravo," said Henri. "What are you singing?"

"Oh, it's a song Herbert taught me. It calms the cats down."

"Is it French? What does it mean?"

"Yeah, Herbert's from Quebec. It's just a children's song about a little black cat. Isn't that right, Licorice, my *petit chat noir*?"

"*Noir*…as in Madame Noir?" asked Henri anxiously.

"Yeah, I guess so. Noir means black, so in English she'd be Mrs. Black. Not that I speak French."

No it couldn't be, Henri thought desperately.

Just then, Robin came into the tent. "I thought I might find you two here. There's Licorice. What a good boy," she said. She turned to Henri. "What's wrong with you? You look like you've seen a ghost!"

"Something like that—a memory from the past, anyway."

Billy and Robin listened incredulously as Henri told them about Mrs. Agatha Black of Dutch Elm Farm.

"Now that you mention it, Madame Noir joined the circus only recently," said Robin. "Just before you came. But Henri, do you honestly think that Agatha Black would go to the trouble of creating a disguise and joining the circus just to follow you?"

"Yes, I do. She's had it out for me from the first day we met." Henri knew he must sound like a puffed-up, self-important idiot.

"But why?" Robin asked.

"I don't know. Maybe I have something she wants, something she needs."

"Henri, you're a kid. What could you have that she wants?" asked Billy.

Henri gave a knowing glance to Robin, and then, taking a deep breath, he said, "Well, I can talk to insects."

"What?" said Billy, looking completely puzzled.

"He can talk to insects," said Robin.

"I heard that the first time, thanks. I still don't understand."

Henri stood up and walked over to one of the gas lamps that lit the tent. As usual, moths fluttered about it, mesmerized by the light. Henri made a muttering sound that was unintelligible to the other two. The moths moved away from the lamp and flew to Robin and Billy, where they started to fly in a circle around them. Henri went to three more lamps and made the same sounds. Again, the moths moved from the light and joined the circle until it appeared as if Billy and Robin were surrounded by a whirlwind of moths. Henri made another sound, and still more moths came from every corner of the tent, joining the crowded dancing circle.

Billy stood with his mouth hanging open. Robin's smile stretched wide across her face, and she hopped from foot to foot in her excitement. Henri made another sound, and in an instant, the moths dispersed and everything was as it had been the minute before.

"OK," said Billy. "Henri can talk to insects," and he smiled. "But why does Agatha Black need Henri to talk to insects?"

"And let's say that she and Madame Noir are the same person," Robin interjected.

"So what? She wants Henri to call insects for her so she can eat them and get fat?" asked Billy, and they all laughed.

"I doubt it," said Henri. "But I wonder if there's something in my ability that would be helpful to her. She seems to be making a collection of insects. Maybe she needs me to help her find something in particular." Suddenly Henri thought of all the books on Southeast Asia in Madame Noir's tent. Could she be looking for *Goliathus hercules*?

"All for an insect collection? Who could be that obsessed?" asked Billy.

"My Great Aunt Georgie collects buttons, and she's obsessed," responded Henri. "The whole house is covered from floor to ceiling in buttons. I think there are different reasons that people collect. Great Aunt Georgie just loves buttons. In a way, they hold memories for her, but imagine if a person could become rich and famous because of something they discovered or collected. Isn't it quite possible they would use any means to achieve it?"

"I suppose," said Billy. "But Madame Noir hasn't done anything to you, has she, Henri? Have you ever even talked to her?"

"No, I haven't. You're right. Maybe she's just biding her time."

"But what about the torn butterfly wings? You said you thought that was some kind of warning," said Robin.

"I don't know what it means, though," said Henri.

PROFESSOR YOUNG

So startling was the thought that Madame Noir and Mrs. Black might very well be the same person, Henri hadn't even had the chance to discuss the upcoming split of the circus with Robin and Billy. The thought of it depressed him. It occurred to him that they might not even have heard news of the split yet.

In the morning, Henri walked to town to mail two messages. One was to his mother and the other to Great Aunt Georgie. He decided to write postcards, because beyond letting them know that the flea circus was heading to Mexico, he really had only one urgent question for each of them. To his mother, Henri asked if his father had any interest in insects. To Great Aunt Georgie, he asked if she had seen Mrs. Black recently.

Since he was at the post office, Henri checked to see if there was any mail waiting for him. To his astonishment, there was already a reply from Professor Young, the entomologist. Henri ripped it open.

Dear Mr. Bell:

It would be my great pleasure to meet you and discuss insect communication. I can be found in my office at the university on Tuesday and Thursday afternoons between 1:00 and 4:00 p.m. I do hope this time will suit your schedule. I look forward to meeting you.

With kind regards,

Dr. Daniel Young

Tomorrow was Thursday! If he could catch the train, he could visit Professor Young and be back in just one day. Henri raced back to the circus to ask Maestro Antonio if he could have the next day off.

"Not a problem, Henri. You have the show running like a well-oiled machine. Just let the fleas know you'll be gone and that I'll be in charge for the day."

"'Let them know?'" Henri asked. Did Maestro Antonio know that he was talking to the fleas?

"Henri, it's a joke, but I swear those fleas perform so well that I often wonder if you haven't found some way to communicate with them!"

Maestro Antonio had just seen a sneak preview of the new show, and he was so enthusiastic that he declared they must have a new banner painted.

"I want it to say, 'Maestro Antonio's Amazing Menagerie of Insects. The Greatest Little Show on Earth!'" the maestro had said.

The train trip the next day was uneventful. Henri arrived at the university and quickly located the entomology department. Since he was early, he sat on a wooden bench outside Professor Young's office. When he heard the clock chimes strike one, he stood up and knocked on the door.

"Come in," said a voice.

Henri opened the door and stepped inside. There was a name-plate on the professor's desk that read *Dr. Daniel Young*. Behind the desk sat a man of about sixty years of age. His hair was white and rather long. He wore reading spectacles that rested on the end of his nose, and he was intently making notes, glancing from time to time at an open book on his desk.

Behind the professor towered shelves and shelves of thick leather-bound books with gilt lettering. On a table at the side of the room was a glass tank. Henri noted that it contained the patent leather beetles, *Odontotaenius disjunctus*, the insects that the professor had written about in his book.

Professor Young looked up from his writing. "I'm sorry," he said when he saw Henri. "I forgot that you knocked. How can I help you?"

"I'm Henri Bell, sir. I wrote to you."

"Ah, Mr. Bell. It's a pleasure to meet you." He rose up from his desk and shook Henri's hand heartily. If he was at all surprised that Mr. Bell was ten years old, he did not show it. "It's always a pleasure to meet people who share common interests."

"Ah, yes," said Henri, glad that Professor Young hadn't thrown him out of the office.

145

"So, you wanted to discuss insect communication. Did you see over there? I have some *O. disjunctus*. Would you like to talk to them? They're quite chatty."

"Um…sure." Henri walked over to see the case. Professor Young removed the lid and made a clicking sound, which Henri immediately understood to mean, "Are you hungry?" He grinned. Clearly the professor could talk to insects too!

Henri bent his head down. "Hello, everyone. I am Henri Bell. Do you like it here?"

"*The* Henri Bell. Oh my goodness! It's Henri Bell. Everyone come out. Henri Bell, he's here!" said one of the beetles.

"Oh, I can't believe it. Finally, a human we can understand!" said another.

"But I just heard the professor talk to you. I understood him perfectly," said Henri surprised.

"Oh, him," said the first beetle. "He can say that and a dozen other things, but that's all. He's like a parrot. Just says the same things over and over again. Conversation is very dull with him."

"Oh," said Henri. He turned to the professor, who had a very serious look on his face.

"Mr. Bell, I have recorded fourteen distinct combinations of clicks that these beetles make, yet I did not understand your clicks. Clearly they are responding to you. Please tell me what you are talking about," said the flustered Professor Young.

Henri didn't want to insult the professor so he chose his words carefully. "Well professor, I think that there may be more than

146

fourteen different clicks, but they aren't perceptible to your ear. The beetles have noticed that your, um, vocabulary is limited and they're, um, a bit disappointed since they would like to get to know you better."

"Really! Well, Mr. Bell, do continue to speak with them. I would like to record the conversation—the clicks—for my research." He swiftly walked to the desk and returned with pen and paper.

Henri leaned back over the case. "You know, the professor is trying very hard, but he's not a young man. I think he can't hear you properly. That's probably why he has never learned to say anything else, but he wants to."

"Oh, let's not talk about him anymore. Let's talk about you, Henri Bell. What brings you here?"

"Well, I want to find out how it is that I can speak to insects, and I was hoping the professor could tell me."

"Wasting your time. He won't have a clue. Now, we hear you're running a circus. I'd like to join. Can I?"

Henri felt rather uncomfortable. He was looking for answers, not recruits. "I'm sorry. We don't have any unfilled positions at the moment, but if we do I'll know where to find you."

"Great, great!" said the beetle.

Henri turned to the professor, who was still scribbling. "Wonderful!" he said. "Could you give me a brief synopsis of the conversation?" He stood with his pen at the ready.

"Oh, well. Um, they know me, or I should say they know *about* me. Most insects seem to. I'm currently working in a circus, developing an insect show and, um, some of them asked if they could join."

"Amazing! Now would you mind if we sit down and I can repeat back the clicks I recorded? You can tell me if I've got them right." He looked at Henri expectantly.

"Well, Professor Young, that might take a long time, and I have to get back to the circus today."

"Oh." The professor looked rather disappointed. "Could you come back tomorrow?"

"It's a traveling circus, sir. I'm afraid I can't."

"Oh. Yes, well…perhaps I'll read it in your book then. You are writing a book? Or will you be presenting a paper? Maybe at the next Entomological Society of America conference?"

"No, professor. I'm not writing a book, and I won't be giving a paper, whatever that is. Sir, I'm just a kid. I'm ten years old. I can speak to insects, and I was hoping you could tell me why."

They moved away from the case and sat down, the professor behind his desk and Henri in the chair in front of it. There was silence. Professor Young stared at Henri for a few seconds, and then he said, "Mr. Bell."

"Please call me Henri, sir."

"All right, then you must call me Daniel. Anyway, Henri, you are a most unusual person. How long have you been speaking to insects, if you don't mind my asking?"

"About seven months," said Henri. "A fly spoke to me first, and I just responded to him. It's only recently that I even realized I was speaking another language. I just thought they understood English."

"Can you speak all insect languages—or perhaps I should ask first: is there one language that is understood by all species?"

"I think there is one language, but there are perhaps different dialects. Do you have any idea why I can speak to them, sir— I mean, Daniel?"

"Henri, I have spent nearly forty years of my life trying to communicate with insects. Today I am humbled to meet a young man who has surpassed my own skill in such a short time. Why or how you've done it, I can only speculate. You must have acutely sensitive hearing and an aptitude for language."

"Um…I don't think I have any aptitude for language, sir. I only just scraped by in Latin class."

"Yes, well, Latin can be a bit of a challenge. Perhaps your interest in insect languages is far greater than your interest in Latin." The professor smiled.

"That would be true," said Henri.

"I am a scientist. It is my job to interpret and explain things, but I am at a loss. You have a gift, Henri. Perhaps in time we shall know the answer. I suggest we keep in touch and that you inform me of any developments."

Henri looked down at his hands and flexed them. They felt stiff today. He had really been hoping the professor would know the answer. "Sure. We can do that. What about *Goliathus hercules*? I read about it in the newspaper. Do you think it's real?"

"I do. There's a lot of speculation, but usually there is at least a grain of truth behind a myth.

"I think that *Goliathus hercules* is an insect with some unique characteristics. I have read that it has gold-tipped horns, and that its ferocious nature has inspired the armor of the Japanese Samurai warrior. You see, Henri, we humans look to the glory of nature for inspiration. Let us consider the legend of scarab beetle, sometimes called the dung beetle. Do you know that the ancient Egyptians revered the scarab?"

Henri shook his head no.

"It was an important symbol. The ancients observed the lowly beetle rolling a perfectly rounded ball of dung upon the ground. They recognized that just as the sun rises in the east and sets in the west, so the dung beetle moved its spherical burden across the earth. Thus a mere beetle became the symbol of that giver of life, the sun. Often the most famous rulers in history have been compared to the sun, so great is their power. So even the lowly dung beetle is a remarkable creature and this *Goliathus hercules*, well, he must be quite extraordinary. I believe he exists, and you are just the man to capture him and show him to the world!"

THE GREATEST
LITTLE SHOW ON EARTH

Henri had a lot to think about on his train ride back to the circus. Yet, he didn't have much opportunity because Professor Young had insisted on coming with him to see the world premiere of the Greatest Little Show on Earth. While the professor was not able to give Henri any insight into why he was able to speak to insects, he was certainly not the fool that the patent-leather beetles made him out to be.

He was a wealth of information and had numerous suggestions as to types of insects Henri should seek out for the circus. For example, if he wanted a spotlight, he should get a type of luminescent click beetle. "Order *Coleoptera*, family *Elateridae*, and you would be needing genus *Pyrophorus*, Henri. Those click beetles have luminescent spots on the hind corners of the pronotum. Why, they provide so much light, you could read a book in the dead of night for several hours! They are found in various parts of South America."

Now it was Henri who found himself rapidly scribbling notes as the professor suggested more and more insects he should consider for the show. "You must travel to Siam," exclaimed the professor. "You can audition some of the most splendid singers in the world because there, you will find the greatest diversity of cicadas. Order *Homoptera*, suborder *Auchenorrhyncha* in the superfamily *Cicadoidea*."

That evening the flea-circus tent was filled to capacity with eager spectators. Robin, Billy, and Professor Young sat front and center. Andre, the World's Strongest Man, Herbert Kramer the Lion Tamer, and Hope and Charity, the Conjoined Twins, were also there. It was already clear that Henri and the maestro would have to do more than one performance that evening because so many people had been turned away. They entered the tent for the performance and the audience fell silent.

"Ladies and gentlemen, you are in for a real treat tonight! I am Maestro Antonio, as you all know, and this is my assistant extraordinaire, Enrico!" There was an enthusiastic round of applause. "Tonight my Amazing Flying Flea Circus is transformed into Maestro Antonio's Menagerie of Insects, and you are about to see the Greatest Little Show on Earth! Enrico, dim the lights!"

As soon as the lights were down, out flew hundreds of fireflies in formation. In unison, the synchronous fireflies spelled out:

WELCOME TO THE GREATEST LITTLE SHOW ON EARTH

After that, they rose and fell like real fireworks bursting into flowers and pinwheels of fire and light. The audience was enraptured, exclaiming with *ohs* and *ahs*. When the last light went out, they cheered and clapped wildly. When the applause died down, the spectators sat expectantly in the dark as Maestro Antonio began his presentation.

"Ladies and Gentlemen, consider the lowly insect. Perhaps you have never given them much of a thought beyond how annoying they can be—that pinch of the mosquito, the sting of the wasp. Tonight, however, you shall walk out of this tent and say insects are one of the most amazing creatures on this great earth! Did you know that there are estimated to be thirty million— yes, thirty million—different species? That represents more than ninety percent of the life forms on this planet. Not only are they the most numerous animal on earth but also the most diverse, as you will discover here tonight. Have you ever stopped to consider that they might be great singers and musicians?"

With that, the lights came up and the music started. Within the glass tank sat an orchestra of cicadas, crickets, katydids, and grasshoppers playing a tune that sounded a bit like the organ music played on the merry-go-round. This had taken a long time to develop because the insect musicians only knew their own songs. Henri had taken them for many rides on the merry-go-round to hear the tune that he had been punch-drunk with dizziness by the time he got off.

As the orchestra concluded their introductory number, Maestro Antonio announced, "And now our company of dancing butterflies and moths will perform 'Waltz of the Flowers' from Tchaikovsky's *Nutcracker Suite* in an aerial ballet."

Henri wasn't sure that Tchaikovsky would have recognized his own composition as sung by insects, but it sounded sweet and melodic. There was a whirling of kaleidoscopic color in the air as the partnered butterflies moved perfectly in time to the music, and as the song approached its conclusion, the luna moth gently rose from the bottom of the case and appeared in the center as if he himself were the sugar plum fairy.

The ballet ended and the orchestra started into a lively tune as the circus performers entered, riding on three large scarab beetles that lumbered in just like the elephants in the big top. The insects riding on the beetles' backs waved colorful flags.

The rings of fire act remained a crowd favorite. Giovanni pulled the chariot, but now five fleas rode in the back of it, balanced one on top of the other and waving flags in four of their six arms. As Maestro Antonio announced each act, he also gave interesting little facts about the insect performers.

Another innovation for the circus was costumes. As all the fleas had attended at least one big top performance, they knew that costumes were essential. Fabio insisted that he would no longer be performing "naked," and when the others heard that, they demanded costumes as well. This was no easy task as the fleas were very small. Henri had chuckled to himself as he watched the fleas strutting about showing off their costumes before the performance began.

For the final act, Umberto came out to the center ring and stood in his new lion tamer outfit to put the supposedly furious tiger beetles through their paces. Henri had also found some stag beetles with menacing-looking pinchers. Neither insect was in fact vicious, but the audience didn't know it, and the beetles put on an excellent act. They snapped, leaped, and eventually let Umberto "tame" them. He had them jump up onto spools of thread, stand on their hind legs, and form a pyramid. To the audience, he appeared to be the brave and invincible lion tamer.

When Umberto's act was over, the scarab beetles reappeared, and the performers jumped up on their backs again to leave the ring. They waved to the crowd as the musicians sang the closing number. As they exited, the lights dimmed once again and the fireflies returned for an encore spelling of *Thank you, come again* before bursting into cascading waves of lights.

The insect performers, Henri, and Maestro Antonio—all received a standing ovation. Everyone wanted to see the insects. If the performers had been humans, the spectators would have asked for autographs. Robin's little sister, Olive, tugged at her mother's sleeve and begged to have her very own dung beetle. Maestro Antonio was in deep discussion with Professor Young, who was explaining, "There is some debate as to which beetle is the strongest in the world. I would say that one could make a case for *Onthophagus taurus*, a type of dung beetle with two horns; however, others feel that the single horned *Trypoxylus dichotomus* is the true title holder." Henri could see that the maestro had pulled out the notes Henri had provided him in preparation for the show and now he was adding more facts.

Robin and Billy pushed their way up to Henri. "Fantastic show!" said Robin, and she gave him a hug.

"Great! Really great!" said Billy.

"Thanks," said Henri, but he felt low, like he felt on Christmas Day when there were no more presents to open. He felt like there was nothing to look forward to. Tomorrow the circus would split up. Robin and Billy would go to Florida, and he would be going to Mexico with the detestable Madame Noir. His mind flashed back to the mourning pin piercing his father's picture. Once again he felt troubled. Just what was her connection to his father?

"Don't look so sad. I know the circus and the side shows are splitting up tomorrow," said Robin as if she could read his mind. "But time will pass by quickly and we'll see you in the spring!"

"That's right," said Billy. "Hey, what did the professor tell you? Does he know why you can speak to insects?"

"No," said Henri casting his eyes downward. "He doesn't know." And then he thought of *Goliathus hercules* and what the professor had said: *You are just the man to capture and show him to the world!* Suddenly Henri was convinced of two things. First, this was *his* quest. He would be the one to find *Goliathus hercules*.

Second, Madame Noir wanted to find the gigantic insect too. She expected Henri to lead her right to him. What else could all those insects and books on Southeast Asia mean? And somehow his father was mixed up in it all.

Henri looked back at Robin and Billy with a broad grin on his face, but his smile slowly vanished as he glanced beyond his friends, toward the back of the tent, and saw Madame Noir standing alone. She stared at Henri and then smiled, a smile like someone showing their teeth to the dentist. Henri went cold. He knew that smile. He was sure of it. Madame Noir turned and walked out of the tent.

PART III

It was so easy, really. The web was spun and the boy had walked right into the trap.

She needn't go to Mexico with the rest of the side show folk. There was no point. Everything was moving along perfectly, and all she had to do now was bide her time. Madame Noir looked into the mirror and gave herself a smug, congratulatory smile. The boy's independent spirit and his willingness to embark on an adventure all played perfectly into her hands. That foolish courage that others so much admired would be his downfall. Not only was Henri Bell setting out on his so-called quest to find Goliathus hercules, but he also entertained the childish notion that while others had failed, he alone would find his father.

Who knew where his father was? Who really cared? Certainly she did not! He had very conveniently disappeared with no "special" assistance from her. How perfect that he should vanish in the very place that she wished to lure the boy. She couldn't have planned it better. Ugh! Love and sentimentality—qualities that make a person weak and vulnerable. Qualities that make it easy to manipulate a person. Suddenly the fortune-teller threw back her head and laughed. If anyone had seen her, they would have been quite shocked, for never had Madame Noir seemed in such good spirits.

It had been so easy to steal the picture of Henri's father from his Aunt Georgiana, put it in the mourning pin, and then strategically place it in her insect collection for the boy to find. It had been an accident, an indiscretion, the night the children caught her "collecting" insects. She hadn't meant for them to know, but it turned out to be a happy accident. After that episode, she didn't need to be a fortune-teller to know that it was only a matter of time before Henri's interest piqued and he would snoop around. That pesky, nosy girl, Robin, had goaded him into further investigation.

Upon seeing the insect stabbed with the mourning pin holding his father's image, the boy must have been frantic with fear. Off he would run on his heroic mission. He would go alone, just as he had come to America and just as he had joined the flea circus. Away from familiar soil, the protection of family and of friends, he would be easy prey. She would follow Henri Bell, and he would lead her to Goliathus hercules.

Right now, he was a useful tool, but dangerous too. Once she— not he—had captured the mysterious creature, she would decide what to do with the boy. He was the only threat to her grand plan, a plan in which her control would be so great that all creatures, man and beast, would bow down to her in fear and submission.

She raised her hands up to her head and, with a quick tug, lifted off the ridiculous wig. Madame Noir was no more. The person who stared back in the mirror had beady eyes, a hooked nose, and hair drawn back so tightly in a bun that it distorted her features. She grinned at her image, the kind of awkward, toothy smile you give a dentist inspecting your teeth. Out loud, she said, "Agatha, so good to see you." She gave a short chuckle. "My work here is done. Now I must wait, watch, and be ready for the real adventure to begin!"

ADIOS

The side show performers had steadily traveled southward in search of warm weather. Now they were in Oaxaca, Mexico. To Henri's surprise he was actually beginning to enjoy himself. This was due in large part to the absence of Madame Noir. She had completely vanished from the circus! On the day they were to leave for Mexico, her tent had disappeared and she hadn't left a note.

Unfortunately Henri had no doubt that he would eventually meet her again. He had no idea of her motive but when at last he embarked upon the long journey to British Malaya—the last place his father was seen and the home of the mysterious insect *Goliathus hercules*—he suspected he would be reunited with the detestable Madame Noir, or Agatha Black, or whatever she would be calling herself by then. While he had no desire to confront her, Henri was anxious to get to Malaya. Unfortunately that was far easier said than done.

Awaiting him on a recent visit to the post office was an envelope postmarked London, England, and addressed to him in his mother's handwriting. It was with bitter disappointment that Henri discovered that someone had tampered with his mail, completely removing the contents. The only thing Henri knew for sure was that his mother was home now. Was Father with her? His gut said no and if that was the case he must continue the search. But how was he to raise the funds for such a journey?

In the meantime the show had to go on! The first performance of the day was about to begin when he noticed that Sophia was nowhere in sight. This was unusual—normally she could be found on the circus stage insisting on a last-minute rehearsal. She appeared a short time later looking quite drowsy.

"Sorry, Henri! Overslept. I'm feeling tired these days."

"Maybe it's the heat?" suggested Henri. "Is there anything I can get you? Are you hungry?"

"No thanks, Henri. I'll be fine. Just need to wake up, do a few leg springs, and get the old joints moving." She did a few short jumps in the air and looked much more like her old self.

The day's shows went smoothly. But at mealtime, she couldn't be found.

"Where's Sophia?" There was some murmuring, but no one knew. Henri called in a louder voice, "Sophia, where are you?"

A feeble voice called back. "I'm over here." Sophia lay on her side by the edge of the stage. She did not get up. The other fleas bounded over to her.

163

"Put her on my hand," commanded Henri. He lowered his hand, and the other fleas very gently lifted her up and placed her on his fingertip. "Maria?"

"Yes, Henri."

"Please come alongside. I may need you." Maria jumped up beside Sophia, gently holding her as Henri raised his hand out of the case. He walked over to his trunk, which was stowed under a bench and, with one hand, pulled it out. Henri opened the lid and retrieved an old matchbox. He pulled out a bit of cotton batting, placed it inside the matchbox to make a comfortable bed and then gently lowered the fleas down into the matchbox. Maria carefully lifted Sophia down onto the soft cotton. Sophia let out a satisfied sigh.

"Sophia, you're sick. You can't fool me anymore."

"I guess I can fool you, Henri, because I'm not sick. I'm dying. Not of a disease. Of old age. Tell him, Maria."

"She's right, Henri," said Maria. "We've lived a good life with you and the circus, but we are old. You've taken such wonderful care of us that we've all lived nearly three times as long as we would have on our own, but the time has come. These old legs just don't jump the way they used to."

"Don't look so sad, Henri," said Sophia in a barely audible voice. "We've had fun. I have done things and met insects I never expected to. I wouldn't have missed it for anything! Thank you, Henri. It's been a pleasure knowing you."

Henri could scarcely speak. "Thank you, Sophia, for all your hard work and all the things you have taught me. I'm going to miss you a lot."

"I want to sleep now, Henri. Take Maria back to the others and close the box. I'll see you in the morning."

Henri did as she told him. It was a bit like taking orders from Great Aunt Georgie. He couldn't disobey. And that was the last time Henri spoke to Sophia.

In the morning, he opened the box. Her body was still. The life had gone out of her. Two days later Maria passed away, followed soon thereafter by Liora, Giovanni, and Umberto. Only Fabio remained, and, being a true showman, he gave his last gasp on the stage. As he was shot out the cannon, he bounded from wall to wall ringing the bells to chime out the tune to "La Cucaracha," especially for their Mexican audience. At the successful conclusion of his act, he did not rise from the floor to take his final bow. With his death, the last of the original fleas was gone.

The fleas had enjoyed their fame in the circus. Each of them had children and so Fabio Junior took over his father's act, but to Henri it wasn't the same.

He insisted on a send-off for his friends. It wasn't exactly a funeral but it was a solemn occasion. On a morning when the circus insects normally would have been rehearsing, Henri gathered them together. He had placed the bodies of the deceased fleas in the old matchbox and put it in the center ring. Henri spoke fondly of his departed friends.

"I remember my first day at the circus. Sophia took charge right away and…"

"Henri!"

Henri jumped and turned to see Maestro Antonio, his head poking in the door of the tent and a look of complete astonishment on his face.

"You really can speak to insects, can't you?"

"Umm…well…yes," Henri stuttered. He had been careful to keep all communication between himself and the insects private, but now he had been caught.

Maestro Antonio walked toward Henri. "I have been saying it for months. It's as if you can talk to those insects, and it turns out that's exactly what you are doing!" He chuckled. "Henri, it's time I heard the whole truth. How is it that you can speak to insects? Where are you from? Are you really a boy?"

IT'S ALL INSECT TO ME

Yes, of course I'm a boy!" exclaimed Henri but as he said it he realized he wasn't so sure.

Before the maestro could ask anything more Henri blurted out his whole story.

"I'm not really an orphan," he said and began to tell Maestro Antonio about his father's departure to British Malaya and his subsequent disappearance. Henri explained how his mother sent him to live with Great Aunt Georgie in America and how his life changed the day he spoke with Dom, the fly. He retold the story of the spectacular rescue of the insects in the stream, which had catapulted him to hero status in the insect world. Speaking carefully, Henri shared his suspicions of Agatha Black, aka Madame Noir, and the highly coincidental links to his own story. He finished by telling the maestro how desperately he wanted to travel to British Malaya to search for his father and capture *Goliathus hercules*.

Maestro Antonio looked dumbfounded. At last, he said, "But you haven't explained how it is that you can speak to insects."

"It's just something I am able to do. I thought Professor Young would have an explanation, but he doesn't. All I know is, one day I just opened my mouth, spoke to a fly, and the fly understood me. It seems as if I can speak with and understand anything with six legs. I really don't know. It's a gift, I guess, and a complete mystery," replied Henri, shrugging his shoulders.

"I don't know quite how to say this, Henri," said Maestro Antonio with a look of concern, "but has it ever occurred to you that you might be an insect, or at least turning into one?"

No! It couldn't be, thought Henri. Everyone said he had his father's eyes and his mother's smile. There was definitely a family resemblance. But a biological connection to insects could explain his acute hearing and eyesight. That wasn't all. There was the stiffness in his joints, and recently Henri had noticed that his complexion was becoming quite green and that he was losing his hair! If he was turning into an insect, how long did he have before he would no longer be a boy?

"Tony, it all makes sense in a peculiar way. Um…have you noticed any changes in me lately?"

"Well, you've been looking a bit greenish, kind of sickly. I thought maybe you had picked up a tropical disease of some kind down here, but there's something else too. Your eyes, they seem to be getting bigger and bigger. I hope you don't mind my saying this, Henri, but, um, you seem to be going bald."

Henri groaned and put his head in his hands. Maestro Antonio patted his back and said, "Henri, this is crazy talk. How can a boy turn into an insect? I'm sorry that I ever suggested it. Please forgive me."

Henri looked up. His lips trembled, but when he spoke, his voice was firm and clear. "No, I think you're right, Tony, and if it is true, then I may not have much time left. I have to get to Southeast Asia and find my father."

They sat in silence for some time. At last Maestro Antonio said, "You know, Henri, I have an idea! The insect circus is popular. If we add a few more shows each day it won't be long before we have enough money to get to us to British Malaya."

"What do you mean, 'we'?"

"You're a kid. You're not going to get very far by yourself. First we'll go to London, taking along the Amazing Menagerie of Insects and perform the show to raise a bit more money. While we're there we'll announce that we're going in search of this Goliath…uh…that Hercules type insect. Then we can approach universities and scientists to endorse and maybe even sponsor our trip. Of course we'll look for your father too," assured the maestro.

Henri was stunned into silence for so quickly had the maestro formed a plan.

Maestro Antonio continued, "You know I actually find insects quite fascinating, Henri. Insect communication, why it's revolutionary! We are pioneers in the field! What we're doing should be recognized not just for its entertainment value but as a scientific achievement! You know Professor Young and I have become pen pals. I've been reporting to him on our travels and the various new insects we've added to the show. In his last letter he called me an excellent field researcher. Well I think it's time I went even farther afield!"

Henri sat waiting for Robin and Billy with a mixture of antici-pation and dread. He feared they would notice the change in his appearance. Two months had passed since he had last seen them. At last in the middle of the afternoon with their chores completed, his friends excitedly bounded into the flea circus tent.

Taking only a moment for her eyes to adjust to the darkness of the tent, Robin exclaimed, "Henri, you've been sick! You look terrible! Have you seen a doctor?"

"I'm fine, I'm fine. Don't fuss."

"You're lying. Look at him, Billy. He looks like he's been dreadfully ill!"

Billy eyed him from head to toe. "She's right. You look awful."

"Thanks a lot," retorted Henri. With a sigh he said, "All right, sit down, I've got some news." Slowly, he explained the very strange changes to his body. "Maestro Antonio thinks I might even be turning into an insect," he concluded.

"What!" they both exclaimed.

"That's impossible, Henri! Stop it!" commanded Robin. She turned her back and started to cry. "You should see a doctor," she sniffed.

Henri moved toward her and rested his hand on her shoulder. "Please, Robin, don't cry. I've resigned myself to my fate. Anyway, who knows how long this transformation or metamorphosis or whatever it is might take? It could be years; maybe it will never happen at all. I have things to do, and now I'm motivated to get them done!"

"What do you mean?" asked Billy. "What things do you have to do?"

"For one, search for my father!" Henri explained how his father had gone missing in Malaya and how his mother had gone off to look for him.

"I'm so sorry, Henri," said Billy. "That's terrible."

Henri nodded, looked downward, and was silent. The awkward silence was broken when Henri remembered that he had not yet told Robin and Billy what he considered to be his most interesting piece of news. He looked up and announced that Madame Noir had vanished from the circus. "And according to my Great Aunt Georgie, Mrs. Black, aka Madame Noir, has not been seen at Dutch Elm Farm in many months."

Henri pulled out and read from his great aunt's most recent letter: "It's very good of you to ask about Mrs. Black's health." Henri made a face and continued reading. "Coincidentally, I'm sure, Agatha departed on a trip about the same time you joined the circus. You will recall she was experiencing some respiratory problems. I received a very nice card from her saying that she has gone to a healing spa in the Southwest where the climate is much drier and more suitable for asthmatics."

Henri snorted. "Unlike my Great Aunt Georgie, I don't believe it's a coincidence that Agatha Black disappeared around the same time I joined the circus. And I think it has something to do with *Goliathus hercules*," replied Henri.

"Who's he? Another sideshow performer?" asked Billy.

"No! He…I mean, it could be a she too…" spluttered Henri.

"Oh, like Albert Alberta, the half man, half woman?" asked Robin.

"No! No! No! Can I please finish my sentence? *Goliathus hercules* is an insect, an insect from the jungle of Southeast Asia, the very same area where my father went missing. Robin, I told you about it a long time ago."

"Oh, I remember," said Robin. "The Bigfoot of the insect world," she added skeptically.

"Well, some would say that, but Professor Young thinks it exists, and Tony and I are going to find it before Agatha Black does!"

Henri knew he must sound a bit crazed. What interest could Agatha Black possibly have in *Goliathus hercules*? It barely made sense even to Henri, but his visit to Madame Noir's tent had made it clear that she was interested in insects and Southeast Asia. And then there was the skewered insect on the mourning pin bearing his father's picture. Henri gave a shudder.

"If you're going to Malaya, how are you going to get there and why is Maestro Antonio going?" Robin wanted to know.

"Well, we've saved our money, of course, and we have a plan to raise more. First we'll go to London, taking along the insects to perform the show there. Then Tony thinks we should approach universities and scientists to endorse and maybe sponsor our trip. We're even writing a paper on insect communication with Professor Young to be presented to the British Entomological Society!"

"A paper?" asked Billy.

"It's an academic essay about our research," replied Henri. "Presenting papers and publishing them is how you gain credibility in the worlds of science and academics. Professor Young says this will be important for us if we're to find sponsors. He's helping us, and he says it's good for his reputation too."

"What does Maestro Antonio know about insect communication?" scoffed Robin just as the maestro himself walked into the tent.

Seeing them, Maestro Antonio drew himself up and, in insect language, said, "Your mother eats poo!"

Henri collapsed in a fit of laughter. This was a popular insult in the insect world, although generally not said to flies, as it is usually true.

Of course, Robin and Billy did not understand, and Henri refused to translate.

"You can speak Insect?" asked Robin in surprise.

"Yes," said the maestro proudly. "Henri's been teaching me. I can't articulate everything I want to say yet but I'm making rapid progress. I'll show you why." The maestro opened a trunk and pulled out a metal box with wires, buttons, and an attachable earpiece.

"This newly invented device…what's it called again, Henri?"

"A hearing aid."

"Yes, hearing aids are going to replace the ear trumpet in this modern world. At great expense, we have purchased one. You see, part of what was slowing down my progress was my inability to hear the insects. I can speak with them, but I can't hear them the way Henri can. But now, with this device, I'm able to. I've been practicing with our circus performers, and they tell me I am becoming quite fluent!" He beamed. "I expect Henri has told you of our upcoming expedition. It won't be long before we're ready to head out upon our adventure!"

"Henri, I want to come too," said Billy. "I want to come on the expedition to Malaya to find your father and that big insect."

"Me too!" said Robin.

"Don't be crazy," replied Henri. "It's too dangerous. I don't want you risking your lives for something that doesn't involve you!"

"I'm an orphan," said Billy. "I can make decisions for myself. To be honest, I don't want to be a lion tamer. I want to explore and make discoveries too!"

"I feel the same way as Billy," said Robin. "I was born into the circus. I've never had a choice, but now…well, I'd gladly leave. I want to help you, Henri."

"Whoever heard of running away from the circus?" remarked Maestro Antonio.

"Are you two sure? We can't promise that you'll come back in one piece," Henri said in his most serious voice, but really he was overjoyed that his friends wanted to come along.

"Yes!" Billy and Robin replied.

Before any more objections could be made Billy said, "OK, so it's agreed. I think that we should learn to speak Insect too. When can we start?"

"How about after the last performance tonight?" suggested Henri.

And so it was that Billy and Robin learned to run the insect circus because it was best way to learn the language. They came to the tent during their free time; Henri provided basic instruction, and the rest of the insects acted as their tutors. Maestro Antonio, Billy, and Robin would never have the kind of hearing to become as fluent as Henri, but they progressed nicely with the help of the hearing aid. Robin turned out to be the best of the three because she worked harder at it.

With Robin and Billy assisting, the insect circus was able to perform more often and thus it was possible to quickly save money for the expedition. Sometimes Maestro Antonio and Henri even left them in charge. Of course, there was some unintended hilarity as Billy and Robin learned how to work with the insects. On May fifteenth, Billy asked the fireflies to spell out *Happy birthday, Robin* at the conclusion of the day's show. He failed to make sure they knew the spelling or the order of the letters, which was a mistake—after all, the fireflies couldn't actually read. Thus, as they reached the finale of the show, they flew out in formation to spell *Harpy barfday, nibor.* Robin said it was the thought that counted.

By the time the circus's season was drawing to a close,

Maestro Antonio announced that they had enough money to go to London and on to British Malaya! At the conclusion of their final show, Henri, Maestro Antonio, Robin, and Billy packed their bags and the insect circus. They were taking the train to New York and from there they would travel by steamship to London. It was a most extraordinary group that gathered on the railway platform to send them off. Tears were shed by Robin's family as well as by Hope and Charity the conjoined twins and Gertrude the Fat Lady. Herbert Kramer the Lion Tamer had taken up a collection and the adventurers were presented with an odd assortment of gifts including a lucky rabbit's foot, an umbrella, and a fly swatter! As they waved to their friends from the window of the train, the whistle blew, and with a blast of steam the train started to move. As they pulled out of the station Henri saw that Andre the World's Strongest Man held Theo the Human Caterpillar above his head. He waved one last time, closed the window, and smiled. The quest was truly about to begin!

A LONDON REUNION

The door to the old apartment opened. Henri took one look at his mother's face. In an instant he knew that for both of them Father's absence had created a hole, a gap that could not be filled, a chasm so deep and wide it could not be crossed. A piece of the puzzle that would have made their family whole was missing.

Now, as Henri stood looking across at his mother, he felt like a stranger. They were both older. Henri was twelve years old. It had been two years since he had seen his mother, and four since his father had gone missing. It was a bittersweet reunion because in all the letters that had crossed the ocean, there had always been hope. Father would come home, and they would be together again. They had willed themselves to believe that he would be found, but that had not happened.

Henri looked deep into his mother's eyes, and to his relief, he still saw hope. They would persevere, keep looking and do whatever needed to be done to locate his father.

Without a word she embraced her son, and they stood clinging to each other for a long time. She did not remark on his appearance. She seemed to be preoccupied with the fact that he was home. Henri was glad he didn't have to make up an excuse, although he was prepared to if she did ask. He certainly was not going to tell her the truth. She had enough worry in her life already.

With tears in her eyes, she thanked Maestro Antonio for looking after her son. She embraced Robin and Billy and said it had given her great comfort to know that Henri had such good friends.

They sat down to have tea in the dining room. Henri's mother produced maps of Southeast Asia and British Malaya that they immediately began to pore over. They had been folded and unfolded so often that some were falling apart at the creases. Each map was marked with circles, Xs, and a few question marks.

"Mrs. Bell, can you explain your notations on the maps?" asked Maestro Antonio.

"Well, the places marked with an X are the first I visited. They were obvious places—the plantation where George was employed and the state capital that he visited frequently. The circled locations are places that he had mentioned in letters and postcards, places I knew he visited. I went to all of those too…but nothing," she said in a defeated voice.

"And the question marks?" asked Henri.

"Those are places that I didn't visit but would have liked to. They are very remote areas, dense forest into which it just wasn't possible for me to go alone."

"Then that's where we should start!" said Henri. "Mother, we are organizing a scientific expedition in search of *Goliathus hercules*, a mysterious insect that, coincidentally, is found in the same area that Father went missing. Nobody has captured one alive, and we intend to do so. At the same time, we will be looking for Father."

Maestro Antonio took over and told Henri's mother of the insect circus they had brought to London and the paper they would be presenting to the British Entomological Society in three months' time. "We are...um...or really, I should say, Henri is an expert on all matters to do with insects. With Henri as our leader, no one is better prepared than we are to set out on the quest to find *Goliathus hercules*—and your husband."

Henri gave her an encouraging smile.

"Well, I insist you all stay here with me while you make your preparations!" said Henri's mother.

Robin shared a room with Henri's mother, Billy shared Henri's room, and Maestro Antonio had the chesterfield in the parlor, which he shared with the insect menagerie. Sometimes at night, Henri could hear the maestro as he tried to shush the peeps and calls of the performers. "Confound it! Can't a human get some rest? We're not all nocturnal, you know!"

Next, they set about finding a small theater to present Maestro Antonio's Amazing Menagerie of Insects—the Greatest Little

Show on Earth. It was hard to find a place with the intimacy of the old circus tent, but they were finally able to rent a church basement near Piccadilly Circus. The new space was larger than the old circus tent, and so it was decided they would have to revamp the act, making it even more spectacular than ever.

Maestro Antonio and Henri had decided that their first performance should be by invitation only. Professor Young had written letters of introduction to many of his colleagues in the entomological world. Fifty learned guests in all were invited to see a staggering display of exceptional communication between man and insect. In addition, they had invited reviewers from the three major London newspapers.

Opening night arrived. With everyone seated, the lights dimmed. The synchronous fireflies flew out and spelled the welcoming words:

Next, the fireflies moved into position to form a glowing, floating Union Jack. The insect orchestra began their first number, "God the Save the Queen," and the entire audience felt obliged to stand. At the conclusion of the song, the fireflies burst into pinwheels, shooting stars, and tumbling cascades of light. The audience burst into thunderous applause.

Then the lights went up to reveal a boldly patterned wall of color. As the music began, the audience could see a figure moving away from the wall that had until now been camouflaged in the pattern— it was a girl entirely covered with butterflies, moths, grasshoppers, and cicadas! As she danced to the music, the winged creatures slowly ascended from her dress and joined her in the dance. Gradually, the patterned wall behind Robin dissolved

as other insects took flight, so that they all waltzed around her in a whirlwind of color and magic. As the orchestra reached the last notes of the song, the luna moth rested on her forehead, and other smaller butterflies came to alight upon the top of her head to form a crown. Then Robin made an elegant curtsy and exited the stage with the colorful entourage in her wake.

After that, Henri and Maestro Antonio walked onto the stage to introduce the circus performers. The new aerial acrobatics routine with orange grasshoppers acquired during their stay in Mexico received wild applause. They could fly higher and farther than the flea trapeze artists ever could. Then Billy came out and refereed a wrestling match between a flea and a junebug. Despite the flea's diminutive size, she won the match when the junebug called out "Uncle!" Maestro Antonio had figured out a way to set up the hearing aid so that it amplified the sound enough that the audience was certain they had heard the junebug give up in defeat.

At the conclusion of the show, Maestro Antonio and Henri stepped forward. In his booming voice, the maestro announced, "Thank you for attending the British premiere of the Greatest Little Show on Earth. It has been our pleasure to entertain you. But friends, we have a bigger mission than this. All of nature's magic you have witnessed tonight is the result of my colleague Henri Bell's research and dedication to insect communication.

"In six months' time we will embark on an expedition to British Malaya to capture and bring back the mysterious *Goliathus hercules*!"

There was an audible intake of breath at this announcement.

Oh, many have sought to find it, but none have succeeded. Well, now I present the only man up to the job: Henri Bell.

"We are looking for sponsorship for our expedition. I invite you to contribute and share in the scientific glory that will come to all associated with our endeavor."

The next morning the three newspapers reported on the show. Each gave a glowing review. For the next three months, every show was sold out and contributions to the expedition came flowing in. Queen Victoria herself requested a performance of the insect circus at Buckingham Palace. After the show there, she declared herself to be very amused and gave her royal endorsement and support for the expedition.

In early June, Professor Young arrived in London a few weeks

before they were to present their paper to the British Entomological Society. Henri and the maestro had already raised
enough for their journey to Malaya, but they were anxious for the
approval of the scientific community.

Everything was going so well—far better than any of them
had dared to hope. There was just one thing that bothered
Henri. One evening, as the show concluded and the audience
was leaving, Henri spotted a tall woman dressed in black near
the back of the theater. She glanced up and smiled. Henri could
not see her face, for she wore a mourning veil over her hat, but
he recognized the smile immediately.

SCANDAL

Truth be told, Henri found their paper to the British Entomological Society a bit dull. He and Maestro Antonio had left it to Professor Young to present the information academically. They had made astounding discoveries, but when Professor Young presented it, it was all Henri could do to sit up straight and not nod off in front of the large audience. Maestro Antonio sat beside him with a glazed look on his face.

"As I have previously indicated, my early research noted fourteen distinctive clicks made by *O. disjunctus*," the professor read. "However, Mr. Bell was able to decipher an additional fifteen, making a total of twenty-nine recognizable and distinct sounds. Used in combination with one another, this gives the species a total of 812 possible phonetic combinations. I shall now begin the elocution of the twenty-nine distinctive clicks. Number one..." And so on and so on, it went.

Nonetheless, the professor's presentation brought a tremendous round of applause. Now Henri and Maestro Antonio were to give a practical demonstration. They would take requests from the audience who would ask that the insects perform various tasks and maneuvers.

Henri and Antonio rose and stood beside the table next to a tank of various insects waiting to be summoned. They had agreed to speak the language in voices that the audience could hear, although from the insects' point of view, this was the equivalent of bellowing.

The chairman selected a man in a tall black top hat who introduced himself as Dr. Pratt from the Entomology department at Oxford University.

"Could you please have one of the large scarab beetles fly from the tank and land on the top of my hat?" he asked.

"Sir," replied Henri. "I could make such a request, but as an entomologist, you yourself will know that these large beetles are not able flyers. I do not believe one could make it the entire distance without stopping to rest. I would recommend that you select another gentleman or lady who would be willing to serve as the midway stopping point before it proceeds to your own hat."

"Very well observed. You are correct," said the man in the top hat as he scanned the audience. A number of people had their hands up, offering to volunteer. He selected a man in a bowler hat whom he addressed as Professor Chadbourne.

Professor Chadbourne rose to his feet.

185

Henri chose one of the large scarab beetles and clearly and audibly gave the instructions through a series of clicks and hums. He raised his hand, and the beetle took off, wildly flying off-kilter, up, down, and from side to side, before successfully landing on top of Professor Chadbourne's bowler hat with a bit of a thud. The beetle took a quick break and then launched itself in the direction of Dr. Pratt's hat in the same less-than-graceful style. He landed with a plop, and the audience clapped enthusiastically. Dr. Pratt walked up to the stage so Henri could remove the scarab, and they shook hands.

The chairman next selected a short, squat older gentleman who had not a hair left on his shiny head. "Please make your request, Mr. Heathrow."

"Yes, thank you, Mr. Chairman. Well, as you can see, I am a little lacking on top." He patted his bald head. "I wonder if you would be so kind as to provide me with a living wig of various insect species," he said.

"Of course, sir," said Henri. Together, he and Maestro Antonio selected a number of insects that, upon receiving their instructions, flew directly to the man's head and landed nimbly. Eventually, they covered the top of his head, nicely giving him the most fantastic and elaborate hairdo. It was as if he had braids and a topknot! Maestro Antonio invited Mr. Heathrow to come to the stage and model his new hairstyle, which he did with an enormous grin on his face.

The chairman then selected a woman, a Mrs. Blackburn. From his vantage point, Henri could only see the top of a very elaborate hat adorned with bird feathers and even a stuffed wood pigeon. When she stood up, Henri saw that her face was obscured by a mourning veil. She was exceptionally tall and wore a stiff, black silk dress. His stomach turned.

"Please proceed, Mrs. Blackburn," said the chairman.

"Thank you, Mr. Chairman. I do have one small request, but first if I may, I would like to make an observation. We have listened today to a very learned dissertation on insect communication, and I have no quibble with the facts stated. I do wish to note that the authors fully admit Mr. Bell actually hears the insects in full clarity. Am I the only one here who finds this odd? Such an ability suggests powers far beyond a mortal being!"

The audience looked absolutely shocked. What was Mrs. Blackburn suggesting?

"I have investigated Mr. Bell, and for the past two years he has traveled in a circus sideshow. During this time, he has gone through a remarkable transformation, or should I say, *metamorphosis*. He began as a normal-looking little boy, but I say—look at him now! Mr. Bell, I have one request: would you mind removing your hat?"

Maestro Antonio appeared tense. Professor Young seemed perplexed. Sitting in the front row, Henri's mother, Robin, and Billy looked outraged. There was nothing Henri could do. He calmly removed his hat and put it on his lap. In the last three months, he had lost all his hair. His head was as shiny as Mr. Heathrow's with one exception. On either side of it, he had two bumps, each the size of a quail egg.

"You see!" exclaimed Mrs. Blackburn. "He is a freak! A sideshow freak! This is not a boy! Perhaps he is a changeling! Look at his green pallor and his head. What is that forming on the sides? Horns? Perhaps we are sitting with the devil in our very midst! I, for one, shall not sit here listening to the enticements of evil!" With a dramatic turn and a swish of her skirts, she marched out of the lecture hall. There was a hush and then a murmuring.

The audience was shocked, although it was unclear whether they were surprised by Henri or by Mrs. Blackburn's behavior. A dozen or so people stood up and exited the hall. Henri knew that suggesting someone was a changeling, the offspring of trolls, ogres, and other malevolent creatures, was a serious accusation, but surely none of these academics would believe Mrs. Blackburn, would they? Henri continued to sit, nervously turning his hat in his hands.

It seemed as if utter chaos was about to break out. It was Maestro Antonio who raised his hands to calm the crowd. His many years in the circus had taught him how to deal with unruly crowds.

"Ladies and gentleman, we have come today to hear of the latest breakthroughs in science. We are believers in facts, logic, and the scientific method. I fear to say that Mrs. Blackburn is surely no scientist, for she clings to old wives' tales. Will we let superstition and prejudice guide us? Mr. Bell has the great misfortune to suffer from a grievous condition—alopecia—better known as hair loss. I see nothing sinister in this. It is our great hope that modern medicine will in the near future help him and that he will sport a healthy head of hair. In the meantime, he can wear a hat or, like Mr. Heathrow, enjoy a living wig, if he so chooses."

There were some chuckles from the crowd.

"Please, Mr. Bell, I think none of us will object if you put on your hat."

Henri did not hesitate.

"As to the unfortunate bumps on his head, it is true that he had hoped to hide them. They are the result of a particularly virulent reaction to chicken pox. Sadly a couple of his spots became infected, causing the skin to rise. He has the coincidental misfortune that they should appear symmetrically on either side of his head. While Mrs. Blackburn thought they were devil's horns, I would not be surprised, at this meeting of entomologists, if you thought he was growing antennae!" Maestro Antonio gave a hearty laugh at his little joke, and most of the audience joined in with him. "Might it be possible to return to our demonstration, Mr. Chairman?" the maestro asked.

The chairman appeared a little unsure, but as he looked out into the audience, many raised their hands, hoping to be selected.

At the conclusion of the demonstration, there was resounding applause. The chairman took to the podium. "Ladies and gentlemen, superstition and prejudice have no business in our learned halls. Tonight the British Entomological Society and the Geographic Society announce that we are endorsing and supporting Mr. Bell and company on their search for *Goliathus hercules*. We wish them Godspeed!"

Many in the audience stood up and cheered. Henri and Maestro Antonio waved to the audience as Professor Young uncharacteristically raised a celebratory fist. Finally, the validation they had sought was theirs.

Now that Henri's changing form had been pointed out, Professor Young was concerned, although he also was professionally interested.

"It's a first, Henri! Man transforms into insect! I understand that it is, um…a little disturbing—perhaps a tad inconvenient—but just think: perhaps you'll be able to fly! Wouldn't that be remarkable? We must record this metamorphosis for the scientific community."

Henri allowed the professor to weigh him, measure his growing antennae, and question him on his health each day. The professor had pointed out that perhaps, if Henri were able to change from human to insect, it might be possible to reverse the process as well. Henri desperately wanted to believe that. While he liked insects very much, he wasn't so sure he wanted to be one.

Henri's mother never spoke of his condition. She was her usual loving and attentive self. Henri once recalled that when he was very small, he had asked her whether she had wanted a girl or a boy while she was expecting him. She had responded that it made no difference. All she wanted was a happy, healthy baby. "What if I was a fox? Would you still love me?" She had laughed and said, "Of course I would love my baby fox." However, a fox is cuddlier than an insect.

The day of the departure to Malaya drew ever closer. The party would say good-bye to Henri's mother, the professor, and all the menagerie insects that would return with Professor Young to America. He promised to care for them, and their offspring could await Henri and the maestro's return.

At last, everything was ready. Maestro Antonio and Henri had met with various members of the Entomological and Geographical Societies and had agreed to gather specimens of plant and insect life. Billy and Robin dealt with the practical matters such as gathering tents, camping equipment, rain gear, more maps, two cameras, and notebooks.

On a rainy evening in September, the expedition party gathered at Waterloo Station. From there, they would travel by train to the south coast, over the English Channel by ferry, and on to Paris by train again, where they would catch the Orient Express to Constantinople. It would be at least a four-month journey overland, along the old trade route known as the Silk Road, before they turned southward to British Malaya.

The train whistle blew to signal its impending departure. Henri moved to his mother. She hugged him close to her, but she did not cry. "Promise to write, dear."

"Of course, I will. Don't worry."

"I won't," she said firmly. "Henri, I believe in you. I know you will be successful. I love you."

"Thanks, I love you too."

Henri turned to Professor Young. "Good-bye, professor. Don't worry: Tony will keep up the measuring and recording."

"Good grief, son! I'm not worried about that. Take care of yourself, Henri." And for once, he dropped all formality and embraced Henri.

With that, the travelers boarded the train and entered their compartment. As the train pulled out from the station, Henri leaned out the window for one final good-bye. As he did so, he noticed someone else leaning out the window one carriage down—someone in a large black hat with feathers and a veil.

Henri drew back inside immediately and slammed the window shut.

22

CAT AND MOUSE

She's the Woman of a Thousand Faces!" Billy joked when Henri told the group that Agatha Black—aka Madame Noir and Mrs. Blackburn—was aboard the train.

"Ha-ha," replied Robin. "Does she think we're little children who don't know any better? Fooled by her every disguise?"

"No," said Henri. "She's trying to torment me. It's a game to her, and she seems pretty confident. Why else would she continue to show up in these ridiculous costumes?"

"You're right, Henri," said Billy. "These are the actions of someone toying with their prey. Like a cat playing with a mouse."

Mrs. Blackburn did not emerge from her compartment until they reached Constantinople. When she stepped off the train, she was enveloped in black from head to foot in a burka. Among the devout Muslims of the city, it would have been the perfect disguise, had Mrs. Blackburn not been so tall. Henri laughed mockingly when he saw her step down on the platform; however, Mrs. Blackburn turned out to have the last laugh, for they quickly lost sight of her in a sea of anonymous women concealed in black.

The expedition traveled through Arabia by camel. It was not until they reached the lands of the Silk Road trade route that Henri would sight his nemesis again. They had given up the camels and now traveled by donkey cart. This was necessary in order to transport their many trunks of equipment and supplies over rocky, treacherous terrain. The donkeys were slow, and one day, a palanquin—a chair carried on four poles—and its uniformed bearers caught up and passed them. For the next three days, over desolate, dry earth, the palanquin was always in sight. They speculated on who might be traveling inside.

"Maybe a princess?" suggested Robin. "The daughter of an emperor?"

"Why does it always have to be a princess or something out of a fairy tale?" complained Billy.

"If it were a princess, I expect there would be an army escorting her. This person only has eight in her party," replied Maestro Antonio.

They set up their tents each night upon ground that was not really desert but was nonetheless wasteland, rocky and unforgiving. On the morning of the fourth day, they saw just who rode in such grandeur. It was a woman—a tall woman in a black tunic. Her head was covered in an elaborately embroidered black cloth, and she wore a veil so that only her eyes and forehead were exposed.

"I can't believe it!" said Robin.

"I can!" said Henri. "I'm going over there to settle this once and for all!"

Maestro Antonio put on his hat and joined him.

However, they didn't get very far. They were within thirty yards of the camp when they were stopped by the four palanquin bearers, who held raised swords. A finely dressed man approached and bowed.

"Good morning, gentlemen. My name is Khan. May I be of assistance?"

"Yes, you may. We would like to speak to your mistress," said Maestro Antonio.

Khan smiled. "I am sorry, but that is not possible. It is not appropriate for a woman to meet with strange men."

Henri spoke up. "Could you give her a message?"

"Certainly," replied Khan politely.

"Please tell her we're watching her," said Henri.

Khan looked perplexed but nodded.

"One other thing," said Henri. "What is your mistress's name?"

"In our culture, it is impolite to address someone by their given name," said Khan. "The lady you speak of is the emperor's wife's cousin's brother-in-law's sister."

Henri and Maestro Antonio looked at each other and then burst out laughing. "And I'm the King of Siam!" said Maestro Antonio.

Khan frowned and said, "She's a very important person. Please wait while I deliver your message."

A short time later he returned with the message that the emperor's wife's cousin's brother-in-law's sister sent her regards and invited them to travel to Tashkent with her party. She was making the journey so that she could purchase the finest Chinese silks at a workshop in that city.

"We'd be delighted to join her," said Henri. He figured there was no harm in following and if she was indeed Agatha Black in disguise, they might get a better idea of her intentions. They trailed the palanquin for another four days before finally entering Tashkent, the city known as the gateway to the Orient and famous for its beautiful mosques.

They had to leave their carts at the outskirts of the city to follow the palanquin through the narrow, dark streets. The old quarter of the city was like a labyrinth. Streets meandered and forked so that Henri and the others soon lost their bearings. This made Henri nervous. Perhaps they were walking into some kind of trap. His anxiety became even greater as his ears picked up a sound—a sound so awful, he stopped dead in his tracks.

"What is it, Henri?" asked Billy.

"Don't you hear it?" replied Henri, putting his hands to his ears. Henri sank to his knees. "They're crying! They're screaming in pain! Oh, it's terrible!" Tears started to well up in his eyes.

"Who, Henri? Who's screaming?" cried Robin.

"I don't know," groaned Henri. "It's coming from that direction." He pointed to the way the palanquin had gone.

"Come on!" said Maestro Antonio. He and Billy grabbed Henri under the arms and lifted him to his feet. They dragged him through the streets until they came to a gate with a sign over it.

TASHKENT SILK FACTORY
ESTABLISHED IN 1805

Supplier to His Imperial Majesty the Emperor
& the Khan of Mongolia

They could see the palanquin had been set down in the courtyard. Henri could barely stand.

"Maybe we shouldn't go in," said Billy, looking at Henri.

"We have to!" cried Henri.

"This could be a trick!" said Robin.

"I don't care! I can't let them hurt them anymore! I can't let them kill them!" Henri stumbled into the compound. The others followed warily.

Henri looked around frantically. All around the courtyard women sat at looms weaving, while others dipped silk threads into dye baths of brilliant colors. The courtyard was festooned with beautiful, shiny silk fabrics, hung to dry. Some of them still dripped with dye. They flapped in the breeze like long multi-colored flags. It was a festive sight, but Henri still sensed pain and death. On the right, they saw Khan and the emperor's wife's cousin's brother-in-law's sister standing by steaming pots. Khan walked toward them. Henri stood rooted to the spot with his hands over his ears.

"Welcome to the Tashkent Silk Factory. Here you can see how silk is made." He looked at Henri with some concern, obviously wondering if he was trying to slight him with his

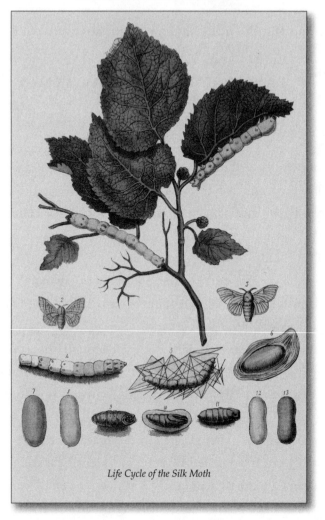

Life Cycle of the Silk Moth

hands placed over his ears. He must have decided to ignore this peculiarity, for he continued, "Do you know how silk thread is made?"

They all shook their heads.

Khan led them to a corner of the courtyard where trays of

leaves were set out. Upon the fresh green leaves, thousands of caterpillars munched happily. "These are silkworms, the caterpillars that make silk. They eat only mulberry leaves. When it is time, they will spin their cocoons."

He moved over to show them some nearby branches where caterpillars wound the silk thread they produced around their body. This created a cozy protective home, where they would transform themselves and later emerge as silk moths. Some of the cocoons were complete. Attached to a branch, they appeared as unmoving white capsules of about half a finger's length. Henri watched and tried to listen to Khan, but he still held his hands over his ears, trying to keep out the horrible screams.

Khan directed them back to where the emperor's wife's cousin's brother-in-law's sister stood partially obscured by great billows of steam coming from the pots. "Here is where the silk thread is unraveled," said Khan. They watched as a woman with about six cocoons in her hand prepared to drop them into the boiling pots.

Suddenly Henri understood. "Stop!" he yelled. "You'll kill them if you do that!" He reached out and grabbed the woman's hand. Everyone looked startled except the emperor's wife's cousin's brother-in-law's sister. She stared intently at Henri.

"But how will they reel the silk thread?" asked Khan in a reasonable voice. "The water softens the gum that holds the cocoon together."

"Don't you see? The boiling water kills the silkworm. It can't survive that," replied Henri.

"It's true," said Khan, "but I think it is a small price to pay to have the most luxurious fabric in the world upon the emperor's wife's cousin's brother-in-law's sister's back. Today we have come to order a thousand yards of the finest silk this workshop produces."

Henri was outraged. "Just how many silkworms will die for that?"

Khan turned to the woman who held the cocoons and spoke to her in an unfamiliar language. "She says they will need one million cocoons to produce that much cloth." Henri still held the woman's hand. Now he turned it over, pried open her fingers and removed the silk cocoons. He was shaking with anger. "One million dying is a small price to pay? Maybe to you, but not to them!" He held up the cocoons. "I hear them screaming. It is an agonizing death!"

Robin, Billy, and Maestro Antonio looked horrified, for they now understood that what Henri had heard were the wails of silkworms being boiled alive. They heard a laugh and looked from Henri to the face of the emperor's wife's cousin's brother-in-law's sister, still veiled in the steaming mist. Khan approached her, and she whispered into his ear.

"She says you are very sentimental. She is sorry that you are upset. She thought this might be an educational visit."

Henri was ready to leap at the emperor's wife's cousin's brother-in-law's sister and toss her into the big, steaming pot of boiling water, but he was held back by Maestro Antonio and Billy. Henri struggled, but they were too strong for him.

As gently as they could, they forced Henri out the factory gate, finally releasing him once they were on the street.

"W-why didn't you l-let me at her?" he stuttered in anger.

"She's the emperor's wife's cousin's brother-in-law's sister—royalty, in other words. They probably would have locked us in prison and tossed away the key if you had hurt her," declared Maestro Antonio.

"She is *not* royalty!" retorted Henri. "She's Agatha Black! You know she is! Masquerading once again!"

"Henri, we all know that, but Tony is right. The people around here seem to think that she is royalty," Robin said.

"What do we do now?" asked Billy.

"We wait!" snapped Henri. "And then we follow her."

Grimly, they agreed. They retreated down the street, hiding in a very narrow and smelly alley until the palanquin passed. Stealthily as they could, they followed it to the marketplace. At last, it stopped.

Henri watched as the emperor's wife's cousin's brother-in-law's sister emerged from the palanquin and walked over to a stall that had shelf upon shelf of tiny, very ornate cages, too small for a bird. Henri recognized them right away from his days of polishing buttons for Great Aunt Georgie. They were cricket cages. At once, the most sorrowful sound came to his ears. It was the saddest song in the world. There were different voices, but they all sang the same story. A tale of once-happy, pleasure-filled days until the cricket was captured and forced by man to sing its song. The songs spoke of lonely, gray days trapped in the beautiful barred prison cell. It was a lovely song, but so sad.

After the emperor's wife's cousin's brother-in-law's sister pointed to a cricket, the shopkeeper used a sharp stick to poke the cricket, which was its cue to begin singing. She tested the voices of at least a dozen crickets before finally purchasing six of the best singers. In their individual cages, they were packed into the palanquin. The shopkeeper gave her his stick. The emperor's wife's cousin's brother-in-law's sister returned to the palanquin and pulled the curtain. Immediately, the crickets began to sing. Henri, Robin, Billy, and Maestro Antonio all understood the sad song. They winced as they imagined the crickets jabbed with the stick, ordered to sing their melancholy tale.

When the palanquin was gone, Henri approached the stall. He gazed at the caged crickets and turned to the others. "We're buying them all," he said. No one objected. Maestro Antonio hired three men to help carry the cricket cages to the city out-skirts. There they opened the doors, and as they did so, he said, "You're free. Run away from here." Many simply hopped away as fast as they could, but others stopped to ask which human had freed them. "Henri. Henri Bell," was the response.

"Thank you, Henri Bell, for your great kindness. We shall not forget this, and I will tell all my kind of this selfless deed," said one. And that was the beginning of Henri's fame in the Orient among the six-legged folk. He was a beacon of light, a reason for hope as a "Black" cloud crossed the continent.

They continued to track Agatha Black, aka Madame Noir, aka

Mrs. Blackburn, aka the emperor's wife's cousin's brother-in-law's sister, following her to every site of insect atrocity known to man. In each country, she assumed a new identity, although why she bothered, they couldn't understand.

"Maybe she just likes to dress up?" suggested Robin.

"She's toying with us," retorted Henri.

In India, they trailed her to a workshop where the wings were torn off live jewel beetles to make hair ornaments Mrs. Black had braided into her long hair. In Burma, she feasted on wok-fried cicadas, popping them into her mouth like they were peanuts. In Thailand, she commissioned a fancy serving tray covered in a mosaic pattern of butterfly wings.

Agatha Black's cruelty seemed to know no bounds. Her capacity to inflict pain and suffering upon insects seemed insatiable. It was obvious she took malicious pleasure in watching their pain. It disgusted Henri. He burned with a hatred so strong that sometimes he could think of nothing else. He knew he could not rest until he had captured *Goliathus hercules*, found his father, and put an end to Agatha Black!

INTO THE GREEN

The air in Kuala Lumpur was thick with humidity and exotic scents. Nothing in Malaya was dull, Henri noticed. People wore flowing garments in a rainbow of colors. The vegetation was the most dazzling bright green, and trees were laden with fruit so enormous that one would have thought they were grown expressly for giants.

They were all relieved now that they'd arrived in the capital of British Malaya. Still, Henri had trouble sleeping at night. Just south of Bangkok in Siam they had lost track of Agatha Black. He awoke again and again from nightmares of Mrs. Black's horrific crimes. Billy had taken to wearing binoculars around his neck and was constantly scanning the horizon for any sign of "the old hag," as he referred to her. Maestro Antonio put his energy into recording their journey and making notes on the landscape, plants, and animals they encountered.

It was clear that Mrs. Black was heading to British Malaya like they were, though the maestro wondered why she didn't just rush ahead and find *Goliathus hercules* herself. "She's obviously capable," he remarked. "And wickedly smart. She could have all the fame and glory to herself."

"Lots of people have tried to capture *Goliathus hercules* before, but no one has succeeded," said Billy. "Maybe she wants to ride our coattails into the jungle and snatch him right up from under our noses."

"I think it's more than that," said Robin. "She doesn't just want to capture it. Maybe she needs Henri to speak to it. But why?"

"I think Robin's right. She needs me for some reason, but at the same time she's trying to wear me down. That's what all this torment is about."

They decided to start in Kuala Selangor, which was north of Kuala Lumpur and near the coast. Henri felt drawn to the area because it is the one other place in the world where synchronous fireflies can be found. Having worked with the fireflies in the circus, he was keen to meet their cousins. If they found nothing there, they would keep traveling inland to a vast, uncharted jungle to the west where the oldest rainforests in the world could be found.

As they waited for the rainy season to end, they looked for a reliable guide to hire in Kuala Lumpur. Foreign explorers and adventurers like themselves tended to congregate in a few restaurants and social clubs around the city. In one such place, a restaurant called the Golden Horse Palace, they met a well-known explorer named George Maxwell. He had written a book called *In Malay Forests*. He was just the man to help them find a guide. Mr. Maxwell was intrigued as he listened to Henri describe their mission.

"There seems little doubt that *Goliathus hercules* is a member of the beetle family, order *Coleoptera*," Henri said. "And physically it's one of the most intimidating-looking insects to walk the earth. Its head is crowned with shiny, black horns tipped with gold!"

"You're a tad late," said a rather belligerent-looking, red-faced man sitting nearby with a group of men dressed in safari khaki.

"Excuse me?" said Henri.

"I said you've missed the boat!" replied the man. He smirked at his friends, and they laughed in return.

Maestro Antonio spoke up. "Are you saying that someone has announced the capture of a live specimen?"

"Well, a few weeks ago," said the red-faced man with emphasis. "A tall woman...What was her name?" The man turned to his friends.

"Was it Blackburn?" asked Robin.

"Yes! That's it, but she should be called Mrs. High and Mighty! She waltzes in here announcing that she's on an expedition to capture *Goliathus hercules*. Says she's even got the blessing of Her Royal Highness Queen Victoria! She was waving around a piece of paper and showing it to anyone who would look. I didn't bother looking, myself, because, after all, would the queen really send someone on such a fool's errand? Mrs. High and Mighty is flapping about in her black dress and starched petticoats like she's on her way to the British high commissioner's funeral, not off into the jungle!" He let out a hardy laugh. His friends chortled along with him.

Henri turned to his companions. With his elbows on the table, he rested his head in his hands. He felt defeated.

"Cheer up, Henri," said Billy resolutely. "They didn't say she had caught *Goliathus hercules*, although I have to admit she's got a head start on us."

"I take it that she is your rival in this venture?" asked George Maxwell. They all nodded. "Every explorer has a rival, a competitor with whom they are racing against to reach their destination or goal. Sometimes it is a friendly rivalry—"

"Not in this case!" interjected Billy.

"I gather that. Bitter adversaries have been driven to despicable acts, including slandering the competition, sabotaging the

207

other's equipment, and even murder!"

"All excellent ideas," muttered Billy under his breath. He received a sharp elbow from Robin.

"But I caution you not to lose sight of what's important. Don't concern yourself with Mrs. Blackburn. She is a distraction. In order to successfully complete your mission, it will require your complete attention and all of your energy. Don't let her needling divert you from your goal."

"That's exactly what she's been trying to do," said Robin with vehemence.

"We haven't come all this way to give up now," said Maestro Antonio. "Remember, Henri, capturing *Goliathus hercules* is just one part of our goal."

"You lot must be those circus people Mrs. High and Mighty said were on her tail," the red-faced man chortled.

"Just what else did she say?" asked Henri sharply.

"She said you're a bunch of sideshow freaks, and I have to say that you, young man, look rather peculiar. I predict your little party won't last a week in the jungle."

Henri, Billy, and Maestro Antonio stood up. "Don't let him goad you," implored Robin.

The red-faced man continued laughing and then said, "You know, once you capture *Goliathus hercules*, you could head south to the Dutch East Indies. You can pick yourselves up a garuda— half man and half bird. Put them both in your sideshow!"

"After that, they can go to Tibet and capture the yeti!" said one of his companions who wore a monocle.

"I think it's time we departed," said Mr. Maxwell.

The party gathered their possessions and moved toward the door without a word to the jeering table of men. Henri paused. "I'm sorry, I think I left my notebook at the table. I'll just be a moment. You can wait outside for me."

"Make it quick, Henri," instructed Maestro Antonio as he ushered the others out the door. Henri turned back to the table, fiddling with the buttons on his shirt as he walked. He stopped briefly at the vacated table and then moved to stand in front of the red-faced man and his companions.

"Gentlemen, we never formally introduced ourselves." He held out his hand to the red-faced man who reluctantly took it and then Henri shook the hand of the monocled man. "I'm Henri Bell."

"Harry Staunton," said red-faced man.

"Albert Perkins," said the monocled man.

Henri turned to the other two men in the group. "And you two?" he asked. With lightning speed, another set of arms with clawlike hands emerged from Henri's shirt and grabbed their hands. All the men screamed, jumping up and knocking down chairs and drinks, and the two in Henri's grasp wrestled to remove his viselike grip.

Henri released them at last. "Oh, well. Another time, then," he said. "Perhaps I'll see you gentlemen when we return with *Goliathus hercules*. I know you'll want to be the first to congratulate me. And thank you for the suggestions of other adventures, but you must understand that insects are my passion."

Henri retracted his extra set of limbs, quickly buttoned his shirt, and with a little bow, turned and exited the Golden Horse Palace.

Henri did not mention the hand-shaking incident to his companions. There was no denying it: in Henri's present form, he was half man and half insect. His fully formed antennae were usually tucked under his hat, his eyes were the size of saucers, and he had sprouted another set of limbs out of his chest. "Who couldn't use an extra set of hands?" Billy joked, but still, it was terrifying.

Unless he was alone with Robin, Billy, and Maestro Antonio, Henri kept these extra limbs concealed under his shirt, although he had to make a conscious effort not to reach out to grab things with them. His hands were becoming more clawlike than anything else. Even Maestro Antonio could no longer explain away his deformities with hushed whispers of "thyroid problem combined with an extreme case of arthritis." Henri's days in public seemed numbered.

"Don't listen to those blowhards at the Golden Horse Palace, Henri," Mr. Maxwell had told Henri. "Great scientists and explorers must possess imagination. It's what allows them to speculate and theorize. Those four dullards are men of means who call themselves adventurers, but all they do is hire others to track big game, and then from their lofty, comfy perch atop an elephant, shoot the creatures. Hardly sporting! They're fools. I believe

Goliathus hercules exists because where there's smoke, there's fire, Henri. So many learned men couldn't have just dreamed up this creature."

He suggested that Henri's party hire its very own jungle guide. Mat was from one of the jungle tribes and knew the rainforest environment well. While he made no claim to have ever seen *Goliathus hercules*, he knew the stories and tribal legends of the creature. "There is usually some measure of truth to such tales," George Maxwell pointed out.

Once hired, Mat helped recruit the other men, including cooks, more guides, and porters to carry the supplies. At last they were ready to begin the walk to Kuala Selangor. No one had ever thought the quest would be easy, but even before the expedition party had reached the jungle, they were already miserable. It was beastly hot, and the rain continued daily, even though the rainy season was officially over. Often it was hard to tell whether they were wet with rain or perspiration. No one complained, but no one looked happy either.

The tents, which had often seemed a cozy refuge, were now stifling hot, damp, and smelly. It was Maestro Antonio who broke first. "Ugh!" he yelled one night. "I can't get a moment's peace because of this infernal buzzing!"

Everyone was finding it difficult to sleep because of the high-pitched noise of the mosquitoes. They had assumed that they wouldn't have any trouble with mosquitoes—one wave would arrive, and Henri would negotiate with them. But no sooner had that lot gone than they'd be replaced by another group, and the procedure would start at the beginning again.

This misery was compounded by leeches. One only needed to stand still for a minute and the leeches, sensing a warm body and juicy blood, would find their way to the legs of the unsuspecting victim. So stealthy were they that none of the party ever saw or felt the bloodsuckers attach themselves. Robin took off one of her hiking boots at a lunch stop and found nearly half a dozen sucking at her toes. She screamed and tried to pull them off.

"They're vile," exclaimed Robin in tears. "Henri—try to talk to them."

"I can try, but I don't think it will work. I'm only good with six-legged creatures. These don't have any legs," and he was right. His reprimands did no good.

On the eighth day of their journey, they arrived to a great welcome at their final stop before entering the jungle. The people in this remote village were farmers, but they frequently entered

the forest to hunt for game and collect plants for herbal remedies. The expedition party was paraded through the village as honored guests to the house of the headman, who happened to be Mat's brother. It was wonderful to change into dry clothes, and that night everyone slept well under the protection of the house's thatched roof and bamboo walls. It was decided that they would stay a few days to regain their strength and good spirits.

The next morning, village elders gathered in the headman's house and regaled them with tales of *Goliathus hercules*. Several wore charms around their necks, which they claimed were made with the elytra of the insect. Excitedly, Henri, Billy, Robin, and Maestro Antonio examined the charms, and it seemed possible that indeed these were authentic. Robin and Billy brought out the cameras to document their first finding related to the quest. Maestro Antonio feverishly sketched, and Henri pulled out the five-year diary to make his first-ever entry.

Yet no one wearing the charms claimed to have seen *Goliathus hercules* alive. They'd found the pieces alongside the path that follows the river to the next village, a three-day walk from theirs. When Henri asked the elders why they thought they had never seen one alive, some responded that it was too clever to be seen, while others said that it was possessed by a spirit that made it invisible.

"Surely it must have unique and exceptional camouflage," said Maestro Antonio. "How have people who live in the jungle and wear amulets with its wings not seen one alive? Or…perhaps they choose not to see it?"

On their final night in the village, an old man was carried to the headman's house. He told a story from his childhood of a boy killed by *Goliathus hercules*. "No one saw the insects attack the child, but his body was found in the jungle," he said. "How do we know it was the giant insects and not a tiger attack? Well, here is the very strange part. All around him were the remains of several of the creatures. It was as if the boy had interrupted a fierce battle between the insects themselves! What kind of barbaric animal attacks its own kind?"

A low murmur arose from the crowd that had gathered to hear the story. Then the old man lifted his left hand. He was missing his index finger.

"My finger, bitten off by the demon you call *Goliathus hercules*! I was a young man. I was climbing a tree in the forest. I had seen a bird's nest, and I wanted to collect the eggs. As I reached up and put my hand upon the next branch, I felt the most unbearable pain! My hand was wet and pouring with blood. I thought that I might faint. Scurrying away, I looked up and saw the beast. Don't let anyone tell you it doesn't exist! This creature was about the length of my hand and wearing a golden crown!"

THE CAVE

Henri lay awake the night before they entered the jungle. This had all been his idea, and his friends were putting themselves in harm's way for something that might well be a fool's errand. Between *Goliathus hercules* and Agatha Black, someone was bound to get hurt.

And where was his nemesis? Henri had no doubt she was lurking somewhere. He rolled over on his mat, sleep unattainable. It seemed that he was finally within reach of capturing *Goliathus hercules*, but he'd made no progress in finding his father. He could not leave Malaya until, good news or bad, he knew the truth about him. He had uncovered nothing new despite numerous inquiries in Kuala Lumpur. Here in the village no one could recollect seeing a British man walking into the jungle. Henri's only hope was that if his father had come to Kuala Selangor, he might have entered the jungle through another village.

Henri turned over again. It was hard to get comfortable. The problem wasn't the hot weather. In fact, it suited him. No, it was a considerably more serious issue that caused his discomfort now. Where should he put his extra set of limbs? When he slept, they always seemed to be in the way so that he could not find a relaxed sleeping position. In the day, he tucked them under his shirt, but then it felt like he was wearing a straitjacket.

The people in the village immediately recognized Henri's insect-like qualities, but rather than being repulsed, they were amazed. To them, he was the living embodiment of the popular character Serangga-orang, hero of a dozen tribal legends. Serangga-orang, or Insect Man, was a wily inhabitant of the jungle. In the tribal tales, he was a master of disguise whose cleverness got him out of scrapes with tigers, crocodiles, and pythons. He had a beautiful singing voice that allowed him to entrance his enemies and escape harm every time. And so Henri had become a celebrity in the village. He was like the Pied Piper. Wherever he went, he was followed by at least twenty children. At times he got tired of his audience and would shoo them away, but before long they would creep back to observe him again.

At last Henri succumbed to sleep, but it was interrupted by nightmares in which he was Serangga-orang trying to outwit his sworn enemy, Agatha Black. This time she was a bat that flew toward him with her mouth open wide as if to swallow him in one gulp. Instead of flying away upon his new wings, he opened his mouth to sing the song that would enchant her, but for some reason he couldn't utter a sound.

The shriek of a bat woke Henri. No one else moved, and he knew that it was only his acute sense of hearing that allowed him to discern the bat's call. Despite the tropical heat, he felt a chill run down his back.

In the morning the expedition party set out. The jungle was a very noisy place. From high in the trees, monkeys swung from branch to branch, often screeching back and forth to one another. The high-pitched voices of cicadas provided a constant drone broken only by birdcalls and crickets' and grasshoppers' chirrups.

They walked slowly so as not to miss a thing. Reaching a mossy clearing, they were delighted to see many large grass-hoppers hopping and flying about. Their wings varied from pink to blue to purple. The party decided to have their lunch there. Robin and Billy brought out the cameras while Maestro Antonio took out his journal and watercolor paints. As they ate lunch, one of their local porters reminisced about a nearby cave he had visited when he was a child. It was near a waterfall where he had gone swimming. "That might be a good place to investigate," said Henri. Earlier sightings of *Goliathus hercules* had noted that the creature seemed to like damp conditions. What could be better than a cave?

After lunch Mat and Abdul, the porter, led Henri, Robin, Billy, and Maestro Antonio toward the cave. The bush was so dense that they were frequently brought to a standstill as the leaders hacked at the growth with their machetes.

The heat of the day had reached its peak and it was nearly four o'clock by the time they arrived at the mouth of a large, very dark cave. Trees and bushes obscured the entrance. Again, Mat and Abdul pulled out their machetes and began to hack away at the vegetation. When enough had been cleared, the party entered with lanterns lit. Mat tied a rope to one of the trees near the entrance. As they walked into the dark nothingness of the cavern, he let the rope out so that they wouldn't lose their way when returning. They could always follow it back to the light and fresh air.

"Ew! It smells disgusting in here," complained Robin.

Mat laughed. "It's the bats. Or I should say, it's their *droppings* that smell. You'll get used to it."

Henri and Maestro Antonio lifted their lanterns up, exposing hundreds, if not thousands, of silently sleeping bats hanging from the ceiling of the cave. Robin wasn't the only one who shuddered as Henri recalled his dream of the previous night.

"Do you think anything else lives in here?" asked Billy as they walked farther into the cave.

"No big animals. There are probably cave toads and some blind snakes that feed on the bats," said Mat. "Nothing that would be interested in people, I don't think."

Suddenly there was a light—a small pinpoint of bright, greenish light. Everyone tensed. A moment later, there were several more lights, and then a second later, there were hundreds all blinking in unison!

"Fireflies!" exclaimed Billy. They all laughed. Much to the surprise of Mat and the porter, Billy, Robin, and Maestro Antonio, Henri called out the traditional insect greeting of

"Are you hungry?" A thousand responses came back, all in the affirmative. They laughed some more. Henri began an earnest discussion with the fireflies nearest him.

"Greetings! My name is Henri Bell. My friends and I are on a quest, a quest to find *Goliathus hercules*. Do you know where he or she is to be found?"

"Why do you wish to find the demon?" came the response.

Henri was startled. *Goliathus hercules* must be quite a tyrant if even other insects referred to it as a demon. He wasn't sure how to answer their question. Why did he want to find *Goliathus hercules*? He supposed because it was a challenge. No one had ever succeeded. Wasn't that the reason that all explorers faced hardships and risked their lives, simply to do something that had never been done before? How could he explain that to the fireflies?

Rather than answer, he responded with another question. "Why do you call him the demon?"

They laughed. "You shall see soon enough! Follow us to the end of the cave. We must hurry. They sleep. It is safe now." Then they flew off deeper into the cave.

Henri told the others the gist of his conversation, and they cautiously moved farther into the cave, following the light of the fireflies. As they moved farther and farther back in the cavern, they saw something glowing a greenish-yellow. They had reached the end of the cave. Hanging from the wall and upon the floor were the largest beetle pupae they had ever seen. Lit by the glow of the fireflies, they had a ghostly appearance. There were at least one hundred of the silently slumbering creatures.

"It's them!" whispered Henri as he shone the light upon the unmoving masses.

"They're huge!" whispered Billy.

"They look like corpses all lying side by side," whispered Robin.

"I saw a mummy in the British Museum, and these remind me of it," said Maestro Antonio. "It was all wrapped up tight, just like these."

"Do you think we can take photographs? Will we wake them?" asked Billy.

"I don't think you can wake them," said Henri. "This is their last stage before they emerge as fully grown adults. You can see their horns and their legs, but I don't think that they can move until they have gone through full metamorphosis. It's like they're in a deep sleep."

"I agree," said Maestro Antonio, "but I think we should be careful. We don't know anything about their, um…parenting style. There may be adults around to protect the pupae from any harm."

Carefully, they shone the light around the cave, checking for any movement or sound beyond that of the fireflies. None came. "Nothing," said Henri, "but I think we should make this quick just in case. This would be a bad place to be ambushed." And he wasn't just thinking of *Goliathus hercules*. The bats had disturbed him. There was a menacing presence in the vicinity. He could feel it!

Quickly they set up the cameras, and Maestro Antonio and Henri pulled out their journals and began to feverishly sketch and record the details. Mat and the porter, Abdul, kept watch. Slowly, Henri noticed the light was dimming. He looked up and saw that the fireflies were leaving. He called to them, "Where are you going?"

"The hour has come, Henri Bell. Danger lurks. We must not tarry here! Good-bye, good luck!" they called out.

In twenty minutes, they had completed their documentation. The fireflies' warning had set the party on edge. What danger was associated with the hour? Would the adult *Goliathus hercules* return at dusk? Hastily they exited the cave, not wishing to find out.

SERANGGA-ORANG

They began the march back to their camp. Everyone was excited that on their first day in the jungle they had come remarkably close to their quest and lived to tell about it! Arriving to camp exhausted but exhilarated the cave explorers sat down to eat.

"We're on the right track! We found the pupae, and where there are babies, there must be parents, right? Why don't we set up camp near the cave tomorrow?" suggested Billy.

"Yes, I suppose it is a good place," Henri agreed reluctantly, but he didn't like the idea of being near the bat cave at all.

"What does *Goliathus hercules* eat?" asked Robin. "From the stories the other night, I think he might be a carnivorous beetle. I think we should put out some bait."

"Good idea," said Maestro Antonio. "The old man got bitten climbing a tree, so perhaps we should put the bait in a tree and keep watch. It may be that they're nocturnal so we should keep watch at night."

Henri had to agree it was a good plan, and what he particularly liked was the fact that they would lure *Goliathus hercules*. They would be in control. Henri instructed Mat to hang the bait—the remains of a chicken carcass left over from dinner—on a teak tree just beyond the camp. He assigned the men in shifts to watch it all night long. Henri himself took the first watch. Unfortunately, nothing seemed to find the bait attractive that evening.

They broke camp in the morning and moved up by the cave. During the day, they roamed the area, recording even more new species of insects. Much to their disappointment, as night approached, it started to rain. They reset the bait and settled in for a long, miserable watch. Maestro Antonio and Henri took the first shift. But once again, their shift ended with no sign of *Goliathus hercules*.

Henri returned to his tent and had just fallen into a deep slumber when he was awakened by a bloodcurdling scream.

The scream was followed by the sounds of yelling and people running. Henri leaped out of the tent and hurtled toward the hubbub. The rain was still pouring down, and there was much confusion. Mat was there with Abdul cradled in his arms, blood streaming from Abdul's face.

"What happened?" yelled Henri. In a few moments, Billy and Maestro Antonio were standing beside Henri, looking down at the unfortunate man.

"He says he was sitting, watching. He heard a noise, so he got up with the net and slowly walked toward the tree. He doesn't know what happened next, but something bit him!"

Robin brought the first-aid kit and convinced Abdul to move his hands away from his face. They all saw the something, whatever it was, had bitten his nose full-on, leaving a deep gash that would cause a scar.

In the morning, four porters accompanied Abdul back to the village. Two of them informed Henri they would not be returning.

It rained again that night, and with the rain, the mosquitoes and leeches returned. Along with wet clothes and damp tents, patience was running thin and so was the goodwill of their party.

"Let's give it another two days," Henri told his companions as they gathered in his tent. "If it continues to rain, then we'll go back to the village and wait until it stops. Then we'll head out again." Everyone agreed this was a reasonable plan.

Just then, Mat came bursting in. "Henri! Everyone! You must see!" He opened his hands and laid before them the elytra of nearly a dozen beetles. They were black, edged with flecks of gold!

"It's from *Goliathus hercules*! They're just like the things the men had around their necks as charms," shouted Robin.

"Where did you get them?" asked Billy.

Mat explained that as two of the porters who had accompanied Abdul returned to the camp, they had come across a goat carcass. "The goat must have strayed from the village. The *Goliathus hercules* ripped it apart! Savages," he muttered. "The men, they found these littered about the remains."

"I don't understand," said Robin.

"Remember the story the old man told about the boy who died?" replied Maestro Antonio. "It's as if the creature goes mad with bloodlust! In the thrill of the kill, they tear apart their own comrades! I've read of piranhas—a kind of fish in South America—with a similar bloodthirsty nature."

Henri, looking thoughtful, announced: "I have a new plan. I'll be the bait!"

"No!" was the resounding response from his companions.

"Henri, that's crazy. Even in the insect world they're called demons!" said Robin.

"I've made up my mind." Henri took off his shirt, and his third set of limbs was exposed.

Mat gasped and then said, "Don't worry, Serangga-orang has never been defeated! He will outwit them."

When night fell, Henri moved away from the camp and closer to the mouth of the cave. Hidden behind trees and makeshift palm screens, the entire expedition party nervously waited, ready to spring if, and only if, he gave the signal.

Henri had decided he would reveal his true self to *Goliathus hercules*. He wore no shirt and no hat, thus exposing his most obvious insect traits. It was still raining. With his nervous energy, Henri didn't feel like sitting or standing in one place. He strolled about, walking in circles and carefully listening for any approaching sounds. At last the rain slowed and finally stopped. A wind picked up, moving the clouds away to expose a full moon.

As he gazed up to look at the moon, he heard them! They approached from the opposite direction of the cave.

It was hard to know how many. They weren't close enough yet to see, but the moonlight would make it much easier. These beetles talked among themselves in voices perceptible only to his keen ears. There was nothing sinister in their conversation. They spoke of the things insects always talk about—food! Henri was so excited he would at last see this creature of myth and legend that he could have laughed in delight if only he weren't so scared that he might be tonight's meal! They must have picked up his scent, for they seemed to move without hesitation or detours.

Goliathus hercules had no idea he could hear them, Henri realized, so he would have the element of surprise! It seemed an eternity until

Actual Size

226

he saw the first fleck of gold twinkle in the moonlight. It was like a sparkling wave coming toward him, the beetles' numbers indistinguishable as they moved as one. When they were about twenty feet away he spoke: "Greetings, *Goliathus hercules,* king of all insects."

The wave stopped abruptly. There was some muttering. Then an authoritative voice responded, "Greetings, stranger. Now prepare to die!" The wave moved forward again. Robin was right.

There would be no small talk. These were insects of action and very few words. Instinctively Henri took a quick step back, but before he could say anything else, there was a terrible high-pitched shriek.

Startled, Henri turned toward the cry. The advancing mob paused too. The sound had come from the cave. To his amazement, hundreds and hundreds of bats were hurtling out of its opening. Among them, a tall figure emerged from the mouth of the cave. In the moonlight, Henri could see the long black dress and the smile, the smile like someone showing their teeth to the dentist. Agatha Black!

No! thought Henri. It wasn't as if he hadn't suspected she'd appear. But now that he faced both a rampaging horde of carnivorous beetles and his archenemy at the same time, Henri wasn't sure who he should defend himself against first! Either way, things didn't look good.

Another shriek pierced his ears. The bats soared high in the air and then dove down to scoop up the large beetles. Henri could hear the shouts of the *Goliathus hercules*: "It's a trap, it's a trap!"

The bats attempted to fly off with the beetles, but their prey was heavy and fought back with deadly ferocity using their powerful mandibles. A few bats managed to get off the ground, but they were quickly forced to drop their snapping prey in midair. Henri watched as one of the monstrous creatures fell toward earth, spreading open its wings, for all beetles are able to fly. Catching the air, it flew remarkably well for such a large species.

Now, in the moonlight, Henri witnessed *Goliathus hercules*'s true bloodlust. The species could not only defend themselves; it could inflict great pain. They were not able to follow the swift bats, but this did not prevent them from continuing the fight. When they saw one of their comrades battling on the ground, they flew with precision, dive-bombing to skewer the bat with their gold-tipped horns. Mortally wounded, the bat flailed about. A quick snip with their powerful mandibles brought an end to its suffering.

Henri realized that *Goliathus hercules* was not cowardly. The beetles were not satisfied to escape. They reveled in the battle and fought to win! Suddenly Henri thought of mercenaries—skilled, hardened soldiers who would fight anywhere for a price. Clearly there was no insect more vicious than *Goliathus hercules*.

Is this why Mrs. Black was interested in them, creatures that mimicked her own true nature? Did she just want the fame and glory that would come with the capture of one of them? Or did she have a much grander plan, perhaps a job for the ultimate insect warrior?

In that moment Henri realized that if he must choose whom to fight, it would be Agatha Black. *Goliathus hercules* was a terrible creature, but only in the way a tiger might seem horrifying to an innocent rubber-tapper about to become its lunch. Mrs. Black was the more dangerous of the two because she was a conniving, power-hungry bully whose cruelty knew no bounds.

As Henri's thoughts raced, it was as if he stood still in the eye of a hurricane. Caught in the fierceness of the fight, *Goliathus hercules* had completely forgotten about him. The bats took no notice of him either as they swooped, attacked, and retreated again and again. Surely someone—Agatha Black, no doubt—was interfering with Mother Nature. *Goliathus hercules* could not possibly be a normal meal for bats. With wings extended, the beetles were the same size or larger, and far better equipped to do battle. For the bats, this was a suicide mission. They stood no chance of winning.

Out of the corner of his eye, Henri saw Agatha Black enter the fray. She walked calmly toward the center of the skirmish, an ornate metal cage in one hand. Her other hand was covered in a thick glove, like the kind a falconer might wear. She bent down, and with a quickness he had observed long ago when she was collecting insects by night, her hand darted out and picked up the leader of the beetles.

"No!" cried Henri, and he launched himself at Agatha Black.

He knocked her to the ground with a thud. She gave a surprised cry. Perhaps she thought he wouldn't dare touch her, but he had made his decision—he would fight her. For months now, she had tormented him. His anger and hatred of the detestable woman gave him a strength he had not even realized he had. She struggled hard and screamed at him to let her go. It was difficult for Henri to hold her down because, after all, she was a grown woman and he was still a boy; however, he was determined not to let her get away.

It turned out Billy was right—an extra pair of hands *is* very useful. Using the hands he was born with to restrain her, he used his new limbs to pry open her gloved hand. Mrs. Black gave a cry of horror as she saw his new sharp claws.

Henri turned to the beetle leader he had just freed from her hand. "Get out of here!" he shouted.

The beetle's shiny black eyes caught the moonlight. He stared at Henri for a moment, taking in his curious form, considering him. Henri thought the insect must have been wondering: just who was the enemy? Was it the bats, Mrs. Black, this very strange insect-man, or all of them? He must have been unsure, for with a toss of his regal horns, the huge beetle opened his wings and launched himself in the air. His encounter with Henri and Mrs. Black had no doubt caused him to reevaluate the situation. Henri heard the giant beetle call out to his comrades, "Retreat! Retreat!" The beetles, so summoned by their leader, abruptly ceased fighting and turned.

Henri cursed to himself. Why was Mrs. Black here? Why did she have to spoil everything? If she hadn't turned up, he might have had a chance to reason with *Goliathus hercules*, for the beetles had momentarily paused. In a moment of inspiration, Henri called out to the rapidly departing insects: "*Goliathus hercules*, run, fly away from here! This woman is evil. Tell all your kind that tonight Serangga-orang, your insect brother, came to fight for you!"

Henri turned his attention back to Mrs. Black. He might not have captured *Goliathus hercules*, but at least he had his nemesis trapped! Up close, she smelled distractingly like sulfur, a noxious scent. He shook his head. He must not lose his focus. It was his job to make sure that she was taken care of so that she would never bother him or maim or kill another insect again!

However, he couldn't continue to hold her down by himself. He needed help!

He shouted for the others to come to his aid, but another shriek pierced the night, completely drowning out his call. The sound seemed to have come from Agatha Black. But it was a completely inhuman utterance, and while she struggled beneath him, all that came from her mouth was a steady stream of very unladylike words.

He had just managed to pry the cage from her fingers and toss it aside when something struck him in the face. Suddenly the bats had taken aim at Henri. Again and again they dove at him, relentlessly pelting him with their bodies until he had no choice but to let go of Mrs. Black and shield his face from their claws.

Agatha Black easily pushed him off and jumped up.

"Now!" cried Henri again, which was the signal to this companions that he needed help. But he could not look up to see if they were coming because the bats continued to attack him.

He could somehow still hear the swish of Mrs. Black's dress. With his head lowered and his arms protecting his face, Henri raised himself up and tried to follow the sound of the stiff silk skirt. His antennae moved about as if they had a will of their own, attempting to locate his enemy. He took a few blind, tentative steps, but quickly became confused as the swish of the dress was drowned out by the sounds of running feet and shouting voices.

Again a piercing cry rang through the air. The bats abruptly ceased to strike him and soared high in the sky.

SCENT OF DANGER

Now Robin was at his side. "Henri, are you OK?"

"Agatha Black…Did you see her? Which way did she go?" Henri looked frantically about.

"Tony, Billy, and Mat went after her."

"I have to follow them. We can't let her get away!" shouted Henri. By now, clouds had drifted over the moon and they stood in pitch dark. With all the commotion, Henri and Robin had no idea which way to run. Echoes of distant voices bounced off the trees, confusing them so that they dared not go too far for fear of losing their bearings. And then Henri caught the scent—the smell of sulfur.

"Do you smell that?" he asked Robin.

"What smell?"

"Like sulfur, like someone striking a match."

Robin sniffed the air. "No, I don't smell anything like that."

Standing motionless, Henri took a deep whiff of the heavy night air. When he opened his mouth and breathed in, he realized he could actually taste the aroma of at least a dozen scents upon the breeze. His antennae waved about, searching, searching for the scent of Agatha Black. For the first time, Henri completely gave in to his insect instincts. He knew which way to go!

Grabbing Robin's hand, he turned toward the cave and started running, drawn by the rotten-egg smell of sulfur. At the cave entrance, they stopped. The scent was there, but it was not fresh. Moving to the right, Henri now noticed an overgrown path heading into the jungle.

"This way!" he yelled. Moving as quickly as they could in the dark, they stumbled along the path, frequently tripping over tree roots. Henri knew it was a foolhardy venture. They had no idea which way they were going. Aside from Agatha Black, there were other dangers in the jungle such as tigers, snakes, and *Goliathus hercules*! It was dark, and the only weapon they had was Robin's machete. Neither of them had any practice wielding it. What were they going to do, anyway? Chop Mrs. Black into pieces?

Where were the others? Henri had no doubt that Agatha Black had come this way. He could smell her evil nature as strongly as the circus fleas could smell the fresh blood of their evening meal.

Rage propelled Henri farther into the jungle, pulling along Robin, who did not protest. She understood that they had come this far and there would be no giving up. He had just pulled Robin up from the ground, her knees a bloody mess, when they heard the unmistakable swish of silk. Mrs. Black was just ahead of them! Sniffing the air, Henri found the sulfurl-ike smell to be oppressive. She wasn't far away.

They began to inch forward when Henri suddenly stopped. There was a new smell in the air. A delicious one—the smell of warm cinnamon buns with icing and a little butter. It was heavenly, and it was just off the path toward the left. Henri started moving toward the enticing smell.

"Henri! What are you doing? Where are you going?" whispered a frantic Robin.

Henri stopped. He blinked. He wasn't quite sure, but he wanted to follow the delicious smell. He licked his lips and continued walking off the path.

"No, Henri!" cried Robin. She tugged on his arm, trying to pull him back, but Henri pushed forward. Suddenly Robin felt his arm slip from her grasp, and he vanished! It was pitch dark. Putting her arms out before her, Robin grabbed at where Henri had just stood, but she brought back only a handful of leaves. "Henri! Henri! Where are you?"

In response came a brittle laugh and then the swish of stiff silk. Raising her machete, Robin called out, "Show yourself, you old hag! Come here! I've had enough of you! What have you done to Henri?"

But Mrs. Black did not reveal herself, although it was clear she had been within feet of them. Robin heard the rustle of silk moving farther away.

"Argh!" yelled Robin in frustration. She raised her arm and

considered throwing the machete in Mrs. Black's direction. Could that work? Once Roberto, the knife thrower at the circus, had invited Robin to come to practice. Robin had thanked him politely but declined. She told Henri later that it just hadn't seemed useful at the time.

Robin lowered her arm. Should she throw the machete and miss, she might just lose it in the thick undergrowth, and then she would be alone without any kind of protection. Stomping her feet in agitation, Robin turned from the sound of the departing Agatha Black and back toward the place where Henri had disappeared.

She stared into space. How could Henri vanish? It was impossible. He must be there. Perhaps he had fallen down a hole, struck his head, and was unconscious. Gingerly, she tested the ground, inching out her foot. She couldn't move forward because of the dense foliage. She would have to hack her way through. Robin raised the machete in the air.

Just as she was about to bring down the blade, the clouds cleared and moonlight revealed large podlike plants. The pods surrounded her and were nearly as tall as she was. And to the right, one was shaking! Scared though she was, Robin moved toward it. Tapping on the outside of the pod, she called, "Henri?"

From inside came an incomprehensible muffled sound. It seemed like a lifetime ago that they had stood in Madame Noir's tent, and the Venus flytrap had bitten Henri, but that memory convinced Robin. "Henri! I know you're in there! Don't worry, I'm going to get you out!"

She didn't dare hack at the pod with the machete for fear of injuring Henri, but the membrane was so thick her hands could not rip it open, try as she might. Eventually Robin was forced to hack at the stalk. It had a tough, woody stem, and Robin had to chop frantically for ten minutes before the pod fell to the ground with a thud. The carnivorous plant, now dead, released its grasp and Robin pulled a dazed and damp Henri out of the pod.

Offering her hand, Robin pulled Henri to his feet. "It was a trap; Mrs. Black planned for that to happen. Come on; let's get out of here."

Henri felt foolish. The scent of the giant pitcher plant had lured him. What was his

Carnivorous plant, the giant plant (foreground), is the one believed to have trapped Henri

strength was also his weakness. His insect qualities gave him superior eyesight and hearing as well as an astonishing sense of smell and taste, but his heightened senses made him vulnerable to dangers like the pitcher plant. Its aroma confused his mind, and he had lost all sense of purpose. He would not let that happen again! "Thanks," said Henri.

"No problem. You would have done the same for me. We'll keep this between us."

They returned to camp and sat waiting impatiently for Billy, Tony, and Mat to return. It was a tense wait. At last Billy, the maestro, and Mat returned—just the three of them. No Agatha Black. Henri sank to the ground, his head in his hands. "She's gone! She's escaped!"

Grimly, they nodded.

Henri blamed only himself. If only he hadn't let go of her! If only he had resisted the seductive scent of the pitcher plant! He had nothing! Not *Goliathus hercules*, not his father, and now he had failed to defeat Agatha Black!

Crying out in frustration, he bellowed to the sky, "You can run for now, but I know you'll be back…and next time, I will win!"

PART IV

It was in the whispers of the wind on every call, every chirrup, and every growl. The news traveled hundreds of miles in less than twenty-four hours. Something was wrong. Something in the natural order of the forest was dangerously askew.

The cave bats had never before attacked the mighty Goliathus hercules. For centuries, the two had lived side by side without conflict. Clearly the bats had been the provocateurs, but the motivation to attack the warrior insect was unclear. It was cause for uneasiness.

Two hundred miles away from the scene of the confrontation, the whispers, instead of fading upon the breeze, had elevated to a full-scale screaming match!

"Who is this creature who speaks our language and calls himself Serangga-orang?" cried the Biggest One.

"Why did they retreat? It is shameful! I say we go out and destroy the intruder!" exclaimed the Shiny One.

"Calm yourself, brother. Calm yourself," said the Old One.

"Tell me again. What did he look like?" asked the New One.

"They say he has six legs and long antennae," said the Pointy One.

"Nothing remarkable in that. What else?" asked the New One.

"He is pale with a green tinge. Large, yet somehow not fully formed," said the Pointy One.

"A nymph, perhaps?" suggested the New One.

"I don't know," replied the Pointy One irritably. *"Perhaps."*

"By himself...hmm..." said the New One.

"And what did he say?" asked the Old One.

"He said, 'Tell all your kind that tonight, Serangga-orang, your insect brother, came to fight for you!'" responded the Pointy One.

"We do not need his help! None dare to interfere with us!" cried the Shiny One.

"It seems that is not true, brother, for there was another there. A two-leg veiled in black brazenly snatched up the Leader. It is possible that had this Serangga-orang not intervened, the Leader would have been at the two-leg's mercy," reasoned the New One.

"Hmph!" came a snort from the Shiny One.

"We will not seek out trouble; however, if trouble comes to us, then of course we will defend ourselves! We shall bide our time, brothers. We will go about our business as usual, but we will be watchful. We will be ready. It is decided," said the Old One.

Across the great jungle expanse, all its creatures braced in anticipation and nervously waited. The balance of a complex and sophisticated order had been tampered with. There would be consequences— deadly ones, perhaps.

CLOSE FRIENDS

Miss Robin Sayers
British Malaya

June 4, 1893

Chairman, British Entomological Society
London, England

Dear Mr. Chairman,

As Secretary and Registrar of the expedition, it is my sad duty to inform you of the death of Mr. Henri Bell on May 25, 1893. Mr. Bell perished during his brave attempt to capture Goliathus hercules. *I will do my best to apprise you of the unfortunate events of May 25, but I confess that the shock of Mr. Bell's loss leaves me quite devastated.*

On the night in question, Mr. Bell decided the only way to lure the insects out of their lair was to offer human bait. He proposed that he alone should await the bloodthirsty hordes. We pleaded with him that such a sacrifice was unnecessary, but Mr. Bell insisted and we reluctantly agreed.

Mr. Bell not only spoke to the legendary and mysterious Goliathus hercules, *but he survived this encounter! I believe he would have successfully captured a specimen had he not been disrupted in his negotiations by an unscrupulous collector whom you know as Mrs. Blackburn. This beastly woman has dogged our every footstep. I will not tarnish Mr. Bell's memory with further mention of this odious woman, but I implore you that if you have any influence over her, please request that she cease and desist. It is our expedition alone that is officially sponsored, and her interference has cost us dearly.*

The disruption caused by Mrs. Blackburn created considerable commotion as it provoked the insects into combat, unnecessarily risking Mr. Bell's life. Fortunately he was successfully able to extricate himself from the situation. At the time Mr. Bell's injuries appeared minor, a few cuts and bruises.

Upon his return to camp, Mr. Bell was discussing our next strategy when he fell ill with a fever and sweats. Despite our best efforts to save him, Mr. Bell stopped breathing approximately six hours later. In investigating his death, we discovered that during the skirmish, Mr. Bell was pushed up against an Upas (Antiaris toxicaria) *tree, more commonly known as the poison dart tree. Given his other injuries, the poison in the tree's sap quickly entered his bloodstream resulting in death.*

I know you will find this news most shocking and tragic! The remaining expedition party members have agreed that we will continue the expedition in honor of our esteemed colleague. I hope you agree that it is a fitting tribute.

Your faithful servant,
Robin Sayers

"Let me see it," said Billy. He picked up the pages and began reading. Occasionally he snorted. "Can't you make it a little more dramatic?"

"If you don't like it, then you write it!" retorted Robin.

Just then Henri walked into the room. "What's not to like?" asked Henri.

"Speak of the devil! He's risen from the dead!" Billy dropped to his knees in mock terror.

"He says your death by poison dart tree is not dramatic enough," said Robin.

Billy smiled. "I was thinking a tiger attack or maybe cannibals might be good!"

"I don't care," said Henri. "Just kill me off."

"Henri, this is ridiculous," said Robin. She grabbed the letter from Billy, tore it in two, and then scrunched it up into a ball. "I will not lead others to believe you are dead! You're going to want to be around when we bring *Goliathus hercules* back to London and savor the glory. Besides, your mother will be brokenhearted if she thinks you are dead. She's already lost her husband. We'll find another way to explain your appearance."

Henri looked down, sighed, and pulled off his cap so that his antennae stood up on his head and sniffed the air as if they had a mind of their own. "You're right, but only because I don't want to hurt my mother. Though how she can love me looking like this, I don't know."

Maestro Antonio entered the room. "Henri looks fine," he said. Robin and Billy raised their eyebrows.

"I don't want to cause alarm," said Robin gently. "But Henri does not look fine, or at least not fine for a human being. Beyond an extra set of limbs, antennae, a greenish pallor, and enormous eyes, he's, um, getting shorter. We used to be the same height, but now he only comes up to my shoulder. Also, his voice…it's changing."

"All boys find their voice changes around his age," responded Maestro Antonio.

"I didn't mean like that. He sounds a bit tinny, kind of hollow. And sometimes it's hard to hear him."

Maestro Antonio looked at Henri and said a little too casually, "I hadn't noticed." Henri realized now that Tony was trying not to upset him or hurt his feelings.

Maestro Antonio continued. "So we need to come up with some kind of explanation, do we? The solution is obvious, and I'm surprised that two people who grew up in the circus haven't thought of it yet." He turned to Robin and Billy, who both shrugged.

"Makeup and costumes, of course!" declared the maestro. "A little powder will take care of the green tinge. Hats and wigs will hide the antennae. A proper-fitting suit will mask the, uh… additional appendages. As to Henri's diminished stature and the timbre of his voice, we can put him in a wheelchair and explain that he has rickets." He clasped his hands together and said, "So that's settled. Frankly, we have more pressing issues. Let's discuss our next attempt to capture *Goliathus hercules*. I'll not have Agatha Black defeat us. And shall we go back to Kuala Selangor or venture into the jungle?"

Maestro Antonio was right. The expedition must go on, but Henri was so shaken by his nearly catastrophic encounter with the pitcher plant that his confidence was shattered. His ever-increasing insect nature made him susceptible to dangers he would never have considered in his more human form. He wanted to be the leader of the expedition, not the weak link!

He also couldn't ignore the fact that his metamorphosis was speeding up. Maybe soon his friends wouldn't have to come up with explanations for his appearance at all because he would be fully changed into an insect! Maybe the only excitement in his future would be an audition for the circus's insect orchestra!

He had to stop the process, but how? Was it possible to reverse it? Perhaps it was a new disease. It might take years before a solution or a cure could be found.

Ever since they had left the jungle empty-handed, Henri's mind had been consumed with these gloomy thoughts. They had not returned to Kuala Lumpur. Accompanied by only their guide, Mat, the party had instead gone northward to the Cameron Highlands. They were staying at the plantation of a British tea merchant they had met at the Golden Horse Palace in Kuala Lumpur.

The house was perched atop a hill with a panoramic view of rolling acres of tea bushes. Above the heat and whine of the mosquitoes in the jungle below, the climate made it the perfect place to rest and nurse their weary bodies and exhausted minds. And in Henri's case, a broken heart because he had found no sign of his father.

It was hard to keep up hope. There was absolutely no reason to believe his father was alive. Maybe he had simply walked into the jungle one day and never walked out again. Was it misadventure? The jungle was a wild and unforgiving place that could easily envelope and consume a man. Or had he simply chosen to abandon his family without explanation?

Henri looked up to see that Mat had entered the room. "Ah, are you making plans?" he asked the explorers brightly. Far from being disappointed over the failure to capture *Goliathus hercules*, Mat was jubilant that they had made contact and lived to tell about it. Unlike the others, he showed no concern over Henri's appearance. To Mat, serving the living embodiment of the legendary hero Serangga-orang was an honor. Now he turned to Henri.

"Serangga-orang, you look very serious. I know you will think of a way to defeat the evil one and capture *Goliathus hercules*," he said.

Henri couldn't help but smile back at Mat. Serangga-orang, half man and half insect! The jungle was his domain, and he was master of it. With wit and agility, he defeated his foes and came to the rescue of the weak and the lost. Suddenly Henri realized how much he'd given in to self-pity. It was time to snap out of it! He had to balance his two natures and live up to the name of Serangg-orang.

Henri's Great Aunt Georgie would have described Mat as the type of person who saw the glass as half full rather than half empty. Henri laughed to himself as he remembered her expressions, things like "You can't judge a book by its cover" and "A picture is worth a thousand words." Just then another came to mind—a bit of advice she had written to him in a letter he had received just before the jungle expedition. At the time, he hadn't really understood it, but now he did. He turned to the group.

"My Great Aunt Georgie told me, 'Keep your friends close and your enemies closer.' That's what we're going to do."

"But, Henri, we have tried to do that," said Robin. "As soon as we discovered Mrs. Black was following us, we tried to pursue her rather than the other way around."

"That was true until we reached the jungle. We should never have gone in without knowing exactly where she was. For the time being, we need to go after Agatha Black first, and then *Goliathus hercules*!"

Of course that was easier said than done. Still, everyone was pleased to see Henri's mood brighten. Whether he realized it or not, they all considered him their leader.

"But there's something else. We haven't been keeping our friends close either," said Henri.

"What do you mean, Henri?" asked Billy.

"I mean that we have a million or more allies that we have not called upon," said Henri "and the time has come to ask for their help!"

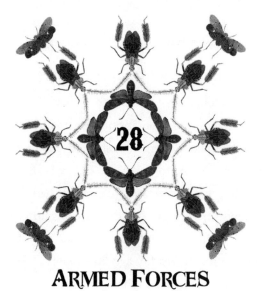

ARMED FORCES

They had a plan. Now came the preparations to carry it off. The expedition would continue onward to the vast, uncharted central jungle region. Mat left the very next morning, heading south toward the remote village of Kuala Tembeling where he would hire guides, porters, and cooks. This was the gateway to the uncharted jungle. Billy went with him for since he'd learned about the poison dart tree, he wanted to find out more about how they could use the plants and trees of the forest to aid their quest. Or, as Billy muttered under his breath, to "do away with the old hag." By accompanying Mat, Billy would have ample opportunity to learn as much as he could from him, and also, perhaps, some secrets from the tribal people of the jungle.

As for Henri, he, Robin, and the maestro were in charge of building and coordinating the insect army. "Do you think I'll have any trouble convincing them to join us? It's not their battle, after all," asked Henri.

"I would think a simple recitation of Agatha Black's numerous crimes should convince them that she's an enemy to the entire insect world!" replied Antonio.

They needn't have worried. Just as it had happened in America, news of Henri's heroics freeing the crickets of Tashkent had spread like wildfire. He had only to introduce himself, and the insects readily agreed to help.

His success emboldened Henri. "In the past I haven't had luck speaking to creatures with more than six legs, but we could add a lot to our arsenal if we could recruit them. Many of them are venomous. I suggest we speak to insects that share the same environment as centipedes and millipedes. Maybe they're bilingual?"

So they decided to look in one of the nearby mining caves. They brought along the hearing-aid machine. Unlike Henri, whose ability to speak insect came from sheer instinct, Robin seemed to have a talent for picking up foreign languages quickly. While she agreed that recruiting beyond the six-legged world was a good idea, the thought of sitting in a cave with some of the ugliest and most terrifyingly poisonous creatures known to humans was unappealing. However, for the good of the expedition, she quelled her fears.

They entered the cave with lamps ablaze. They didn't have to go far before they encountered a large dung beetle on the cave floor. They set up the hearing-aid machine so that Robin and

Maestro Antonio could tune in to both sides of the conversation. Henri introduced himself, Robin, and Maestro Antonio.

"Henri Bell, come to my cave?" the beetle said. "Well, if I had known, I would have tidied up a bit. Shame on me! But it is an honor, sir, to meet you."

"We were wondering if you are conversant with some of the other creatures that live in this cave, such as millipedes, centipedes, spiders, and perhaps scorpions." Henri said.

"Oh, well, of course. We've all grown up here in the neighborhood. Folks just flip-flop between the languages. Not a problem."

"Could you be our tutor in this other language?" Henri asked the dung beetle. "Of course, we would pay you. How about a selection of your favorite foods?"

"Uh, Henri, you *do* know what she eats?" Robin whispered.

"We'll worry about that later, Robin," whispered Maestro Antonio hastily.

"Well, that's a very nice offer," said the beetle. "I've never taught before, but I'm willing to give it a try."

"Great!" said Henri. "Robin will be your first student."

"Thank you," said Robin, turning to the beetle. "I'm…really looking forward to the lessons," she said with a little shudder, but the beetle seemed not to notice.

For the next week, Robin attended her lessons each day. It turned out that insect and millipede language had similarities like those between French and Spanish—languages in the same family. Robin also overcame her fears of the cave inhabitants. In fact, she was becoming a bit of a celebrity, as more and more creatures came to have a look at her. They were shocked that she had only two legs and assumed that she must have been in a horrible accident to be so severely handicapped. Eventually she was able to persuade the multi-legged creatures to stand in solidarity with their six-legged friends against Agatha Black.

While Robin continued her lessons, Henri and Maestro Antonio made forays out into the countryside to recruit the insect army. The only insect types they hadn't asked to join were butterflies and moths as neither Henri nor Maestro Antonio could think what use they could possibly be in battle.

But just two nights before the trip to the jungle, Henri, the maestro, and Robin were discussing plans when they heard a light tapping on the window of the plantation house parlor. They looked up to see a flurry of moths beating their wings and bodies against the window. Henri opened it, and a soft white cloud of hundreds of moths sailed into the room. From somewhere in the cloud came a voice. "Henri Bell?"

"Yes, that's me."

"I'm Art. This is my family," said the moth who had been designated as their spokesman.

The cloud sailed around the room, moving from lamp to lamp, drawn to the bright light.

"Be careful!" said Henri. "You shouldn't get too close!"

"Yes, yes, I know. It's these youngsters. Come away from there! Darn fools. We'll be fine. We've faced greater dangers tonight."

"What greater dangers?" asked Henri.

"Bats! But we outsmarted them!" replied Art.

"Really?" said Henri, now very much interested. "I would love to hear about that."

"Oh!" Clearly Art was flattered that Henri asked. "Anyway, word's been going around the forest that you're recruiting an insect army, but you haven't come and asked us to join!" He sounded a little hurt. "I told them let's go and volunteer our services."

"That's very kind of you," said Henri. "But first, what's this about outsmarting bats?"

"Oh yes. Just an average night. We easily outmaneuvered them. Some fancy flying, a couple of rolls, a few quick drops, and a little trickery too."

"Trickery?"

"We tossed them back a few clicks!"

"Tossed them back a few clicks?' What do you mean?" Henri asked.

Robin and Maestro Antonio could only hear Henri's side of the conversation without the hearing-aid machine, but Robin quickly picked up the gist of the conversation.

"Henri, I think I understand. I've been researching bats and they navigate by something called echolocation. A bat makes a series of calls or clicks, and then based on the returning echoes, it's able to judge the distance to its prey."

Turning to the moths, Robin said in insect language, "When you click, you're mimicking their sounds. It confuses them, doesn't it? They think they're hearing their own echo bouncing off another object."

"Oh!" said Art. "She speaks insect too. Yes, you're right," said

253

Art. "That's exactly what we do. The bats get disoriented, and then they just give up the chase in frustration. It works most of the time."

Henri smiled at Robin. "He says you're right." Turning back to the moth, he said excitedly, "Art, I would like to accept your offer and have your family join our army."

The moths all beat their wings in delight. With that, the last and perhaps most valuable member of the force was selected for battle. Simple confusion of the enemy might work just as well—or better—than threat and brute force.

EMBRACING SERANGGA-ORANG

Mat and Billy sat under a primitive lean-to on the outskirts of Kuala Tembeling, waiting for the arrival of Henri, Robin, and Maestro Antonio. As soon as they saw them, Mat and Billy jumped up and came running forward.

"Stop! Don't come any farther," said Mat.

"What's wrong?" asked Maestro Antonio, looking worried.

"Nothing, nothing," said Billy. "Everything is good. We just need to get Henri, I mean Serangga-orang, ready for his big entrance into the village."

"Don't call me that," said Henri. "What do you mean by my big entrance?"

Mat and Billy looked at each other, and then Mat said, "The people here are very superstitious, very old fashioned. I tried to explain that you are making a scientific expedition to find *Goliathus hercules*, but they don't understand."

"Mat, are you trying to tell us you haven't been able to hire any men?" asked Maestro Antonio.

"No, no! I just had to explain it so they understand better."

"So he told them Henri is Serangga-orang, and that it is an opportunity for the young men of the village to prove they are brave and strong by joining him on the expedition," said Billy. "Now we have more than enough men! Everyone wants to come along and work with a living legend!"

"Legend! Henri is not Serangga-orang," retorted Robin.

"How do you know?" said Mat. "Henri is half man and half insect. He is brave. He was meant to be in the jungle."

Mat had a point, thought Henri. Much of the story of Serangga-orang fit him. Certainly he had the physical qualities, and he did feel at home in the jungle. He liked the heat and dampness. And he could speak to insects. He could hear them and understand them. Brave? Well, he wasn't so sure about that part.

"So right now everyone in the village is waiting for Serangga-orang, is that right?" Henri asked.

"Yes!" Mat beamed.

"Henri, we need you to look the part," said Billy.

Sighing resignedly, Henri nodded. They had him remove his hat and shirt. His antennae sniffed the air. "I know you're not used to using your extra limbs, but no need to hesitate anymore," said Billy.

As they walked through the village gate, Mat called out something in Malay. People poked their heads out of their small wooden houses, and when they saw Henri, they came running. Soon a big crowd surrounded them, and the party came to a standstill.

"You should say something," whispered Mat. "I will translate."

"Ah...Thank you very much for this friendly welcome to your village." Henri began. "I am overwhelmed by your generosity."

"Say something about the expedition," prompted Mat.

"In a few days' time, we will enter the jungle to search and, I hope, capture *Goliathus hercules*, one of the most fearsome creatures of the forest. I, um, Serangga-orang, hope that many of the strong, brave men I see before me will join me on this quest. Thank you very much."

Mat gave a lengthy translation, which was followed by a round of applause and cheers. As they were led to the headman's house, Henri whispered to Mat, "I know you weren't translating exactly what I said."

Mat looked down. "Sorry. I just changed it a little bit. I said that those who join us would prove to everyone that they are brave and strong. I also said that you know that the forest spirits, the river spirits, and all the ancestor spirits will be pleased, and we will make many offerings to them."

"Oh. Well, I hope you're right and that the spirits are on our side."

Perhaps they were, for on that first evening in the Kuala Tembeling, Mat had news for Henri. Apparently the villagers recalled that several years ago a lone man—a foreigner—had arrived. He wanted to go into the jungle and had purchased a canoe from one of the village families. The next day he paddled off on his own and was never seen again. No one could recall the man's name or where he came from. He did leave one thing, though. In halting Malay, he had asked the people of the village to keep it safe until his return.

Mat pulled out an envelope. Inside were two photos.

"Look, Henri. Is this you and your papa?"

Henri held up one photo. It was of a smiling man and a boy, maybe six or seven years old. They looked like they were in a park. Henri stared and stared. His father had left so long ago that it was hard to recall his face. The boy was familiar, but his resemblance to the Henri of today was only slight. "Can I see the other photo?"

Mat handed him the other photo, which showed a couple, a man—the same man as in the other photo—and a woman. "That's my mother," said Henri with certainty. He turned back to the other photo, the one of him and his father. A tear rolled down his face. Time and distance had obscured everything so that not only was he unable to recognize his own father, but he couldn't see himself in the shy boy looking out from the picture.

The owner of the photographs had never returned to collect them, which wasn't hopeful news. Still, this was the first evidence that his father had been in the jungle, and that gave Henri something to hold on to. He was anxious to go back into the jungle. If luck was with him, they would defeat Mrs.

Black, capture *Goliathus hercules*, and, just maybe, learn what had become of his father.

In the morning the expedition party rose early and, with the guidance of the village shaman, made offerings to the spirits. To the river spirit they asked for calm waters for their canoes. To the forest spirits they asked for protection from rains, winds, and wild animals. And finally they gave offerings to remember the ancestor spirits. These spirits could not help them, but, if not shown proper respect, might become angry and put obstacles in their way.

The jungle was magnificent. The trees rose straight up hundreds of feet, creating elegant columns that seemed to scrape the sky. A canopy of brilliant, green leaves created a roof above their heads. Some leaves were as large as an elephant's ear. Brightly colored birds of red, green, blue, and yellow flew from branch to branch in their heavenly realm, never in their lives having touched the ground. Henri and the others disembarked from their canoes and then stood for a full ten minutes on the riverbank, gaping at the awe-inspiring beauty.

Among the trees were millions of eyes scanning, waiting for signs of unusual activity. The cicadas and grasshoppers were to keep watch and, at the first sign of Mrs. Black or her bats, sound the alarm.

There had been no sighting of Agatha Black in the village, but Henri had no doubt that a rendezvous with his nemesis was just days away. His presence alone would lure her, and she would be sure to show herself if she believed that Henri was on the verge of capturing *Goliathus hercules*. This time, though, he would be ready for her.

As Robin and Maestro Antonio set up the hearing-aid machine, Henri listened to the wind and the voices it carried. The crickets chirped, "All's well, all's well." The cicadas called, "No Black yet, no Black yet." The grasshoppers and katydids trilled, "All quiet on the front, all quiet." Hmm…thought Henri.

Nearby a particularly loud katydid with magnificent wings like a ballroom gown of brown and yellow said, "Good afternoon, Henri Bell."

"Greetings, madame."

"We are so pleased to see you."

"Likewise," said Henri. "Is everyone here and accounted for?"

"I believe so. I myself have seen the bees, wasps, blister beetles, and three battalions of army ants!"

"Impressive!" said Henri. "What about the moths? Are they here?"

"Look behind you, Henri Bell. They come."

Henri turned his head and saw the moths move across the river. Their numbers were so great that a startled Robin and Maestro Antonio looked up from the hearing-aid machine as they heard the beating of a million wings. The men setting up camp shouted out in wonder as they too saw the advancing squadron move like a threatening storm cloud. With their keen eyesight, the moths immediately identified Henri. They moved toward him as one, and Henri heard his friend Art say, "Reporting for duty, sir!"

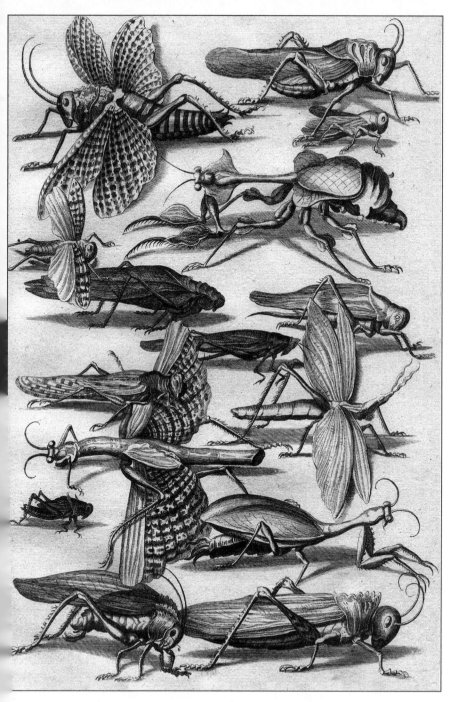

Ground troops amass in preparation for the battle. Illustration created by Maestro Antonio from his recollection one year after the jungle encounter.

With the hearing aid set up, Robin located one of her multi-legged recruits, who reported that the centipedes were positioned in trees around the area. Everyone was in place! Unbeknownst to Mrs. Black and her allies, the ground, the trees, and the air seethed with millions upon millions of creatures loyal to Henri Bell.

They went to sleep that night lulled by the gentle gurgle of the river and the continuous cries of "All's well" and "No Black yet." Henri listened for sounds out of the ordinary—a bat call, the swish of stiff silk—but nothing broke the relative peace. He slept deeply, uninterrupted.

The following morning, as he lay in his tent, it took Henri a few minutes to realize the reports had changed. He hurriedly put on clothes and crawled out of the tent to see the sun just rising. The calls reached his ears.

"Be alert, be alert!" said the crickets.

"Maybe Black, maybe Black!" came the high-pitched cry of the cicadas.

"Something coming from the west," called the grasshoppers.

Henri woke the others, informed them of the new reports, and immediately struck out to get the latest information. He searched and found the katydid he had spoken to the day before. She confirmed what he had heard already. Someone or something was coming from the west. Gazing into the sky, Henri called out for his friend Art. In a minute, the moth appeared, accompanied by a small entourage.

"Something is coming," said Art.

"Yes. I need to know whom, and I need to know when they will arrive. I am going to ask you to gather this information. Don't put yourselves at any risk!"

"I shall personally see to it." And with that, the moth took to the air, calling out for several of his family to join him.

At breakfast, Henri and the others stood by the campfire discussing what to do.

"If it's Mrs. Black and her bats, then we can expect them to attack at night," said Maestro Antonio. "That gives us the rest of the day to ready ourselves."

"I have the spiders building a tremendous web," said Robin.

"And I've found some plants that could help us in battle," said Billy. "Come, I'll show you."

As in any jungle, vines grew abundantly, taking a stranglehold upon trees. One such ivy, known as the Rosary Pea, or *Abrus precatorius*, had beautiful seeds of black and red that produced lethargy and dizziness if ingested. The rengas tree, family *Anacardiaceae*, was, in fact, a shrub. Rubbing against its leaves provoked a reaction similar to poison ivy, something that each of them was all too familiar with. Billy had also located two different types of stinging nettles—one called a nettle tree and the other a Nilgiri nettle, which not only stung but caused blisters.

Maestro Antonio was thinking practically. "There's a clearing over there," he said, pointing to a spot not far from the campsite. "That might be a good place to stage the battle. The stinging nettles and the rengas trees are just to the south of it. Robin's spiders have their web nearby too. I think if Mrs. Black tries to make a run for it, we should force her in that direction."

"What do you think about shooting some Rosary Peas into the air once the battle begins?" Billy said, pulling out a home-made blowpipe. "It will be distracting to the bats, and if they are foolish enough to swallow them, they'll get a dose of dizziness and abandon the attack."

"Good idea," said Henri. "You know, Tony's right. This is the perfect place. The trees surround the clearing so that our air forces can lie in wait. The ground is clear, so the ants and millipedes will have an uninterrupted path. There's only one more thing: is *Goliathus hercules* even in this area? I haven't seen any sign of them. I guess we'll just have to wait and see."

At that moment, the moths fluttered down into the clearing. One rested on Henri's arm. Panting hard, Art said, "Bats! Hundreds of bats! They will come tonight!"

THE BATTLE BEGINS

Whoosh! *Buzz!* A moment before, the clearing, surrounded by majestic trees, had stood tranquilly like the nave of a cathedral. Now it was as if a twister raged in its center. Millions of insects had taken to the sky. The air was choked with the multitudes—bees, wasps, hornets, cicadas, flies, and mosquitoes. Their wings, like crystal prisms, caught the light with dazzling effect. It was ordered chaos.

The ground, too, had come alive, writhing and seething like boiling water. Army ants jostled with crickets, grasshoppers, and millipedes. Standing in the center of it all stood Henri, waving his arms as if he were an orchestra conductor and barking commands like a general.

Robin, Billy, and Maestro Antonio gingerly stepped back from the preparations on the battlefield for fear that with one misstep they might crush a loyal recruit. The most enormous grasshoppers any of them had ever seen, with wings of pink and green, sailed by their noses. Robin felt the soft touch of a light wing against her cheek, and then a gentle breeze as the squadron of moths zoomed by. The bystanders worried that with a single intake of breath they might inhale a fearless fly that had been sent out on a reconnaissance mission. The air was so thick that the sun was obscured. A careless wave of the hand might result in casualties to their own troops.

Carefully Henri departed from the clearing. Robin took his place, the hearing-aid machine in hand. It was her turn to direct the allied forces to their places. Ultimately, when it came to the battle, she would stand beside Henri as his lieutenant, translating any orders into the tongue of the multi-legged. Henri returned to camp to inform Mat and the others that the battle was imminent.

"Have you seen any sign of *Goliathus hercules* yet?" he asked anxiously.

"Not yet," responded Mat. "But we'll keep looking."

Henri nodded. "I think we should make some, um, offerings to the spirits. Whichever ones you think would be best."

"Very good!" said Mat. "The men will be happy to do this."

Henri walked to the river and sat down on the bank. For a jungle, it was unusually quiet—the calm before the storm. Beyond the chorus of "Be alert, be alert," there was an absence of insect calls. Most had settled into the clearing in readiness—waiting, watching. Two magnificent black-and-green butterflies lazily fluttered by. A short time later, six yellow butterflies darted over the water. What a peaceful life, thought Henri. Butterflies were the only species they had not recruited for their forces. They seemed so fragile, so harmless. Suddenly he stood up.

"Hello, hello! Do you mind coming over here?" he called to

266

the yellow butterflies. Very slowly, certainly not taking the most direct route, the butterflies settled on Henri's shoulder.

"You called, Henri Bell?" said one of them.

"Yes, I did. I need some messengers. I have an announcement that I want spread throughout the forest. You must tell it to everyone you meet."

"Certainly, Henri Bell. What is the message?"

"The message is: *Goliathus hercules*—Serranga-orang, your insect brother, is here and wishes to meet you."

"Are you sure?" the butterfly asked. "Tell everyone? What if we don't find *Goliathus hercules*?" The butterfly anxiously flapped its wings.

"Tell it to everyone. Even if you don't meet *Goliathus hercules*, the message will get to them."

With that, the butterflies took to the air. Henri continued to sit by the riverbank, smiling to himself. There were no bigger blabbermouths than insects. If *Goliathus hercules* was in the area, the beetles would know soon enough that he was here waiting for them. In the space of an hour, Henri heard his message in the wind, whispered from tree to tree.

When you are anxious about something, time moves very slowly. At last, dusk was upon them. Quietly the expedition party moved to the clearing, where they hid behind trees and makeshift palm screens. Only Henri and Robin stood in the middle of the clearing. Henri made a quick check. He called out, and there was an angry buzz in response. The bees were ready.

They stood silently, looking westward. The insect chorus still chanted, "Be alert!" It had not changed since the morning. A feeling of queasiness was building in Henri's stomach. He felt like retching but forced himself to take deep breaths. It wouldn't do to show his nerves at a time like this.

He turned to Robin. "I want to thank you for being the best friend I've ever had. I just wanted to say that in case I don't get the chance later."

"Thanks, Henri. Thank you for believing in me and letting me come along. It's been fantastic. You're…You're my best friend too." She took his clawlike hand and held it in her own.

Slowly the moon began to rise. With an intake of breath, Henri let his insect side take over. His antennae explored the night air, searching for *Goliathus hercules* or for Agatha Black, the enemy—whichever came first. He picked up half a dozen scents upon the breeze—the smoldering campfire half a mile away, decaying weeds by the riverbank, the corpse flower's thick and heavy odor, the nectar from the bloom of a frangipani tree, the musty smell of something, maybe a jungle rat, and, finally, Robin's own unique scent. Focusing on the sounds of the forest, he could distinguish the millions of expectant whispers upon the ground, in the trees, and in the air.

Crunch, crunch, crunch. The alarm changed. "Alert, alert, danger, danger!" They all heard it.

"Who is it?" asked Robin urgently.

Henri cocked his head, sniffed the air, and smiled. He had

been mistaken about the musty smell. They came from the east. "*Goliathus hercules!*" They had come! Henri's smile quickly vanished as he heard their approaching voices.

"Bah! Serangga-orang, who is he?"

"How dare he come into our territory?"

"Come to taunt us? Come to challenge us?"

"We'll tear him apart limb by limb and feast on his innards!"

Henri had amassed his forces strictly to defend himself against Agatha Black. Now he was wondering if he should have considered some way to protect himself from *Goliathus hercules*! But it was too late.

In a short time his keen eyes spied the flecks of gold reflected off their horns and elytra moving through the trees. Some walked and some flew. As the first ones entered the clearing, he called out, "Stop!" They did not listen and continued to move forward. It was like a sea of bubbling oil spreading before him. Their shiny black backs glistened in the moonlight. He heard Robin give a little whimper beside him.

"Please, stop!" Henri shouted again.

As the words came out of his mouth, he heard another sound. Like dominos falling upon one another, one by one, it started at a great distance and then sped up, moving closer and closer to the clearing. To those who did not understand, it sounded like a primal scream ripped from the earth's center. For Henri, Robin, Billy, and Maestro Antonio, it was the call they had been expecting.

"*Baaaaats! Blaaack!*" The alarm sounded repeatedly, thunderous and united.

CASUALTIES OF WAR

Goliathus hercules stopped. While they understood the words, they did not know their significance. They looked at Henri, assuming he had caused this tremendous disturbance. They were surprised. He did not look back at them. It was as if he had entirely forgotten about them. This was strange indeed—never had their prey ignored their approach! Instead, Henri's eyes went to the sky.

When at last the cacophony of sound ceased, there was an unsettling, tense silence. Henri called out a series of commands.

"Attention! Enemy approaching from the west! Prepare for attack! Wait for my signal!"

Who was he talking to? they wondered. Perhaps he had gone mad. They saw nothing except a two-leg standing beside him. The two-leg spoke too, although it spoke in a language they couldn't understand but recognized to be that of the multi-legged. Very strange indeed.

Turning back to *Goliathus hercules*, Henri spoke quickly. "I am Serangga-orang. Tonight there will be a battle. We have a common enemy. Her name is Agatha Black. She is evil and has committed countless atrocities against the insect world. She will come with her allies—the bats. You are at risk, for it is *Goliathus hercules* she seeks to capture. The entire six-legged kingdom has united to fight her. I ask you now to join us in the battle."

It was the Old One who stepped forward. He was the largest of the warriors, and Henri noticed the battle scars along his armored body. When he spoke, it was with dignity and authority.

"We will join no one," the Old One said. "We fight only for ourselves. Tonight we fight you, the one who taunts us, humiliates us, and trespasses on our land. Prepare to die, stranger!"

"I will not fight you," said Henri calmly. "In a short time we will all be under siege from a very powerful enemy. I will not divide my army and weaken my position. I have asked you to join us, but it seems you have chosen not to do so. I will not fight you, but if you attack my companions and me, I will defend myself." Almost casually Henri returned to scanning the sky as if he were out for a pleasant evening of star gazing.

The Old One was silent for a moment. Henri's response had been unexpected. This Serangga-orang had announced that he would not fight. Was he a coward or a fool? Well, it made no difference. This kind of impertinence would not be tolerated. Behind him he heard his troops muttering, jostling, anxious to begin the fight.

"Forward!" the Old One yelled.

Henri did not flinch, nor did he look away from the sky. Next to him Robin muttered a few unintelligible words.

As *Goliathus hercules* moved forward, they suddenly found the ground beneath their feet alive and slithering. Like ropes bursting from the ground, millions of millipedes entwined their bodies around the legs of *Goliathus hercules*, causing them at first to stumble and then crash to the ground as they found their legs tied up in elaborate knots. The warrior insects bellowed in frustration, tossing and turning to no avail. *Goliathus hercules* was adapted to fight other creatures head on, but they did not have the flexibility to reach under their own feet.

"Trickery! Cowardice!" yelled the Old One as he lay on the ground bound by millipede bodies.

Henri chanced a quick glance toward the felled creature. "Well done, Robin! We're not fighting them, merely detaining them!"

"Piece of cake!" she called back. Though of course it hadn't been easy to learn millipede language and then corral them to one place so that thousands were at the ready.

Henri returned his gaze to the sky, for at that moment he heard the high-pitched squeals of bats. Thousands of bats approaching! "Bees! Begin evasive maneuvers!" he shouted in insect.

From the trees surrounding the clearing rose three swarms of tropical honey bees. The dull roar of their buzz was enough to give Henri goose bumps, despite the fact that he knew they were on his side. For a moment a cloud of bees obscured the moon and then the swarms began flying in formation, back and forth, swooping high and low, and effectively blocking entrance

272

into the clearing. Henri heard the whoosh of fluttering wings as the bats were forced to land upon the surrounding trees. They dared not enter the clearing, for every creature of the forest knows not to challenge the wrath of a swarm of angry bees.

Yet, no sooner had the bats landed in the trees than they were forced into the air again. The clearing echoed with their wounded screeches. Henri glanced at Robin and said, "I think your centipede army has attacked."

"Yes, I expect the bats won't know what has hit them since these centipedes are usually only found in caves."

So far they had the advantage. In the bright moonlight it was easy to see that the bats were in disarray, flying aimlessly above the clearing.

But then a flash of silver caught his eye, and emerging from the bush into the clearing stood a tall figure, draped in black, holding a machete in one hand, a gilt cage in the other, and a coil of rope over one shoulder.

Agatha Black! Like a bear to honey, she had come. Though she wore a veil of black mosquito netting over her head, Henri still saw the corners of her mouth break into the smile that haunted his dreams.

"Stop! Don't you come any farther, you old hag! We've got you surrounded!" yelled Henri.

"Well, well, well! How very frightening!" said Mrs. Black, but her voice betrayed not the slightest quiver. She continued to walk slowly toward them, protected from the whiny pitch and bloodthirsty bites of his mosquito force by her veil. "Come now.

Did you really think a few bees and some pesky mosquitoes would put me off?"

Then she uttered a high-pitched screech that broke the monotonous heavy drone of the bees. Above, the bats circled three times, returning to formation and swooping into the clearing. They took aim at both Henri and Robin, forcing them to shield themselves with their hands. The force of the bat's bodies caused little pain, but their sharp claws left scratches and cuts. Robin was particularly bloodied, but she did not cry out in pain. The knot in Henri's stomach tightened. He felt like vomiting. Why now? When he had faced his nemesis before, his rage was so great that he had forgotten his fear. Again he took deep breaths trying to master his nerves.

Through his fingers, Henri kept his eyes on the approaching Mrs. Black. She was within twenty feet of them. It was time to call in the reinforcements! He barked out his next command.

"Billy, begin firing! Wasps! Attack now. Sting at will!"

Smaller than the bees, the wasps were fast fliers. They quickly landed upon the flying bats, stung, and left before the bat even felt the first twinge of pain. But pain they did feel, a sharp burning throb that a few seconds later turned to painful stiffness. Some of the stung bats swooped to land upon the nearest trees but quickly discovered their mistake when they felt the grasp of the giant centipedes' jaws.

Billy was delighted to enter the fray with his peashooter. In rapid succession, he launched the colorful but potent Rosary Peas into the air. The bats, thinking the peas were small insects caught in the crossfire, opened their mouths and gulped them whole. In less than a minute, the unfortunate bats were seized with spasms and dropped, stricken, to the forest floor. Henri knew it took all of Billy's self-control not to cheer each time he heard a bat thud to the ground.

As for Agatha Black, Henri had not anticipated the heavy veil that protected her head and face. As always she wore her stiff black dress and gloves, despite the tropical heat. The fabric was impenetrable to the wasps' stings. Now they congregated en masse on the veil, buzzing, looking for a way in. With an evil chuckle, Mrs. Black lit something within the gilt cage she held that gave off a noxious-smelling, thick black smoke. She waved the cage about like an incense bearer, filling the air with choking, eye-stinging smoke. In short order, the wasps were forced to retreat, and again a high, piercing shriek broke the night.

Suddenly the bats seemed to become more and more numerous, and it was clear that this time, Mrs. Black would not make the same mistakes.

"Robin!" screamed Henri. "Look out!"

There was a new contingent of bats now—huge fruit bats!—and Henri pointed as one of the largest bats hurtled toward them. As they braced themselves for impact, the bat tilted its wings at the last moment, craftily gliding to their left low over the ground. In a horrified instant, Henri realized what would happen.

Seeing the struggling leader of *Goliathus hercules* bound by the millipedes, the enormous fruit bat did not hesitate. It plucked the frantic creature from the ground and quickly flew high up and away!

"Robin, they can't defend themselves! Call off the millipedes. We have to let *Goliathus hercules* fight."

As Robin commanded the millipedes to loosen their grip, Henri called out to his friend Art and his family of moths. Instantly they appeared, looking entirely out of place on the battlefield. There is something about fragile, winged creatures that suggests serenity and perhaps a summer day's picnic.

"Art, follow the fruit bat! Try to distract him. We must rescue the leader of *Goliathus hercules*. Hurry!" Henri directed.

"Aye, aye, sir." And with that, the moths flitted away as quickly as they had appeared.

Henri had momentarily forgotten Mrs. Black, and now, as he turned back toward her, he was horrified to see that she was gone.

What? Quickly turning right and left, he could see nothing! The bats were no longer attacking and had disappeared too.

"Mrs. Black! Where did she go?"

Startled, Robin turned to where Mrs. Black had stood a moment ago. Dumbfounded, she stuttered, "It's…it's impossible. C-careful, Henri. Maybe you should get everyone to hold their positions?"

"Cease fire! Remain alert!" Henri commanded, and suddenly the forest was still in a way it had never been before. Henri realized they had all been distracted by the huge bats, the newest recruits in Mrs. Black's army. In that moment of inattention, she had vanished.

Robin and Henri moved so that they stood back to back. Henri's piercing eyes searched. His antennae felt the air. There was a slight scent of sulfur upon the breeze. He tried to pinpoint the location.

"She's here," said Henri. "It wouldn't be her style to just leave. She'll want to prolong and enjoy the moment. She'll want to make me suffer!"

"Sir!"

Henri jumped. Art and the squadron of moths had returned.

"Sorry, sir!" said Art. "Tried to distract the bat, but we just couldn't fool him! The leader…he's dead. Drowned, sir. The bat dropped him in low over the river. Didn't have a chance to get his wings open before he hit the water…current carried him away."

In the silence of the clearing, Art's words carried to all the insects hidden in the trees and brush. A short distance from Henri and Robin, a wail mixed with anger and sorrow arose from the assembled swarm of *Goliathus hercules*. In a moment, though, there was a frightening clicking sound as if a thousand pairs of scissors snipped at the air. It was the warrior insects gnashing their sharp pincers. Defiant whoops and war cries filled the air.

"He shall be avenged! We fight in his name! Forward!"

But above all the noise, one voice arose louder and clearer than the others.

"Brothers! Brothers! Stop! Just for one moment!"

Goliathus hercules became quieter, although there was still some muttering. Henri spotted the speaker, a large and shiny specimen.

"We will avenge our leader and show our might, but it is clear we are dealing with a new enemy. I know that I am new to your ranks, but consider for a moment. This creature, the tall black two-leg, is in league with the bats. We cannot win against such deviousness."

Cries of "coward" and "go home" greeted this pronouncement.

Again the New One spoke out.

"I am no coward and I am no fool! I fight for victory! The only way we will win here tonight is to ally ourselves with Serangga-orang and the rest of the insect kingdom. It is the only way, brothers!"

There was much muttering as *Goliathus hercules* considered the notion. Henri took the opportunity to say, "He is right. Join us and we will double our strength to defeat our mutual enemy. We will win!"

At that moment Henri knew that the one thing that mattered to him more than anything else was defeating and capturing Agatha Black.

He could not succeed in finding his father because he must be dead—after all, he had not returned to the village to reclaim his photographs. As to *Goliathus hercules*, if he could actually convince one of them to return to England with him, that would be a consolation at least. But right now, Henri was consumed with a hatred so great it coursed through his entire being. His stomach was on fire. The nausea had disappeared, replaced by burning, fiery anger. His body tingled with nerves, excitement,

278

and a kind of abandon that was a combination of courage, rage, and wildness.

Henri's thoughts were interrupted by shrill cries from above. He and Robin looked up. Bats! They filled the sky again and circled like vultures high over the clearing.

And then—*whack!* In that moment, as they looked to the sky, Henri felt the air forced out of him. Something tightened around his waist. With a jerk, Henri and Robin fell to the ground, bound by a rope. They were captured, and towering over them stood Mrs. Black!

A VICTORY OF SORTS

Dazed for a moment, Henri felt a bit giddy. He had not expected that a woman dressed so ridiculously for the jungle in a long gown and veil could throw a lasso. It struck him as exceptionally funny. But before he could let out more than a guffaw, Mrs. Black stuffed something, perhaps a lace handkerchief, into his mouth.

"Find this funny, do you, Mr. Bell? I think it is I that should be laughing." And Henri saw her stiff, toothy smile behind the veil.

Mrs. Black turned to Robin. "Well, Mr. Bell won't be able to share his little joke with us. Perhaps *you* have the sense to see the seriousness of the situation. I know you speak insect. Call off your forces!" And she held her machete under Robin's throat in a threatening gesture. "Don't try any tricks!"

Robin looked helplessly at Henri. He nodded his assent. With a gulp she said, "My insect language isn't very good. I'm not sure I can."

"Don't try my patience! I'm not a fool. I wouldn't hesitate to slit your throat," Mrs. Black chortled. "I'm sure that the Geographical Society will be saddened when I announce your death, due of course to a savage attack by the natives, but they'll forget all about it when I show them *Goliathus hercules* captured and alive!"

"Commence Phase Two!" called Robin in insect. It was a short utterance that did not draw Mrs. Black's suspicion. The forest seemed to fall quiet. Luckily when Robin had fallen to the ground, the hearing-aid machine had turned off so that the device no longer picked up insect chatter.

Mrs. Black called out, "Antonio! And boy—lion tamer's boy, whatever your name is—do not contemplate a daring rescue! Any heroics and the girl is dead! Show yourselves!"

Still holding the knife to Robin's throat, Mrs. Black scanned the edges of the clearing. Nothing happened.

"I said to show yourselves or the girl is dead!"

There was a rustling of leaves, and Maestro Antonio and Billy came out into the clearing.

"Move toward the center where I can keep my eyes on you!" commanded Mrs. Black. Above the clearing, the bats continued to circle.

Billy and Maestro Antonio moved slowly. They stepped with caution, for, unbeknownst to Mrs. Black, millions of insects were moving into position. The time was approaching for the army ants to attack. They would have little difficulty moving from the ground, under her skirts, over her laced boots, and upward to more delicate areas!

"Hurry up! Whatever is the matter with you?"

Maestro Antonio and Billy stopped in the center of the clearing.

"Fine," said Mrs. Black. "Now, boy, come…"

"It's Billy."

"Oh! Please pardon my manners," said Mrs. Black sarcastically. "*Billy*, would you mind taking this cage and choosing two nice specimens of *Goliathus hercules*? How about a male and a female? That's a good boy."

"No, I won't," responded Billy. "Get them yourself, you old hag!"

"Children these days! It's Mrs. Black to you." She moved the machete's blade closer to Robin's throat, nicking the skin. A drop of blood—visible even in the dark—rolled down her neck.

"There's no need for violence, Mrs. Black," said Maestro Antonio calmly. "That won't be necessary."

"Shut up! No one is talking to you! Now, Billy, come slowly toward me and take the cage."

Billy walked toward Mrs. Black. In the darkness she could not see him step over a stream of army ants. They were not the only ones mobilizing. Only Henri with his keen hearing could hear the considerable preparations being made. He knew what his own troops were planning, but *Goliathus hercules*? Well, who knew how they would react?

Billy looked down at his two friends tied up on the ground.

Robin lay still, but Henri continued to struggle, coughing violently as he attempted to spit out the lace hankie protruding from his mouth. Billy studied their faces hoping for a signal, something that would tell him what to do. Mrs. Black glanced down and laughed.

"The more he struggles, the tighter the rope gets," she said. She stretched out the hand holding the cage. Billy snatched the cage from her as quickly as he could.

"All right. Off you go!"

With a look as if he were walking to his own execution, Billy approached the beetle just a few yards away. As he got closer, the snapping of razor-sharp pinchers filled the air. Mrs. Black cackled. Despite the noise, Henri was now so attuned to *Goliathus hercules* that he heard the New One say:

"It is just as Serranga-orang said. The evil black two-leg has ordered that two of us be captured."

"No! We will not allow it!" came a chorus of voices and the threatening, slashing motion of pinchers.

"Serranga-orang has spoken truthfully. She is our enemy and we must help him. I have an idea," said the New One. "I will allow myself to be captured."

Cries of protest came from the other beetles.

"No!"

"We owe this Serranga-orang nothing!"

"You must trust me. I have a little experience with the two-leg kind," said the New One, who moved closer as Billy approached.

Billy was just a few feet away from the ranks of the *Goliathus hercules* when he stumbled and fell to the ground. He whispered quickly in insect, "I'm sorry. I mean you no harm."

"Don't just lie there, you clumsy oaf!" screamed Mrs. Black. "Grab one!"

Billy reached out to the nearest beetle, but the insect used its strong pinchers to attack, snipping at his hand and face. "Aahh! No!" he screamed. The giant insects scrambled forward as Billy quickly raised himself from the ground, trying desperately to get away.

Only Henri could hear the New One say, "Just enough to frighten him! That's all! Let him get away!"

Henri was relieved that *Goliathus hercules* wasn't going to kill Billy. What were the beetles up to, though? Billy, bleeding, but on his feet now, hurled the cage away and ran back toward Maestro Antonio.

"You stupid fool! Idiot boy! Retrieve that cage and get back over there now!" Agatha Black shrieked.

"No!" said Billy, wiping blood from his face.

"Are you a coward? Why, I used my own hands on my first encounter with them. If not for Mr. Bell's interference, I would have my specimens already and be the toast of the nation."

Just then, Maestro Antonio spoke up. "I would say that the beetles of *Goliathus hercules* are agitated right now, and I think that Billy has just proved that capturing them by hand is not a wise course of action."

Mrs. Black stomped her foot in exasperation. "Just how were *you* planning to capture them?"

"We were planning to use diplomacy, of course. Henri was going to speak with them and invite a few to make the journey to England."

"Oh, really! Freak that Mr. Bell is, I don't for a moment believe that he has real conversation with insects, particularly these ones! I'll admit that he has some kind of intriguing, hypnotic power over them. But, really, insects are stupid, dirty, mindless creatures! They are incapable of thinking beyond their stomachs!"

As she ranted, Maestro Antonio glanced furtively around the clearing. The army ants continued to move forward, while up above, Art and his family of moths daringly fluttered among the bats to distract them.

"I beg to disagree with you," the maestro said. He would try to keep Mrs. Black talking until everyone was in place. "My own experience suggests that they have complex thoughts, the same as you and me. Henri told me that he encountered a fly that could read, and I found my own fleas to be quite skilled negotiators when it came to compensation for their services. Why, I—"

"Enough! We're not here to debate the intelligence of insects!" Agatha Black hissed. "We are all here to capture *Goliathus hercules*, but I am afraid only one of us can claim the glory. That, of course, will be me! Since you are so convinced of the insects' intelligence, Antonio, step forward and negotiate with them. Now!"

"I would like to do that, Mrs. Black, but I am afraid that my language skills are rudimentary at best. We all know that Henri is the only one fluent enough to discuss this delicate matter with them."

Mrs. Black stamped her foot again in frustration. She looked at *Goliathus hercules* inching forward.

"Tell them to stop. Don't come any closer."

"I could ask them, but they are unlikely to listen to me." By now Maestro Antonio was certain that Mrs. Black didn't understand insect. So he walked toward the mass of beetles and said in insect, "Friends! Prepare to attack the enemy!"

The beetles continued to move forward. With her own life at risk now, Mrs. Black raised the machete and sliced the rope that bound Henri and Robin together. She put her foot on Robin's chest as she leaned over and pulled Henri up. "Get me a beetle or the girl is dead!" She pulled the cloth out of his mouth. "No tricks or I will kill her!"

Henri nodded, and stepped toward *Goliathus hercules*.

"My friends, are you ready?" he said to them. "I need one volunteer."

He saw the New One move forward. Then the shiny beetle opened his wing, flew up, and landed on Henri's shoulder.

As Henri slowly turned back to Mrs. Black, he whispered to the New One, "Wait for my signal." It seemed to him that the beetle nodded.

"Here you are," Henri called out to Agatha Black. "Now let Robin go!"

"Where is the cage? Put it in the cage!" she screeched.

Suddenly there was a deafening, high-pitched shriek and

an explosion of brilliant light like an explosion in a fireworks factory. Mrs. Black screamed. Her bats, blinded by the light, broke their formation and flapped about in confusion. Millions of synchronized fireflies and cicadas had together created a stunning blast of light and sound.

"ATTACK!" Henri shouted.

The beetle on his shoulder took off and flew directly toward Mrs. Black's face. She screamed as the beetle landed on her veil, and with his pinchers, ripped at the cloth. Desperately she tore the veil off.

At last Henri gazed at his uncovered nemesis. The burning hatred and anger he felt for her was so intense that he felt it rising up from the pit of his stomach. He felt sick. He lurched forward and retched spectacularly. Suddenly he felt a release. He dropped to his knees. The anger was gone.

Henri heard horrible screaming! When he looked up, Agatha Black was on the ground, writhing.

"What have you done?! Oh, it burns! You are the devil! It's true! Oh!"

To make matters worse, Mrs. Black was lying in a stream of army ants that started to cover her body and sting her. Meanwhile *Goliathus hercules* had taken to the air and were attacking her like crows pecking at carrion. When she was not clutching her face, she tried to swat the beetles away, but they jabbed at her fingers, ripping her gloves.

"Oh! Help me! Have mercy!" cried Mrs. Black.

Her allies—the bats—were in disarray and did not come to

her aid. Henri found he could not pity her, for she was the tormentor to so many of his kind, but he also could not let the savage attack continue.

"Stop! Everyone! Cease fire! We have won!" yelled Henri in both insect and English.

What a commotion! There was raucous twittering, chirping, and cheering. Maestro Antonio and Billy rushed over to Mrs. Black and, taking her arms firmly, lifted her to her feet. She was a horrific sight—her face swollen and covered in something sticky, her black clothes ripped and bloody. She was a shadow of her former haughty self.

"What are we going to do with her now?" asked Billy in disgust.

"We take her to Kuala Lumpur and let the authorities deal with her!" said Henri.

"Henri," Robin pointed out. "I know she's not a nice person, but I'm not sure she's broken any laws."

"What do you mean?" shouted Henri. "She's responsible for the painful deaths of thousands, if not millions of insects!"

"Yes, I know," Robin was quick to respond. "And I'm not saying it's right, but…that's not a crime in the, uh…human world," responded Robin.

"She threatened to kill you!" said Maestro Antonio. "That is most definitely a crime! Attempted murder!"

"That's right!" chimed in Billy. "And she—"

But he was interrupted by a sound none of them had heard before. A tremendous roar.

A huge tiger had bounded into the clearing. A few of the

villagers in the expedition party ran for cover. Everyone else froze in terror.

The tiger paced and snorted, seemingly unsure what to do. Perhaps he was surprised by his luck to have found several tasty meals all in one place.

"All right, everyone—" Henri broke the silence but Billy interrupted him.

"Henri, I think this is my area of expertise, if you don't mind."

Henri nodded. "Yes, of course. Sorry."

Billy let go of Mrs. Black's arm; the maestro held fast to her other arm. Then Billy slowly bent down and grabbed a piece of the rope that had once held Robin and Henri.

"Everyone listen to me," he said calmly. "I don't want any one to move. Keep looking at the tiger. Don't turn your back on him. Don't say anything. Don't do anything to excite or annoy him. I'm going to try and get him to follow me."

"Billy! Be careful," whispered Robin.

"Sure, I'm going to be careful. This pussy cat wouldn't hurt a fly, would you?" he said gently to the tiger. "You're a good kitty, aren't you?"

He held the rope as he had once held the whip during shows in the big top. The tiger twitched his tail and kept his eyes on Billy.

"Come on, there's a good kitty." Facing the tiger, Billy slowly walked backward toward the trees and dense jungle. "That's a good kitty. Come with Billy."

The tiger moved slowly, seemingly fascinated by Billy and his words. Billy started to sing "*Le Petit Chat Noir*," and the tiger followed him.

Just then, Henri heard a groan from behind him. He turned to see Maestro Antonio doubled over in pain. Mrs. Black had broken away and was racing toward the edge of the clearing. With a roar, the tiger turned away from Billy and leaped in pursuit of the fleeing woman. Mrs. Black reached the edge of the trees with astounding speed. Her feet seemed to barely touch the ground, and then she disappeared into the jungle. A moment later the tiger was gone too.

Everyone heard the snap of branches, the shaking of leaves, a roar. And then, finally, a short, high-pitched scream. Then there was nothing.

THREE MYSTERIES

Mat had led his men in the direction of Mrs. Black and the tiger, torches ablaze. Billy and the maestro followed them. Henri, quite sure that his nemesis was no more, stayed in the clearing and turned his attention to their new allies, *Goliathus hercules*. Robin still stood by his side.

"Thank you for joining us. We wouldn't have been successful in defeating Mrs. Black if you hadn't sided with us," he told them. "I'm truly sorry for the loss of your leader."

"He died in battle," said an exceptionally shiny beetle. "There is nothing more honorable for a warrior. He is at peace."

There was much clicking of pinchers by the assembled group. It seemed to Henri to be the equivalent of applause or cheers.

"Serranga-orang, did you come to our jungle simply to fight your enemy?" asked the New One.

Henri looked down at the beetles. "The truth is that both Mrs. Black and I came for the same thing," he said remorsefully. "You."

There was an angry murmur among the beetles.

"What?"

"What does he mean?"

"He came to fight us?"

"You see! He is our enemy too!"

The air was filled with the renewed clicking of pinchers, this time threatening.

"No! I cannot speak for Mrs. Black, but I never meant you any harm! I wanted to meet you! Where I come from, you are mysterious creatures," said Henri. "Some men, or two-legs as you call them, have a great interest in the jungle and all its inhabitants. We call them scientists. I am a scientist—an entomologist, actually. That's someone who studies insects. My expedition party and I only wished to make contact with your kind, learn about you, and invite some of you to return with us to our land. You could then learn about us."

"Why would we want to do that? We have no interest in you! Two-legs do not belong here!" yelled an angry beetle.

"What can you learn by studying us? How to defeat us in battle? Is that what you intend?" shouted another.

"No, no! I told you. I come in peace and in the name of science. Uh…I suppose that by studying other creatures to some degree, we, the two-legged, learn something about ourselves and have a better understanding of our place in the world."

He was stricken with doubt. For years now he had been consumed by the idea of finding *Goliathus hercules* and proving to the world that they existed, but why? It seemed like a childish idea now. He had never needed to explain his motivation to humans, but as he stood before *Goliathus hercules*, searching for an explanation into the intrusion into their lives, it all seemed quite reckless and selfish. What benefit was there for them? Perhaps they would be sought as trophies in the same way tigers were hunted for their skins and elephants for their tusks. Henri suddenly felt guilty.

He was pulled from his thoughts when one of the *Goliathus hercules* asked, "You said, 'we the two-legged,' but you have more than two legs. What are you? Why ally yourselves with them? As you say, what is *your* place in the world?"

Well, that was a mystery to which Henri wished he knew the answer.

"Yes," said the New One. "You have six legs, antennae, speak insect, and we saw you spit acid into the face of the evil two-leg. But you speak their language too and are closer in size..."

"What?" Henri interrupted. "I did *not* spit acid into Mrs. Black's face!" He tried to recall the battle. He had felt strange, and then he had retched—

"You're mistaken. I was just sick. I vomited," said Henri. He turned to Robin. "They say I spit acid into Mrs. Black's face. Is that true?"

Robin nodded sadly. "Yes. Don't you remember? She said her face was burning."

293

With a groan, Henri turned away from Robin and *Goliathus hercules*. He raised his uppermost set of his arms and held his head. What kind of hideous monster was he becoming? How much longer did he have before he would be completely unrecognizable in not only form but in character too? He must hold on. He must fight to retain his dignity, his—his *humanity*.

He felt Robin's hand gently rubbing his back. "It's all right, Henri. Everything is going to be fine." But she was crying as she said it.

At last Henri opened his eyes. He could not look at Robin because her tears would make him sad, and at this moment he must not waver or seem weak. Drawing a deep breath, he turned to *Goliathus hercules* and said, "I am Serranga-orang. I am half man and half insect. Where is my place in the world, in the hierarchy of man and beast? The people of this area have told stories of my adventures for centuries. I can outwit any creature! My dual nature makes me both master of my jungle domain and a heralded scientist in the cities of the two-legged."

It was a fairy tale as far as Henri was concerned, but for the moment it was the best answer to the mystery of his ever-changing body. Surprisingly the swarm of *Goliathus hercules* bobbed its horns and clicked its pinchers in agreement.

Emboldened, Henri continued.

"Who among you is brave enough and clever enough to join me and come to the cities of the two-legged?"

The New One stepped forward and said, "I will."

There was a chorus of "No!" and "Don't go!"

But the New One said, "I told you before that I have some experience with two-legs. They are inquisitive and not easily defeated. They will only continue to harass us. Perhaps if I go with Serranga-orang, it will satisfy their curiosity and I will have his protection."

"Of course!" said Henri.

"It is my choice, and this is my decision," said the New One.

There was much grumbling, but eventually realizing they could not change his mind, *Goliathus hercules* departed the clearing, leaving their lone representative. Robin retrieved the cage Mrs. Black had brought.

"That won't be necessary," said the beetle. "I come of my own accord. You don't need to lock me up."

With that, he spread his great wings and once again flew up, landing on Henri's shoulder, almost like a parrot.

"No, of course not," said Henri.

Just then, Billy, Maestro Antonio, and the rest of the expedition party returned to the clearing.

"We recovered this. It was snagged on some bushes," said Maestro Antonio. He held up a scrap of black cloth, undoubtedly from Agatha Black's dress. "That's all we could find. We'll look again in the morning."

The search continued the following day, and several more shreds of her dress were inexplicably found higher up in the trees.

"Tigers usually go for the throat," said Billy casually. "They don't toss their prey up in the air. Gripping the throat causes

295

suffocation. Then the tiger drags the carcass to a nice private area and begins gnawing at the rump. Of course—"

"Thank you, Billy! That's quite enough detail," said Maestro Antonio. "It seems like there may have been a tussle of sorts, but there is no evidence to suggest that the tiger actually caught her or that she was dragged away."

"In all the years I worked with big cats, I never saw or heard of anyone outrunning a tiger. I don't know how she did it!" said Billy. "In fact, I find it hard to believe. If she really did get away, it's a mystery to me."

The ship rocked gently back and forth, causing her timbers to creak with each sway. The boat seemed to have the same aches and pains as Henri. He stiffly rose from his bed and moved to the porthole to look out. It was a sunny day. Henri pulled open the round window and felt the fresh breeze. He shivered.

"Please close that immediately," came a polite but authoritative voice in the cabin behind him.

"Sorry!" said Henri, and he quickly shut the porthole. He turned around. Upon the desk in his cabin sat the cage Mrs. Black carried. Its door was open, and beside it, gnawing on a piece of sugar cane, was the enormous beetle—*Goliathus hercules*!

"Care for some breakfast?" he said, looking up at Henri.

"Umm…no, thank you." While Henri quite liked sugar cane, the fact that the beetle had straddled it with his entire body was a little off-putting. It was sort of like someone offering you a sandwich they had accidentally sat on.

Henri got back into bed and raised the covers to his chin for warmth. He continued to stare at the grazing beetle.

"I do wish you wouldn't watch me eat. You know it's rather rude to do that?"

Henri let out a chortle. The beetle sounded just like Great Aunt Georgie admonishing him for his poor manners! It also reminded him of a time long ago when Dom the fly had reprimanded him for reading over his shoulder. Really, insects could be very genteel. They hardly deserved their reputation as dirty miscreants.

His laugh had caused the beetle to stop eating, and the beetle gave Henri a sharp look.

"Sorry, sorry!" said Henri. "I mean no offense. What you said, well, you sounded like someone I know."

The beetle abruptly climbed off the sugar cane and moved closer to Henri. He gnashed his pinchers, cutting at the air with aggressive ferocity. Then he rapidly opened and closed his wings as if to launch himself at Henri. Henri, however, seemed unperturbed by these actions, for in the short time he had spent with the warrior insect he had learned that this was a grooming ritual carried out at the conclusion of a meal.

"Really?" he said. "Of whom do I remind you?"

"My Great Aunt Georgie," replied Henri. "She's a real stickler for manners and proper etiquette."

"She sounds like a very cultured person. Please tell me more about her."

"Well, she's nearly a hundred years old," began Henri, who went on to describe the house on Woodland Farm and Great Aunt Georgie's passionate interest in collecting buttons. Over the course of their journey by ship, Henri discovered that this beetle was more curious than any other insect he'd ever met. Mrs. Black wasn't exactly wrong when she said insects tended to think of their stomachs before anything else, but while this particular member of *Goliathus hercules* had a healthy appetite, he also appeared to be fascinated by every last detail of Henri's life.

Aboard the ship that would return them to England, the explorers had nearly two months to discuss their adventures, speculate on the fate of Mrs. Black, and study their most prized specimen, *Goliathus hercules*.

As was their evening ritual, they sat cramped in Henri's cabin with Henri, Robin, and Billy on the bed while Maestro Antonio sat on the lone chair in front of the desk. The beetle ambled about the desktop.

It was Maestro Antonio who pointed out that the beetle was a rather skillful conversationalist. The insect always managed to extract more information than he ever gave of himself. This, among other things, made Billy suspicious of the creature.

"He's up to something, Henri," Billy said one evening. "I don't trust him. He's not…he's not…" Billy searched for the word. "Wild! He's not wild enough!"

"I really don't know what that is supposed to mean!" replied Henri. "He bit you during the battle! That's not wild enough for you?"

298

"Oh yes. I'm not going to forget that any time soon," said Billy, feeling the scar on his cheek. "I don't know. There's something not right about him. He's devious. He's up to something. Henri, he's nothing like any of the reports you told us about."

"Billy, those were reports by people who sighted *Goliathus hercules*, but they never had the opportunity to study them," said Robin. "We have the chance to show that they're not the bloodthirsty beasts they've been made out to be. I think he's charming!"

The cage was just for show in case anyone else on the ship entered the cabin. Then the beetle would be locked inside, where he would make a great show of acting like the fearsome warrior he was purported to be—rattling the cage and pushing his pinchers through the bars. Otherwise, he was free to move about. Sometimes he flew about the cabin, but more often he paced the desk and peppered Henri with questions about his life and where they were going.

This evening, as the friends talked, the beetle had chewed a pencil but spit out the shavings with a sound of great disgust. He had speared an eraser with one of his horns and caused a great deal of commotion when it got stuck, knocking over a bottle of ink and leaving inky footprints all over the desk. While Billy, Maestro Antonio, and Henri cleaned up the ink, *Goliathus hercules* stood still and let Robin remove the eraser. With Robin he was always at his most "charming," as she described it.

Now he concentrated his efforts on opening Henri's five-year diary. As the others talked and watched him, he successfully managed to get his horns between the pages and easily open the journal. He then strutted onto the open page and sat down.

"Agatha Black may not speak insect, but look at him," accused Billy. "He's reading your diary, Henri! He understands English!"

"Oh really, Billy! He's not reading." Robin lifted the beetle away and, upon doing so, discovered that he had left his "calling card," so to speak, on the page.

"Oh! You're a naughty boy! You know you shouldn't do that," she said in insect.

"Trust me, Henri, he planned that!" said Billy. "How do you know he's not reading? Henri knew a fly who could read."

"That's true," said Henri. "But I think my Great Aunt Georgie taught him. This insect grew up in the jungle, so I don't think that's possible."

"Haven't you noticed? He's always listening. He acts like he understands," replied Billy. He put his head down on the desk so that he was eye to eye with the creature. "You'll see I'm right. I'll be watching you, Prince Charming!"

Henri had to admit that the insect—or Prince, as they dubbed him shortly after that conversation—was rather unusual. Mysterious? Perhaps, but he was the equivalent of a trained soldier. A prisoner of war would never divulge sensitive information. He might just be trying to protect himself and his kind. Hopefully, in time, Prince would come to trust them.

Later that night Henri decided to take a stroll on deck by himself. The sea was calm and the stars glittered in the sky. He thought about their journey to capture *Goliathus hercules*. It had been exhausting, dangerous, and frustrating, but nonetheless exhilarating. But Henri still had so many questions.

Only one mystery had been truly solved. His father, after disappearing four years ago, could finally be declared dead. He had gone into the jungle for reasons unknown and had never returned to collect his precious photographs.

Tears rolled down Henri's face.

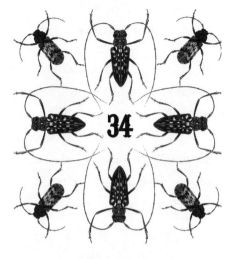

PRINCE

The explorers were within days of arriving in London's port. They had sent advance notice of their successful expedition, and they expected that not only would Henri's mother and Professor Young be there to greet them, but also a number of dignitaries from the Entomological and Geographical societies.

"There might even be someone from the royal palace!" Robin suggested excitedly as she practiced a little curtsy before them.

Billy would normally have taken the opportunity to make fun of Robin, but in his own excitement, he added, "Maybe the news of our capturing *Goliathus hercules* has been leaked to the press. There could be hundreds of people at the dock, all jostling for a view of us and, of course, Prince Charming himself!"

"Speaking of the devil, he's rather busy tearing up that novel you *were* reading," remarked Maestro Antonio, staring down at the busy beetle, who had furtively set about shredding the book to ribbons.

302

"Why, you mean-spirited, conniving, good-for-nothing bug!" Billy grabbed one of Henri's hats that was lying nearby and was about to swat the beetle with it, but Prince was already in the air, flying toward Robin. He landed on her shoulder and affectionately scratched at her neck with his horns.

"As usual! Hiding behind your girlfriend!" said Billy in disgust. "If you weren't so valuable, I would happily throw you out the porthole and be done with you!"

"Billy, you should know better than to leave your book on the desk," said Robin. "Haven't you learned that he loves paper? He just can't seem to resist. I think he does it to exercise his pinchers. He's keeping in fighting form."

"If it's a fight he's looking for, then he's got a willing opponent!" said Billy. "You're right, though; he does have a thing for paper. He reads everything he can get his grubby claws on."

The other three rolled their eyes as if to say, "Not *that* again!"

"But what I notice is he only rips up *my* things!" In insect, Billy said, "What have I ever done to you?!"

Since Henri was the only one able to hear the beetle without the hearing aid, he spoke for Prince. "He asks how he was to know that the paper was important to you?"

"It wasn't just paper! It was a book! A good book about pirates and buried treasure. I hadn't finished it, and now I never will."

Laughing, Henri said, "He says stories are for children. You're almost a man."

"Ugh! Stupid bug!" retorted Billy.

"Don't say that, Billy! He's not stupid," said Robin.

"Look, next time, why don't you ask?" Billy said sulkily.

"He says we were all busy speaking English, and no one was listening to him. He needed the paper to make a nest."

"Ugh!" Billy said in the direction of the beetle. "You're worse than a rodent! Just a few more days! I won't be sad not seeing you every day."

"He says he feels the same way about you."

Everyone laughed except Billy. He just grunted in disgust.

Unlike Billy, Henri was quite fond of Prince. He suspected that the beetle was a practical joker. Spending all day and night in the cabin was very dull, and plotting pranks to rile Billy likely helped pass the hours.

One day Henri showed Prince the insects they had collected during the expedition that were considered new discoveries. The beetle very obligingly told what he knew of each species— its type, its name in the jungle, its habits, and often, a description of how the insect actually tasted.

"Very sweet and juicy. One of those is a great way to start off the day!" and "A little small, but they're salty. Ten or so make a nice appetizer."

Given that Prince seemed to have sampled most of the specimens in his jungle habitat, Henri was left with the impression that *Goliathus hercules* must be at the top of its food chain.

And so Henri and Prince passed the days of the voyage in agreeable conversation. Like Prince, Henri had been confined to his cabin for most of the voyage. His safety was not at issue. Unfortunately, it was his appearance that drew unwanted attention.

Only at night could he steal up to the deck for a breath of fresh air. Usually he didn't stay long because the cool breeze stiffened his joints.

And Henri had shrunk even more! He was now eighteen inches shorter than Robin, according to the measurements that Maestro Antonio regularly took for Professor Young. With the sleeves of a sweater dragging on the ground, Henri shuffled about the deck less like a thirteen-year-old boy and more like an elderly man—or as Billy had aptly described, "like an ancient troll." Robin accused Billy of being insensitive, but Henri appreciated his honesty. He would not be able to make public appearances in the two-legged world for much longer.

Confined as he was, Henri turned to Prince as his confidant. He wasn't sure it was a good idea, given Billy's suspicions, but the beetle was indeed a good listener.

"I'm not really Serranga-orang," Henri confessed one day.

"What do you mean? You're half man and half insect," replied Prince.

"I am right now, but I think I'm becoming more and more insect-like. Serranga-orang is a character from a folktale, a story made up to amuse children and, I suppose, to explain the unexplainable."

The beetle looked at him shrewdly and then said, "I think most would find you unexplainable. How do you know you're not Serranga-orang?"

"Well, I haven't lived for hundreds of years luring my enemies with song and outwitting them with my cleverness."

"How long have you lived?" asked Prince.

"I'm thirteen, and my only enemy, Agatha Black, seems to outwit and escape me again and again."

"Maybe Serranga-orang is what you will become?"

"I'm not sure that's who I want to be. Right now I feel like I would rather be all man or all insect."

"It's less complicated," agreed Prince.

"Some days I think Professor Young is right," said Henri. "I'm on the verge of experiencing something entirely unheard of or imagined. It's like being an explorer or a pioneer. It's exciting! Do you think I'll be able to fly?"

"Perhaps," said Prince. "I can tell you that flying is most enjoyable. One gets a very good view, and it's much faster than walking. It's also a good way to escape one's enemies," he said ominously.

Henri nodded. "That's just the thing. Other days I'm frightened. What challenges and predators are lurking out there? Is there anything you're afraid of?"

The beetle bobbed his horns.

"Man," was all he said.

Once again Henri was filled with guilt. "Sorry. That was a bit thoughtless of me. Don't worry—I'll protect you. I won't let any harm come to you. I promise."

"I know you will protect me as best you can, Serranga-orang," said Prince.

"Would you call me Henri? That's my real name."

"As you wish, Henri."

35

A TERRIBLE GLORIOUS HOMECOMING

O h, Henri!" cried his mother.

She knelt down beside him and hugged him close, then slowly pulled back to look at him. "You've changed…You're so, so…" She stumbled, trying to find the words. "So grown up," she said finally. "I'm so happy you're home!"

She pulled him close again, rubbed her cheek against his and whispered, "Darling, is everything all right?"

"Everything is fine, Mother. I've got a lot to tell you, but not here."

Henri felt her nod. "Of course, dear. Well…I'm so proud of you!"

Henri had been wheeled down the gangway in the wheelchair they had purchased before departing Malaya. His face was powdered white in order to mask the pale green tinge of his skin. He wore a turban on his head to hide his antennae, and gloves covered his claw-like hands. Henri's body was shrouded in blankets in order to conceal his diminished form. It was all part of his disguise as an invalid. Henri had no doubt that he looked ghastly. All in all, he thought his mother was handling things quite well.

Hundreds of people had gathered to greet the ship. Among the crowd, they saw waving banners, some of which read: "Welcome home, heroes!" "Congratulations to the Bell expedition!" and "Greetings, *Goliathus hercules*, king of the jungle!"

Nearly everyone held a little paper flag with a picture of a specimen of *Goliathus hercules* printed upon it. The image was one that Maestro Antonio had drawn and sent to the British Entomological Society chairman with the news of their successful mission. An announcement of their discovery had been published in the newspapers, and readers had been encouraged to cut out the flag and come greet the explorers.

A large and high podium had been erected. The chairmen of both the British Entomological and the Geographical Societies stood near it waiting to greet the expedition party. A dozen very serious-looking dignitaries were seated to the right of a lectern from which speeches would be made. Unable to sit still in his reserved chair, a beaming Professor Young hopped from foot to foot and waved wildly to Henri.

The chairman of the British Entomological Society stepped behind the lectern. "Ladies and gentlemen, we are delighted to welcome back our returning heroes all the way from the distant colony of British Malaya. Let me introduce to you Mr. Henri Bell, Mr. Antonio Ghirardelli, Mr. William Fleming, and Miss Robin Sayers."

As each of their names was called, they waved to the adoring crowd.

"They bring with them a creature of legend. Yes, a creature so very rare, so mysterious, that many a learned scientist did not even believe it existed. Their journey took them into uncharted jungle where deadly creatures awaited! Ferocious tigers stalked them, stealthy crocodiles lurked in the swamps, and snakes able to swallow a man whole dangled from the trees!"

The crowd oohed and aahed at the mention of each animal.

"Persistence against all odds, including grueling weather conditions, tropical disease," the chairman made a nod in Henri's direction, "and hostile natives could not defeat the intrepid party!"

"What hostile natives?" whispered Robin to Billy.

He shrugged. "Makes a better story, I suppose."

"After many months of tracking the elusive *Goliathus hercules,* they at last confronted their quarry in a dense and lonely area of the jungle. In the dead of night, the expedition party was surrounded by a swarming horde of beetles driven mad by the scent of blood. The savage insects came to attack, kill, and feed. With spiked horns raised and razor-sharp pinchers at the ready, they struck! Suffice to say that while our champions prevailed, they have some battle scars as a result of the encounter."

Much to Billy's embarrassment, the chairman pointed to the scar on his cheek. Then the chairman signaled to Maestro Antonio to bring the cage to the lectern.

"Ladies and gentlemen, on this historic day, which you will recall to your children and grandchildren, we formally announce that the expedition party led by Mr. Henri Bell, sponsored by Her Majesty Queen Victoria and the British Entomological and Geographical societies, has discovered and captured *Goliathus hercules*! I present him to you!"

With that announcement, the chairman raised the cage above his head as if he were holding a championship trophy and said, "Three cheers for Henri Bell!"

"Hip, hip, hooray!"

"Hip, hip, hooray!"

"Hip, hip, hooray!"

People cheered, applauded, and threw their hats and flags into the air.

Across the podium Henri looked at his mother, tears of joy streaming down her face. Professor Young now held the beetle in his cage. From time to time, he lifted it to the crowd for another cheer. When he wasn't doing that, he put his face near the bars of the cage and spoke to Prince in his very poor insect language.

"Are you hungry? You. Me. We talk much!" And, "Thank you, thank you! Me happy. You happy."

Henri doubted that Prince was very happy, but at least he didn't snip off the professor's nose.

Henri gazed absentmindedly across at the dignitaries who had risen to their feet for a standing ovation. Suddenly he realized that one of them was a woman—a woman wearing a large black hat. Jolted into alertness, Henri was about to leap up from his wheelchair when Billy stopped him.

"Henri!" whispered Billy. "You're not supposed to get out the wheelchair."

"But Mrs. Black—she's here!"

"What? Where?"

"Over there, where the dignitaries are standing."

Robin and Billy stood up, scanned the group, and then quickly sat down, realizing that they had drawn attention to themselves.

"It's her!" said Robin.

"It's not her! Just a woman in a black hat, and quite an ugly hat too. It's definitely Mrs. Black's style, but it's not her," said Billy. "Come on, Henri. Agatha Black probably didn't get out of the jungle alive. We've been over this a hundred times. Now relax and enjoy the moment!"

But Henri couldn't relax. The speeches and applause went on and on. The chairman of the Geographical Society was now at the lectern and invited the crowd to attend the opening of the British Empire Exhibition in the Queen's building of Earl's Court the following evening. *Goliathus hercules* would be on display for all to see.

At last the welcoming ceremony concluded, and the explorers, along with Henri's mother and Professor Young, were ushered to a very fine carriage that was to take them to their hotel. Henri looked out the window, searching the crowd for a tall woman in black. He felt that sick feeling—the boiling in his stomach that he had felt in the jungle—kindle inside of him. That was not good. He didn't want to cause a scene on the very day of their arrival in the middle of London. He turned from the carriage window and tried to look interested in the conversation of his companions.

"Everything all right, dear?" asked Henri's mother. They were taking tea in their hotel room. Prince was out of his cage, much to the consternation of his mother.

"Oh. Yes, yes. Just a little tired, I suppose," responded Henri.

"Of course. It's understandable. Such a long and exciting day," she said agreeably, but she cast a wary glance at Prince, who appeared to be lapping up tea from Henri's saucer.

Henri took a sip of his tea and began what he knew would be the most difficult conversation of his life.

"Mother, I have news of Father." His mother looked surprised and put down her teacup. "I didn't write to you because I thought it would be better to tell you in person."

From his coat, Henri pulled out the envelope that contained the two pictures his father had left in the village before he had entered the jungle. He passed it to his mother. She pulled out the photographs and looked at each carefully. Tears began to roll down her face.

"I remember when these were taken. Where did you get them?"

"Father left them in the village for safekeeping before he entered the uncharted jungle. He said he would pick them up when he returned."

Henri's mother nodded and put the photographs on the table. She picked up her teacup and tried to take a sip, but as she bent her head down, her tears fell into the cup. She placed the cup back on the table and put her head in her hands. Prince, who had ambled over to the photographs, suddenly opened and closed his wings in rapid succession.

"Stop it," Henri said to Prince in insect language. He got up from his chair and put his arms around his mother consolingly.

"Why? Why did he go? Why would he go into the jungle all alone?" she cried.

"I don't know. It's a mystery." Henri was crying now too.

"What do you think happened? Do you think he was killed by an animal?"

"I don't know, Mother. I don't think we should speculate. There's nothing to be gained from it. It will only make us more unhappy."

As he said it, Henri knew that privately his mother would torture herself, wondering what had befallen her husband, just as he did. Even more hurtful, though, was the thought that Father would do something so reckless and leave his family behind without a word.

She looked up. "You're right, of course. I don't want to imagine it."

Henri knelt beside her, and she put his hands on her shoulders. "Well, I have my son still. We have each other," she said bracingly.

"Yes, Mother, you have me."

They held each other for some time. In the meantime, Prince marched about the tea table. He knocked over the sugar bowl and the little milk jug. Climbing onto a plate of neatly arranged buns, he speared the pastries with his horns and tossed each and every one of them to the floor. Then he snipped off the heads of the flowers that had been placed in a small vase. He seemed to get some satisfaction out of knocking Henri's teacup to the floor where it smashed to pieces. Despite the commotion, Henri and his mother ignored him.

Finally, Henri stood up. "There's something else I need to tell you." He could see her bracing herself. "I suppose you've noticed some changes in me."

She didn't try to deny it but nodded her head and said, "Yes, I have. Are you all right? Have you seen a doctor? We can call for one."

"I'm not sure who can help me. I've talked to Professor Young about it."

"He's not a doctor, Henri. He's an entomologist. How can he help?"

"Well…" Henri removed his gloves and his turban. His antennae sprang up and, as usual, began to explore their surroundings, unbidden by him.

Henri's mother gasped. "What are those?"

"Antennae." Sighing, he said, "I'm afraid it's worse than that, though."

He unbuttoned his shirt to reveal his third set of limbs.

"Ohh!" cried his mother.

With that small cry, two things happened, one after the other. Henri's mother fainted, slumping from her chair to the floor. And then Prince took to the air and began to attack Henri.

SUSPICIOUS BEHAVIOR

W hat the devil is going on here?" bellowed Maestro Antonio.

Drawn by the commotion of crashing plates and Henri's shouts in insect, Billy, Robin, and Maestro Antonio rushed in. They found Henri's mother lying unconscious on the floor among shattered bits of chinaware, and Henri standing in the middle of the room, his face and arms bloodied. Prince whizzed through the air, grazing Henri again and again.

"Stop! Please stop! I will not fight you. I promised I wouldn't hurt you," said Henri in insect. "What's wrong? Please tell me!" Prince took no notice and continued to swipe at Henri each time he swooped by.

"You see! You see! I told you not to trust him!" yelled Billy. He grabbed a pillow and tried to swat Prince with it.

Robin ran to where Henri's mother lay. "I think she fainted!"

The others paid no attention. Maestro Antonio had picked up a pillow too, which he used as a shield, slowly edging toward Henri. Billy continued to run about the room, cursing in insect as he tried to whack the beetle. Sometimes he threw the pillow, but he missed Prince every time. His efforts only succeeded in causing further chaos as he broke a lamp and a china figurine.

Finally, Robin yelled in insect: "Everyone stop! Prince, come here now!"

To everybody's surprise, the beetle flew toward Robin.

"Watch out!" yelled Billy. But he needn't have worried. Prince landed two feet away from her and stood still.

"Prince, what are you doing?" cried Robin in despair.

Maestro Antonio quietly walked over and turned on the hearing-aid machine so that they could all hear his response.

"Nothing."

"Nothing? Nothing?!" said Robin hysterically. "This doesn't look like nothing. Why are you attacking Henri? Why is Henri's mother unconscious on the floor?"

The beetle chose to ignore the first question. Instead he asked, "Will she be all right?" Prince moved closer to Henri's mother. There was a collective intake of breath.

"Take another step, you dirty bug, and I'll finally have the perfect excuse to squash you!" said Billy, pillow in hand.

"Billy! I don't think he means to harm her, do you, Prince?" asked Robin.

"No, I would never, ever hurt her. She's…she's Henri's mother," the beetle said.

316

"All right. I believe you. I think she'll be fine, but why were you attacking Henri?" she asked.

Prince looked at Robin and then at Henri. "I was upset with him."

"Why?" asked Henri.

"I don't want to talk about it right now," the beetle said.

"Someone get a damp cloth. Let's get Henri's mother on the bed," said Robin.

Together Maestro Antonio and Billy lifted her while Henri fetched a cloth for his mother's forehead. They all gathered around the bed, including Prince. In fact, much to everyone's alarm, he flew and landed on the pillow right beside Henri's mother's head.

"How dare you? You must have a death wish," said Billy. "If you hurt her in any way…"

"Stop it, Billy!" said Henri. "Prince, what are you doing there?"

"Nothing!" the beetle retorted sulkily.

"You already caused her to faint once," said Billy. "She'll probably faint again when she opens her eyes and sees your hideous face next to hers."

"You're right. I am hideous." Prince crawled over to the next pillow, but he was still close to her face. "But it wasn't me who caused her to faint. He did." He tossed his horns toward Henri.

"Yes, it's true. I…I told—well, *showed*—my mother what's happening to me. Um…I guess it was a little more than she expected."

"Obviously!" said Prince. "You should have done it more gently."

317

"Well, it's too bad Henri didn't consult with you on the best way to break the news," said Billy sarcastically.

"He should have," said Prince simply.

"Why you—" spluttered Billy.

"Forget it, Billy," said Henri. "Prince, are you going to tell me why you're upset?"

"No."

"I see. I'm sure you'll understand then when I say that it's very difficult to trust you. I would appreciate it if you move away from my mother. If you don't, well, I'll be forced to do something I don't want to do." Henri spoke with a new firmness in his voice.

Resignedly Prince spread his wings, flew back to the tea table and, of his own accord, entered his cage.

"I think it's best if you stay somewhere else tonight," said Henri.

"No! I don't want to. Please let me stay here. I'll stay in the cage. You can even lock it. I—I promise not to cause any more trouble. I'm—I'm sorry for hurting you, Henri."

The beetle did sound sincere. Henri looked at his friends. Robin and Maestro Antonio shrugged. Billy snorted.

"You're hiding something. You can't fool me!" said Billy.

Henri sighed. He walked to the tea table and locked the door to the cage. "Prince, I think perhaps we need some time apart. You and I were cooped up together in the ship's cabin for too long. You'll have to stay with…with Tony tonight."

"Can I come back here tomorrow?" Prince asked mournfully. He looked deflated and smaller in his cage.

"For the next few months you'll be staying in the queen's building at Earl's Court during the exposition. I'll see you every day." Henri tried to sound cheery.

"Will your mother come to visit?" asked Prince.

Henri was surprised by this question. Prince was very fond of Robin, so perhaps the beetle preferred females, but Henri couldn't see how he could have formed an attachment to his mother already.

"I'm sure she'll want to visit once she gets over her shock about me," said Henri.

With that, Maestro Antonio picked up the cage and walked to the door. Robin and Billy helped Henri tidy up the room and then left for the night. Henri pulled a chair up to the bed and sat down beside his mother. He felt worn out and baffled. What was wrong with Prince? Why was he so upset? Had seeing Henri with his mother somehow remind him of his own family he had left behind?

Unable to keep his eyes open any longer, Henri leaned forward in the chair and rested his head on the bed, using his arms as a pillow. He was almost asleep when he felt his mother take hold of his hand. She gave it a squeeze and whispered, "Everything will be fine, Henri. I love you, son."

Henri didn't open his eyes, but he smiled and whispered back, "I love you too."

A STAR IS BORN

This year's exposition, titled the British Empire Exhibition, was primarily focused upon scientific discoveries from the colonies. The insect circus featuring *Goliathus hercules* was the most eagerly anticipated exhibit, but there was also the Indian jungle designed by the renowned taxidermist, Rowland Ward. Many looked forward to a glimpse of the Victoria Diamond, a massive gemstone that had been discovered in South Africa.

There were amusements as well. As Henri, Robin, Billy, and the maestro entered the building, they saw a poster announcing:

Fortune-Telling and Eastern Mysticism
Be serenaded by gypsies!
Authentic Moorish Camp
Exotic North Africa

Rickshaws were for hire to take visitors around to all the attractions. There was even a house of distorting mirrors, just like at the circus.

"It's like going home!" said Robin.

"Indeed it is. Just like old times!" said Maestro Antonio.

The show had opened, as it had so many times before, with the pyrotechnics of the fireflies. Starbursts and pinwheels were followed by the strains of the insect orchestra's rendition of "God Save the Queen." Robin once again performed her dance with the butterflies, and the fleas jumped to new heights in their routine.

Finally, the time had come for the new act! The glass tank that held the three rings of the insect circus was quickly removed and replaced with a wooden table. Upon the table were stacks of colorful paper. Maestro Antonio walked to the center of the stage and began his introduction.

"Ladies and gentlemen, tonight it is my pleasure—no, my honor—to introduce to you our newest performer. Only recently discovered in the deepest jungle of British Malaya, he is an insect so rare, so mysterious, that many believed him to be but a mythical creature!

"But be not afraid! Those who approach him with respect and understanding will discover a noble creature, the rightful king of the jungle! Ladies and Gentlemen, I present to you *Goliathus hercules!*" roared Maestro Antonio.

From the ceiling, Prince descended with his enormous wings outstretched and skimmed the heads of the audience in a menacing fashion. Many people cried out and raised their hands to protect themselves. Prince did two furious circles, and then, with his sharp pinchers, he began to cut the dangling threads that held up little bags of sweets above the audience. There were cries of surprise and then delight as they fell into the laps of the spectators. When all the threads were cut, Prince landed gracefully on Maestro Antonio's shoulder. The audience gasped.

Maestro Antonio remained calm. "Ladies and gentlemen, *Goliathus hercules!*"

There was wild applause and even a standing ovation.

"We actually call him Prince, after Prince Charming," said Maestro Antonio with a chuckle. The audience twittered nervously. "Yes, he is fearsome looking," he added.

At this comment, Prince gnashed his pinchers together, which sounded like a pair of rusty scissors opening and closing. Many in the audience shrieked and grabbed the hands of their companions. A child started to wail in fright.

"Now, now! There is no need to fear him. Let us not forget

that we have dubbed him Prince. And indeed he is as charming as his namesake!

"Prince—and most insects—are preoccupied with many of the same concerns as we humans. They wonder about where they will get their next meal. They are concerned about providing a safe home for their families. And yes, like us, they wonder about the weather!" The audience joined the maestro in laughter.

"Did you know that most insects are quite fastidious in their grooming habits? They are not the dirty creatures they are often portrayed to be! In fact, Prince is really quite cultured."

Maestro Antonio made a little nod toward the insect on his shoulder, and to the audience's amazement, he seemed to bow back.

"Now, as you will no doubt be aware, our expedition party has recently returned from the tropics. I apologize that my appearance today is a tad untidy. I think this would be an excellent time for a mustache trim."

The audience laughed. Maestro Antonio withdrew a small mirror from his coat pocket and looked at himself. Then he gave instructions to Prince in insect, and spectators gasped as the beetle's pinchers carefully and quite expertly trimmed the maestro's mustache.

"Well done! Why thank you, Prince!" said the maestro, looking into his mirror as the audience applauded. I couldn't have done a better job myself."

Maestro Antonio continued: "*Goliathus hercules* is most certainly the king of all insects, and since lions don't live in the forests of Southeast Asia, I think it is quite fair to dub him king of the jungle! What are the qualities we expect of a king? We expect bravery and extraordinary skill on the battlefield. *Goliathus hercules* has both! We will now do a demonstration that will illustrate his agility, his exceptional coordination, and just how sharp those horns really are!"

Billy came out with a slingshot. Supplied with ammunition of red grapes, he shot them quickly and randomly up into the air. Prince took flight from the maestro's shoulder. Zooming above the audience's heads, he easily skewered the grapes on his horns. Once Prince had a grape, he took aim, tossing it off his horn and into the open mouth of Maestro Antonio, who had sat down on a chair and put his head back to catch it.

"Delicious!" he declared. The audience roared in delight.

"And now, ladies and gentlemen, for our grand finale! A king should not only appreciate the arts but also practice art himself, shouldn't he? Insects build hives of wax, nests of paper, and enormous underground cities. Perhaps we humans have not always appreciated their creativity and their efforts, but I believe you will be truly impressed at the virtuoso talent of Prince! Please proceed, Your Highness," said Maestro Antonio with a low bow toward Prince, who had landed on the wooden table among the stacks of colored paper.

Robin, who now stood behind the table, picked up a long, narrow sheet of pink paper and folded it in half many times over. Then she placed it in front of Prince. Suddenly there was a great flurry of little pieces of paper in the air as Prince snipped, poked and chopped at it. When he was finished, he stepped back. Robin picked up the paper and, with a wave, unfolded it to reveal a chain of delicate paper dolls.

The audience cheered. People stood up and yelled "Bravo! Bravo!" and "Encore!"

Robin placed another folded piece of paper in front of Prince, and again he quickly snipped. This time, he had made a lacy snowflake. The audience loved it and called for more and more. Finally, after Prince had cut a dozen patterns and creatures out of the paper, Maestro Antonio stepped forward.

"Is he not a true artist? In fact, is he not the most noble, the most regal, and the most remarkable creature you have ever seen?"

The audience rose to their feet for a standing ovation.

As Robin handed out the paper cutouts to the children in the audience, Maestro Antonio concluded by saying: "It has been our great pleasure to present this scientific and educational spectacle to you this evening. As you depart I remind you to be kind to our six-legged friends. A beetle could be someone's mother and an ant could be—well—someone's aunt. Insects contribute to our lives in ways you may not have considered. I ask that the next time you go to swat a fly or stomp on an anthill, you pause and think of what you have learned here tonight. We should treat all creatures, be they big or small, in the manner we would wish to be treated ourselves. Good night and thank you!"

A Prince Revealed

During the next two months, the insect circus performed daily. Maestro Antonio had decided once again to change the name of the show.

"We'll call it Secret Lives: Mysteries of the Six-Legged World Revealed," he announced. "I think it better reflects our educational mission."

Everyone, including Prince, agreed to the name. An insect had not been so involved in the show since the late Sophia the flea. There had been no further outbursts or acts of aggression from the warrior insect. Nor had there been any sign of Agatha Black. They supposed that a case of the jitters had caused Henri and Robin to imagine they'd seen her that day when they were first welcomed back to London.

As far as the public knew, Henri was convalescing from a variety of tropical diseases, each more horrible than the last. In reality he was always backstage working with the performers. In between shows, Henri worked on writing his account of the expedition, as well planning a butterfly sanctuary the queen had commissioned.

Henri's mother and Professor Young were regular visitors at the Natural History Museum's library, where they scoured obscure books and articles, hoping to find a clue to Henri's mysterious "illness," as they referred to it. They had yet to find an answer, but as Henri's mother said, "As long as there are still books to be read, we have hope!"

When Henri's mother came for her daily visit, Prince would fly or scurry toward her, like a dog eagerly greeting its master. She had recovered from her fright and had grown somewhat accustomed to his landing on her shoulder. She even learned a little bit of insect.

With his latest cut-paper creation clutched between his pinchers, Prince would present it to Henri's mother. He would insist that Henri translate as he described his artwork. Although no one quite understood why, Prince clearly adored Henri's mother. In turn, she was touched by his attention.

"I think they just keep getting better and better. Look at this one—there's so much detail. You see, all the children are flying kites. Some of the kites look like insects. There's a dragonfly and

a butterfly. It's wonderful, Prince," said Henri's mother, smiling at the beetle. "It's funny. There's something familiar about these scenes. I look at them and they remind me of places where I've lived and traveled. They're beautiful."

After the day's last show, Robin, Billy, and Maestro Antonio helped Henri feed the insects, and then they returned to the hotel. Henri, however, preferred to spend the night in the exhibition hall with the circus insects. He seemed to be coming more and more nocturnal in his habits. Sometimes it was a real chore to stay awake in the day, but at night he felt alert and more alive. Back at the hotel, it was very dull to sit alone in his room, wide awake. At the circus, there were plenty of insects stirring and many were quite chatty.

Another reason Henri liked to stay at night was that it gave him a chance to talk at length with Prince, who was no longer locked in his cage because he'd proven himself trustworthy. Now Henri sat down by the table where Prince was perched and took off his jacket and his shirt. It was time to relax. As usual, Prince was cutting out a picture. Henri leaned over to look at it. This time the picture was of a tree and a house and what appeared to be two people in front of the house, a couple embracing.

"I've seen that house before," said Henri. "It looks exactly like our old house here in London! The house I grew up in!"

Prince said nothing.

"Prince? How do you know that house?"

Finally, Prince replied. "I'm sure there are many houses like it. I saw a picture of it in the newspaper."

"Yes, of course. Very strange. Very strange, indeed," said Henri, as much to himself as the beetle.

Suddenly Henri was struck with a thought. "You know, I've been wondering. A lot of your pictures are of people and children. How do you know so much about them? You've never seen a child fly a kite or play ball," he pointed out.

"How do you know I haven't?" asked Prince. "I told you a long time ago that I had some experience with two-legs."

Henri kept thinking. "Wait a minute! I remember another picture you cut of the birds; they were all British birds: robins, finches—not tropical ones. I suppose you're going to tell me that you saw those in the newspaper too!" he said. He stood up suddenly. "Prince, it's time you told me the truth! You've been to England before!"

Just then, there was a great deal of coughing and spluttering. "Henri, Henri! I'm dying of thirst! I need some water!"

It was one of the huge tropical honeybees they had brought back from Malaya. In fact, the expedition party had brought back a whole hive. The bees' ominous buzzing accompanied Prince's dramatic opening descent in the show.

"All right, all right," Henri replied. "Sorry we forgot it earlier. Prince, you stay here while I get the water. Promise me you won't go anywhere! We are going to finish this conversation."

"I promise," said Prince quietly.

Henri picked up a bowl and headed toward the large and picturesque water fountain in the middle of the huge exhibition hall. It was dark, but it made no difference to Henri. His night vision was excellent now. Although there were no people in the hall, it was far from silent. Echoing off the walls, Henri heard the calls of the monkeys in Carl Hagenbeck's monkey paradise exhibit. There was squawking and sniffling from various other creatures that Henri couldn't fully identify, perhaps an anteater or a wallaby. All sorts of strange animals had been gathered specially for the exposition. Near the fountain, a few pigeons still strutted about, hooting.

Henri dipped the bowl into the fountain and started back. He was halfway there when a horrible screech rang out through the hall. Henri dropped the water bowl and ran toward the insect circus room. He could hear a cacophony of insect cries, all in the most agitated state of alarm.

As he crossed the threshold, a horrific sight met his eyes. There stood Mrs. Black.

She leaned over the wooden table. Her mouth was set in the smile that haunted his dreams, but her appearance was far worse than any of his nightmares could have prepared him for. Her face was terribly disfigured by a diagonal scar across her face—a deep, angry red gouge that ran from just above her right eye down to the left side of her mouth. For a moment Henri forgot to breathe.

Then he heard the sound of Prince's pinchers. Henri looked down and saw that Mrs. Black wore a falconer's glove, and in her hand, she held Prince! Gnashing and thrashing in a tremendous effort to escape, the beetle fought with all his might.

Henri did not think. He simply launched himself into the air.

To his complete surprise, a set of wings sprang from his back, and in a single leap he was upon his nemesis. The old sick feeling rose in his stomach, and in an instant he spat venom into the face of his sworn enemy. She cried out and the two crashed to the floor.

In the fall, Mrs. Black loosened her grip and Prince freed himself. Seeing Prince take flight, Henri yelled, "Get out of here! Stay away from her!"

On the floor, Henri struggled to hold down Mrs. Black, but she was far larger and heavier than he. In a flash, she had reversed their positions. Using her weight, she easily pinned him to the floor. She wiped the acidic venom from her face with the sleeve of her dress and then withdrew from her hair the long, sharp pin that Henri had seen in Great Aunt Georgie's parlor so long ago. Now she held it in a threatening manner just above Henri's heart!

"I wasn't expecting you to be here! You always make everything difficult," she panted.

Raising his head, Henri projected another shot of venom toward her face, but Mrs. Black anticipated it and moved her head in time.

She let out of a bark of laughter. "Now, now! That wasn't very nice. There's certainly no need to make a fuss. I have come for just one thing—the beetle. You're going to let me take him, Mr. Bell," she said in a matter of fact voice.

Prince circled in the air above them, unsure what to do. Clearly Mrs. Black held the advantage with Henri pinned to the floor and the deadly pin poised to stab at any moment.

"And why would I do that?" retorted Henri, still struggling. "He's worthless to you. We are the ones who discovered him and brought him back. There will never be any glory for you!"

"It is disappointing that I was not successful," responded Mrs. Black in a conversational tone. "But I have far greater plans for this bug than you can imagine! He is going to come with me… and he will do my bidding."

"I don't think he will!" gasped Henri, still wriggling, still looking for a way to free himself.

"You will make him, On-*ree*. I must admit you have control over six-legged pests. The same way I have control over—well, it doesn't matter. You will make the bug work for me because if you don't, I will reveal to the world just what you are! A freak! Don't think that people haven't noticed the change in you. They're talking, they are wondering, and it would give me nothing but pleasure to reveal the truth! Perhaps I will be celebrated after all when I make the announcement! Maybe I'll get to keep *you* in a cage as one of my pets!" Agatha Black threw back her head and laughed.

Enraged, Henri used every ounce of the strength he possessed and managed to free one of his arms. He quickly reached out and tried to snatch the hatpin from his enemy, but his hand, more of a claw now, was clumsy. He missed.

Startled, Mrs. Black stared down at him, her eyes narrowed. She growled, "I think I have changed my mind. I believe I've had quite enough of you, Mr. Bell!"

She raised her arm, took aim at Henri's heart, and then plunged the pin downward. Henri closed his eyes and braced himself for the pain.

"Noooo!"

That wasn't his voice—it was Mrs. Black's. Henri opened his eyes and to his horror, skewered on the pin, wings wide open, was Prince! Mrs. Black dropped the pin and with it, Prince. She leaped up and, with the abnormal speed he had witnessed once before, raced from the room.

Henri quickly sat up. Prince writhed on the ground.

"Prince! Prince! Oh! I'm going to pull that pin out!" cried Henri, tears streaming down his face. Grasping hold of the pin's pearl head, he pulled it as gently as he could out of the beetle's body.

"I told you to get out of here! Why didn't you go? You should have protected yourself!" shouted Henri in despair.

Prince heaved and gasped for breath. "I couldn't let her kill you, Henri. I couldn't." He had sacrificed himself to save Henri.

"It's going to be OK. You're going to be fine," said Henri unconvincingly.

"Henri, I don't have much time left. I need to tell you something." Prince stopped, caught his breath and continued, "I have been to England before. London was my home. I have been to the house you grew up in."

"What? How?" spluttered Henri.

"Henri," said Prince. "I am your father."

LIFE CHANGES

Suddenly everything made sense—the photographs left in the village, Prince's willingness to leave the jungle, his knowledge of the English landscape, and his keen interest in everything to do with Henri.

"Why did you attack me in the hotel room?" whispered Henri. Rivulets of tears poured down his cheeks.

"I was upset that you frightened your mother…my wife, when you showed her what you are becoming," panted Prince. He let out a gasp of great pain but continued. "I was distressed that you thought that I had just up and left you. I never wanted to do that. This sickness, this disease, whatever it is, it controls you…" His voice was getting weaker.

"Father, Father!" Henri picked up the beetle so he could hear him better.

"Tell your mother I love her. I love you, Henri," and with a last wheezy breath, Prince went still.

Gently, Henri laid him on the floor and curled up beside the beetle he now knew to be his father. The insects of the circus fluttered and hopped about them.

"Henri! Henri! Are you all right?"

But he did not answer them. The floor was cold, but Henri didn't care. Mrs. Black might return, but he could not bring himself to do anything. He cried and eventually fell into a tormented and restless sleep.

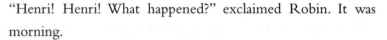

"Henri! Henri! What happened?" exclaimed Robin. It was morning.

And then Robin saw Prince.

"Prince! Prince, is he…is he dead?" she asked.

Henri sat up. He picked up the body of his father and cradled it in his hands. He nodded and felt the tears pricking his eyes again. Stiffly he stood and placed Prince on the table among the disheveled colored papers, his last picture of the house torn in two. Henri picked up the pieces and laid them side-by-side to form the scene.

Henri opened his mouth to speak, but no words came out. They could hear the tropical honeybees buzzing behind him. It was Maestro Antonio who thought to turn on the hearing-aid machine.

"Blaaack!" the bees buzzed.

"She's alive," whispered Maestro Antonio.

"She meant to kill Henri!" buzzed the bees in unison.

Everyone gasped. Robin looked on the ground and saw the pearl-headed hatpin. She picked it up and placed it on the table.

"But Prince threw himself in the way. She killed him!" the bees screamed, and all the insects in the circus began to wail. Their cries were so loud that Maestro Antonio turned off the hearing-aid machine, but there was still a dull roar.

"Oh, Henri!" Robin threw her arms around him.

"Would you like to go your mother's house, Henri?" asked Maestro Antonio.

Henri nodded. He pulled himself away from Robin. He walked to the backstage area, where he found a lidded cardboard box, and returned. Then he picked up some of the red paper from the table and lined the bottom of the box. Robin understood what he was doing. She took off the silk scarf she was wearing, folded it, and neatly placed it in the box. Henri picked up Prince's body and gently laid him on top of the scarf. Then he picked up the torn picture of the house, placed it beside the body, and put the lid back on.

At his mother's house, Henri walked to his old room without a word. He put the box down on his bedside table and crawled into his bed. Robin and Henri's mother followed him into the room.

"Henri, are you sick?" asked his mother worriedly. She came to the bedside and automatically put her hand to his forehead.

"You don't feel hot," she said. She looked at Robin.

"There's been an accident," said Robin.

Henri glared at her.

"Actually, not an accident, really," stuttered Robin "It was Mrs. Black. She…murdered Prince." Robin pointed to the box.

His mother was in tears as she sat down on the bed and drew Henri toward her. He buried his face in her dress and hugged her back. Robin edged her way out of the room to make tea.

Some hours later Maestro Antonio and Billy arrived with Professor Young. How is he?" whispered Billy.

"He hasn't spoken a word yet. I'm really worried," replied Robin. "I'll let him know you've arrived."

A few minutes later, everyone sat at the dining room table. When Henri entered the room, he was reminded of a time before the expedition when they had sat around that very table bursting with confidence and enthusiasm. They had poured over maps of British Malaya and plotted their journey. But now the adventure was over, and all Henri felt was a deep emptiness. Instead of maps, there sat a cardboard box with a lifeless body inside.

Maestro Antonio spoke up.

"We closed the show, packed up all the insects, and took them back to the hotel. The professor dropped by as we were packing, so I sent him with a message to the chairman of the British Entomological Society," he said. "We thought it best not to reveal the true circumstances of Prince's passing. I said that the cooler climate didn't suit his constitution. The chairman will notify the newspapers."

"He was most distressed upon reading the letter," said Professor Young, dabbing at his own eyes with his handkerchief. "He

337

intends to call upon you to express his condolences. Ah! So sad! Prince and I had so much more to discuss."

Henri looked down and took a sip of tea. Then he put down his cup, stood up, and opened the box. From it he withdrew the pieces of the picture Prince had been working on. He quickly replaced the lid.

Henri cleared his throat and finally spoke. His voice sounded raspy as he said, "You don't know everything. Perhaps I should have told you first, Mother, but everyone here is my friend. More than that, everyone here has been my family. Robin, Billy, Tony, you have put your lives at risk many times over to help me find *Goliathus hercules* and my father." He laid out the pieces of Prince's picture to form the scene.

"Mother, last night Prince was working on this picture. Take a look."

Henri's mother leaned over and peered at it.

"Why, it looks like our old house! The one we lived in before George left for Malaya. How would Prince know what our house looked like?" she asked.

Henri stared at his mother, willing her to make the connection, but she looked at him blankly.

"You know how you said so many of Prince's pictures reminded you of places you had been?"

"Well, yes. I did notice that," she said.

"Mother, look at me. What am I becoming?" commanded Henri.

She looked at him. He could tell she was confused.

"You're…you're turning into an insect, Henri."

He nodded.

It was Billy who made the connection first.

"Wait a minute! Henri, are you saying that Prince was your father?" Billy said, standing.

"Yes," said Henri. "He told me before he died."

Henri's mother, tears streaming from her already red eyes, grabbed Henri's hand.

"I think I shall lie down," she said. Henri helped her to her room.

"I wonder why he didn't just tell us in the first place?" asked Billy. They all sat, pondering the question. Would Henri's father be alive now if they had known?

"Maybe he was ashamed," suggested Robin. "Perhaps he would have preferred if Henri and his mother thought he had died in the jungle."

"I guess we'll never know," said Maestro Antonio. "Do you think Agatha Black knew who he was?"

"Maybe she did," said Billy. "One thing is for certain though, she didn't mean to kill him. She intended to finish off Henri."

"I don't understand," said Robin. "Whether or not she knew that Prince was Henri's father, why would she want him? We received the fame and rewards for capturing *Goliathus hercules*, so there would be none for her. If she did know it was him, what was her plan? Kidnapping him? Demanding a ransom?"

"I believe I know," said Henri, who had returned and stood in the doorway. "She said she had 'greater plans' for Prince than I could ever imagine, and that he would do her bidding."

They all sat quietly thinking about everything that had transpired. At last Henri broke the silence. "There's something else I want to tell you," he said. "Last night, I...I flew!"

"Really! How exciting!" said Professor Young, who quickly realized that perhaps that was not the right sentiment. "I mean, how interesting."

Henri finally smiled. "Yes, professor, you're right." He removed his shirt and turned his back to his friends to concentrate. He willed his wings to open, and they did!

"Wow!" said Billy.

"Oh!" said Robin.

Henri's wings stretched out about an arm's length in either direction. They were transparent, which is why no one had noticed them before, but now that they were extended, the group saw there were glints of iridescent sparkles.

"They're beautiful, Henri," said Robin.

"Boys don't want to be beautiful, Robin!" declared Billy.

"I didn't say Henri was beautiful. I said his wings were," she retorted.

"What I find interesting is that your father joined *Goliathus hercules*, but you seem to be changing into something else entirely," remarked Professor Young. "You're a little bit grasshopper, a bit ant, and another part beetle. A hybrid of sorts!"

"Yes, that is strange," said Maestro Antonio. "Could it be a matter of environment? Perhaps Henri's father turned into a member of *Goliathus hercules* because he was in the Malay jungle. But Henri has traveled with the insect circus for several years and associated with a variety of insects…"

"Really, it doesn't matter," said Henri, somewhat impatiently. "The point is that I really think my time is limited. This morning, you probably thought that I couldn't bring myself to speak. That was mostly true, but I am finding it more and more difficult to speak English. My tongue doesn't want to move to make the sounds. I really have to concentrate to speak with you."

"Oh no!" uttered Robin.

"It's a good thing we all speak insect," said Maestro Antonio.

Henri nodded.

"I've spoken with my mother. Even though my Great Aunt Georgie moved to America, she still kept the family house in England. It's a short distance from London, in the country. We thought it would be a nice place to bury Father. Afterward, I think…I think I'll just stay there."

"It will be safer there," said Billy.

Robin nodded her head and looked forlorn.

"Of course, I'd like you all to come with me!" said Henri, seeing her face. "Let's make the most of our time together."

He thought this would make her happy, but instead she began crying.

"Robin?" he asked.

"Make the most of our time together?" she wailed. "Henri, it sounds like you're dying!"

FLIGHT

From London they traveled to Great Aunt Georgie's house in the country. Henri wished that his great aunt was there, but they could not wait for her to make the journey from America. Now Henri, his mother, the maestro, Robin, Billy, and Professor Young stood on the hill behind the house to bury Henri's father.

It was a fine, sunny day, with a gentle breeze rustling the leaves on the trees and wildflowers in bloom. It would have been a gorgeous day but for the sad occasion. As they waited for the funeral to begin, the insects of the circus explored and reveled in the new surroundings. It had been a long time since most of them had been outdoors.

It would have been difficult to explain to a clergyman that the deceased, although a beloved husband and father, was also an insect. Thus, as the eldest among them, it fell to Professor Young to officiate at the funeral.

"My dear friends, we are gathered today to pay our final

respects to George Bell, known to many of us as Prince," he began. "He was the husband of Helena, the father of Henri, and a dear friend to us all. George's untimely demise has brought great sorrow, and he will be deeply missed.

They all took turns saying a few words until it was Henri's turn to speak.

"It's been nearly three years since I decided that I had to find my father," he said. "It turns out that I found him and didn't even know it until the last moments of his life. My father walked into the jungle and into the unknown all by himself. He was brave. He was kind. And ultimately, he was selfless. It doesn't matter if he was a man or an insect. He was my father, and I loved him. I hope that I grow up to be just like him."

Henri's voice broke. "Most of all, I really wish he was here to help me now. Sometimes I feel excited, and sometimes I feel afraid. I wish he could tell me what to expect and show me how to…how to survive."

Henri's mother hugged him. The rest of the party huddled around and embraced them.

They each placed a wildflower on the cardboard box that held the body of Henri's father. Carefully, Billy and Maestro Antonio lowered the box into the grave and then covered it with earth. They didn't have a headstone, so the maestro had constructed a cross out of two pieces of wood. Into the wood, he had carved the initials *G.B.*

Henri dropped to his knees and patted and smoothed the earth as best as he could.

Life in the country was quiet. Occasionally, Henri received visitors. Most of them were of the six-legged variety, but on occasion there was a man or a woman. One of the first to make the journey from London was the chairman of the Entomological Society.

Sitting in his wheelchair, Henri greeted him in his guise of invalid. Henri's stature had diminished further and his pallor, thanks to the makeup, made him look bloodless. Henri's voice was so wispy that it sounded as if he had barely the strength to speak. It appeared as if his body was wizening and the slightest breeze might blow him away.

The chairman was clearly taken aback by Henri's appearance. "I trust you're well—I mean, comfortable," he said. "Please accept my deepest condolences on the death of the specimen of *Goliathus hercules*. Tragic! Such a loss to the scientific community, a loss to the whole country really."

"Thank you," said Henri solemnly. "It's been a difficult time."

"Yes, I'm sure it has. It was your most prized specimen, after all. If only it—"

"I'm sorry, Mr. Chairman. The beetle's name was Prince. Would you mind referring to him as Prince or 'he'?" asked Henri politely.

"Yes, of course. Pardon me. If only he could have lived a few more months, at least until the end of the exposition. It would have been much more convenient for business."

Henri gripped the arms of his wheelchair tightly. *More convenient!* That was an understatement. It would have been more convenient if Prince, his father, had not been murdered! All Henri could do was nod.

The chairman continued: "I presume you prepared and mounted, um, Prince? Have you given any thought to coming back to the exposition? You could put him on display and run the insect circus again. I realize the beetle…um, *he*—was a big draw, but it's an entertaining show with or without him."

"No," Henri said through gritted teeth.

"Well, Mr. Bell, in time I expect you will feel differently," said the chairman. "You know you must think about a home for it—I mean him! I suggest you consider a museum, perhaps the Natural History Museum or a university collection."

Henri could scarcely tell the chairman that Prince was, in fact, his father and that he had buried him on the hill behind the house. But something the chairman said had struck a chord with Henri. With little time left in human form, he must make some decisions. What would happen to the insect collection he had begun since he first discovered he could speak to them?

There were thousands of specimens now. Some were very common and others were quite rare. A few in the collection had performed in the circus, but the majority had simply come to make his acquaintance and never left. Henri had always had a hard time saying good-bye to his friends, and so he kept their remains. Early on he had placed them in cigar boxes, but now they filled cabinets, drawers, trunks, and closets throughout the house.

"You're right," Henri said. "I'm not well. I must consider what to do with everything I have collected."

"Oh, Mr. Bell, I didn't mean to imply that you must rush to any decision. We expect to see you at many Entomological Society meetings in the upcoming year," the chairman replied with forced joviality.

But Henri could read his face. The chairman believed he was looking at a person soon to knock on death's door.

"Thank you for visiting. I'm a bit tired now. I'm sure you understand," said Henri softly.

The chairman rose, understanding that he had been dismissed. "Good afternoon, Mr. Bell. I do hope you're feeling better soon."

Word in the scientific community spread quickly that the explorer, scientist, and collector Henri Bell was not long for this world. A disease picked up in the tropics was causing him to waste away. Eventually, Henri refused all visitors and withdrew completely from public view.

Now with his days free, Henri began to organize his collection. Perhaps it was Great Aunt Georgie's button collection that influenced Henri. From floor to ceiling, the walls of her house had been covered in gleaming rows of buttons that sparkled like jewels in the sunlight. Now Henri arranged his insect collection upon the wall. He paid no attention to order, taxonomy, or any other scientific system; instead, he arranged the insects in patterns—patterns like the one in which the insects had arranged themselves in his room on Woodland Farm. His collection began to look like kaleidoscopic wallpaper, organically growing and creeping throughout the house.

Gradually it became harder and harder to concentrate on the

collection. His insect nature was growing stronger, and each day he wrestled with himself as his desire to be outside flying, sniffing, and exploring increased.

His mother and friends had desperately continued their search for a cure or even the slightest clue to the mystery of his condition.

"Perhaps we should consult a medical doctor," said Professor Young. "We have scoured the entomology libraries and found nothing."

"No one would believe us if we told them what's happening," said Billy.

"They would if they saw him!" protested Robin.

"Robin, we see Henri every day. We see the…the Henri-ness in him, but if you had never known him before, I think…well, I think you'd see a creature, a creature more insect than man. We don't want Henri to be labeled a freak and carted off to a zoo!"

Henri's mother let out a little cry. Robin glared at Billy.

"Don't look at me like that. Look what happened to the Elephant Man. He ended up in a hospital, a freak for doctors to poke and prod!" exclaimed Billy.

"Are you saying you're giving up?" accused Robin.

At that moment the discussion abruptly ceased as Henri hopped—rather than walked—into the room.

"Talking about me?" he peeped in a squeaky voice.

"Yes, actually we were," said Maestro Antonio, looking down at him.

"Look, I know you have all tried your best…"

"And we're going to keep trying!" said Robin.

Gloom descended upon the house. The only person who was not melancholy was Henri. The weather was fine, and he spent more and more time with the circus insects outdoors. They had become his guides and teachers as he learned to adapt to his changing form.

It wasn't long before Henri stopped speaking English, not because he wanted to but because he had become incapable of making the sounds. Luckily, everyone except Henri's mother spoke fluent insect, so they could still communicate with him. Yet it hardly mattered because Henri had become an insect of very few words. He was far more interested in experiencing his new world than talking about it. Each day he became noticeably smaller and more and more insect-like until the time came when none of them could recognize any "Henri-ness" in him. Of course they knew that the grasshopper-like insect that stood on the dining room table was Henri, but only because of his particular insect features.

After spending his days in the nearby field and woods, Henri returned to the house and his room exhausted but exhilarated. As they had done on the ship, everyone congregated in Henri's room in the evening. Now he sat on the desk by the window. Henri's mother and the professor had retired to bed but Robin, Billy, and Maestro Antonio gathered around him.

"It was a beautiful day. I'm sure you had a wonderful time exploring," remarked Robin.

Henri said nothing, though they listened in with the hearing-aid machine.

"Henri? Are you OK? Say something."

Finally Henri said, "I'm sorry, everyone. I'm going tonight." He was calm.

"What?" exclaimed Robin. "No! Henri, please don't go."

"Robin, I couldn't stay if I wanted to. The pull, the call of the wild, whatever you want to call it, it's so strong. Do you think that my father wanted to walk into the jungle and away from his family? No, he didn't, but he couldn't help it."

"Henri, where will you go?" asked Billy.

"Don't worry! I'm not going far. At least I don't think I am. I don't feel an inclination to migrate like a Monarch butterfly. I'll be right out there." With a leg Henri gestured toward the field and woods beyond the house. "I'll be practically in the backyard!"

"Henri. Henri, will…will you come back to visit?" asked Robin with a sob.

"I'll try."

"Be careful out there, Henri," said Maestro Antonio. "You have an enemy. Mrs. Black tried to kill you once. She'll probably try again!"

"I doubt she'll recognize me, but I won't be by myself. Look! Open the window," commanded Henri.

Reluctantly, Billy got up and opened it. Outside fluttered several moths, and the group could hear the chirrups of nighttime creatures—crickets, mostly.

They chanted: "Henri, Henri, come out and play!"

"You see! I'll be with friends. Don't worry," soothed Henri. "But before I go I want to tell you that there's a letter to all of you on the desk in the study. Also, the insect collection, I'm not giving it to a museum. I'm leaving it to all of you."

They all looked surprised.

"We've had a lot of adventures together. One of the things I learned from my Great Aunt Georgie is that part of what makes a great collection is the stories that go with it. You all know how each insect came to be in this collection. They're small parts of my strange story. Someday maybe you'll want to share that with people."

"All right, Henri," said Maestro Antonio. "We'll take good care of it."

"Good-bye. You've been my best friends, and I will never forget you. Say good-bye to the professor for me. Thank him for all his help. Tell my mother I love her and...well, tell her not to be sad. I'll miss you all, but tonight I feel alive! I feel happy. I feel free!"

With that, Henri stepped to the window, spread his wings, and launched himself into the night sky.